ALMOST STRANGERS

A NOVEL

Delsa Winer

Simon & Schuster

NEW YORK   LONDON   TORONTO   SYDNEY   SINGAPORE

SIMON & SCHUSTER
Rockefeller Center
1230 Avenue of the Americas
New York, NY 10020

This Simon & Schuster edition 2002
Simon & Schuster and colophon are registered trademarks of
Simon & Schuster, Inc.

For information about special discounts for bulk purchases,
please contact Simon & Schuster Special Sales:
1-800-456-6798 or business@simonandschuster.com

Designed by Kyoko Watanabe

Manufactured in the United States of America

1   3   5   7   9   10   8   6   4   2

The Library of Congress has cataloged
the Simon & Schuster edition as follows:
Winer, Delsa, 1937–
Almost strangers : a novel / Delsa Winer.
p. cm.
1. Survival after airplane accidents, shipwrecks, etc.—Fiction.
2. Absence and presumption of death—Fiction.
3. Women—Psychology—Fiction. I. Title.
PS3573.I5294 A78 2000
813'.6—dc21
00-025205

ISBN-13: 978-0-7432-1232-8

ALMOST STRANGERS

CONTENTS

PART I

ᴀᴛ ꜰᴏʀᴛʏ, Uʀꜱᴜʟᴀ Kᴏʀɴꜰɪᴇʟᴅ Gᴀɴᴛ ʙᴇʟɪᴇᴠᴇꜱ ꜱʜᴇ ɪꜱ independent of the usual pleasures people seek and connections they covet. She lives alone, although there are men who've had, for a while, resident status. She doesn't own a television, rarely sees a movie. At the news kiosk in Harvard Square she hovers, ghostlike, over the racks. She realizes that some people, Daniel, in particular, consider her pretentious. He doesn't say this; he says she's perfect, but he loves her in spite of it, and in fact her only flaw is that she doesn't know one person in *People.* Books are Ursula's passion.

Immersed one night in *The Times Literary Supplement,* Ursula reaches for the ringing phone. "Ursula," a woman's voice says. "This is Delray, the third-floor nurse at Woodside."

Her old yellow Labrador beside her in bed flicks open his eyelids. She wonders if he instinctively feels it, her sense that something that matters to her more than anything else in her whole life is about to change. "Go back to sleep, Brontë," she tells the dog. "You can't go."

The empty highway speeds by almost unseen, her mind having returned to the night her father was "sent in"—that fatal euphemism. The call came on her answering machine, complete and unretractable, moments after Daniel had hurried away. As she was about to leave for the hospital that time, Ursula had lifted the receiver with the idea of paging her departed lover at the airport, before he could slip back to his wife on Central Park South. But at the busy signal she hung up, relieved.

It suits her image, she guesses, to face a crisis alone.

As a child, Ursula had been compliant and secretive in the way of only children in the city, born to older parents. When she was quite small, she started going with her mother to the vault on the fifteenth of the month. The guard knew Mrs. Kornfield; she signed the card, and then he put his key and hers into the steel door and drew out the gray metal box. He set it on the scratched glass. Ursula was allowed into the booth, although never identified. She would climb on the chair and lift out the thick black books. The books had rigid covers that could not be bent but could be taken apart, but never were, by prying up the metal posts that held the pages. The top and bottom boards of the ledgers were lined with patterned paper, fancy scrolls like a grille. The green-tinted pages had thin red lines. Ursula watched her mother enter the names in her level, unbroken script, names she learned to read: John Deere Credit Company and Gulf + Western and Martin Marietta. Each company had its page and the one facing. Ruth wrote the date and the amount in the column marked Dividend. And there was a column for Date Bought. You never sold bonds, Ruth said.

"People get what they deserve" is another thing Ruth said. Ruth was fair and conscientious. She was proud, proud of paying cash, being American, being decent. When Ursula grew older, decency was very important. Decency was not kissing on the first date and not going all the way until you were married. If you did, Ruth said, you would be ruined. *Ruined,* she emphasized, not rotten in the way of a spoiled piece of fruit. But ruined like a sweater that moths had eaten holes in. Ruth gave Ursula a wrapped book the first time she got the "curse." Though she read the book diligently, to this day Ursula admits she isn't sure how chickens get babies. But in the end that hadn't mattered, had it? Only a month after college graduation, Ursula herself was dispatched to marriage like a gull to the wind. And when her marriage to Jay Gant ended, eighteen months later, Ursula's image of herself as needing nobody was confirmed.

So however it had happened, she thinks now, after all she turned out loose and bold. She slept around—which is the way her mother referred to it; and realizing that Ruth would die of shame if she knew, Ursula felt a little pang of triumph, being loose and bold, yet stricken to the heart.

◆

"I'm here about my mother, Ruth Kornfield."

Ruth has been stably weak and demented for two years. Before that, when Ursula's daddy was alive, Ruth had roared toward senility on Prozac, directing her financial advisor to "roll over bonds" she claimed had matured. But when Charlie died without fuss, as he'd lived, all the frenzy seemed to drain out of Ruth; and like a general without a war to fight, she retired from public life. Her recall of words failed first, although a startlingly apt phrase would pop out when least expected. Now, in her eighty-first year, Ruth's white, vigorous hair flies up from her high brow, her quick brown eyes are slightly quizzical, and her cheek, when pressed against Ursula's, comes away creased like antique satin. Enthroned in her wheelchair at Woodside Nursing Home, Ruth wears the beatific and vacant expression of a plaster saint. Seeing Ursula, she'll clasp her hands under her chin in a childlike gesture of delight. For their roles have been reversed, and Ursula, whose dependence on her mother's praise forever sealed her lips against any appeal for it, oddly found a source of strength in Ruth's relentless decline. She's taken over the financial records and knows enough to roll over bonds when they mature, both of them living well enough on unearned income.

Ursula is told to take a seat. She opens the George Eliot biography that arrived that morning but can't concentrate. Nearby, a fat black woman is horsing around with an equally fat and pleasant black man, trading insults and poking. Ursula is reminded that Ruth is—Ruth *used* to be, before she moved to Woodside—critical of fat people and black people, as if being so were an indulgence. Indulgence of any kind is unacceptable to Ruth. But in the nursing home, when they bathed and diapered her, Ruth clung to their fat arms and covered their black faces with kisses. Once again, Ursula gives Eliot a chance. But she can't concentrate. In an open phone booth a scrawny youth with stringy hair and red-rimmed eyeglasses is reporting tearfully that he has brought his lover into the ER. A gurney slaps through the automatically parting doors with the orderly running alongside pumping an inert chest. The doors open again, and a panting woman carries in a large unconscious child, saying he's "gone mental." The next two hours are filled with the nightly hospital drama familiar, Ursula supposes, to TV viewers, but utterly new and absorbing to Ursula Gant, whose only reference point is Fred Wiseman's documentary *Hospital.* Close to midnight the receptionist suddenly shouts, "Ursula! Through the swinging doors. Room twenty-three."

Ruth is connected to a heart monitor; her face is flushed, she's missing her hearing aid and her teeth. Two student nurses chat across Ruth's body about the May wedding one of them plans; they ask Ursula to step outside.

In the hub of the emergency ward, extras mill around a countertop Christmas tree like actors in a green room. They pay no attention to her. At last, a leading-man type, with a stethoscope draped around his neck, separates himself from the bustle.

"What's the matter with my mother?" Ursula asks tensely.

"Her white count's high. I'll probably admit her." He looks uncertain, as if he's ad-libbing; Ursula can tell he lacks experience. The whole production seems to be suffering from the incoherence of an out-of-town tryout.

◆

Broad-spectrum antibiotics do not touch the infection, which lives its own riotous life inside Ruth, spiking her temperature to dangerous numbers. Nurses rotate as unpredictably as apples and oranges in a one-armed bandit. Ruth is packed in ice like a shipped fish. Needles slipping out of her collapsed arm veins are reinstated in her neck, and oxygen flows unseen through tubes in her nose; nourishment enters from a pouch on a pole, and tainted urine drips into a bottle on the floor.

On the other side of the Marimekko print curtain a beaming white-haired woman calls out to Ursula every time she visits, "Tell your daughter hello for me!" Mae's upcoming procedure for uterine cancer is discussed with no apparent loss of good cheer. On Mae's high-mounted television, well-dressed, handsome, successful men and women anguish over their own problems, largely adultery and murder, from what Ursula overhears.

◆

"Do you know you can measure the oxygen in the blood with a meter on the wrist?" Ursula asks Daniel on Friday when he comes for his weekly visit. Daniel shudders visibly at the mention of body fluids. His wife's high-profile illnesses reduce him to panic; at each crisis he clings to Ursula the Indestructible, whispering that Cissy is at death's door. Cissy's broad-bottomed vulnerability feeds Daniel's guilt. Recently he has been going with her to her psychiatrist, to cure her of the mental suffering he is causing her. Ursula decides now to try to squeeze out a little vulnerability, but it's not in her. Early in their relationship, Daniel used to praise her reasonableness and unshakable sanity; he no longer mentions it. His wife is a screamer, a scene maker, a hurler of expensive objects; he'd told Ursula this two years ago, soon after they'd met.

When Ruth surrendered the financial ledgers, Ursula flew to New York to meet Daniel Dorfman, Ruth's financial advisor. In the corporate headquarters, done in chrome and silver-lining gray, she'd been surprised by the lean, young-looking man in a blue striped shirt, initials DMD embroidered on the pocket, necktie rich and modest. At lunch, he came across as boyishly sweet and unoffendingly confident. He didn't smoke or drink. Ursula didn't know what to make of him. He seemed too eager to be liked.

Jay Gant, her first husband, a plastic surgeon and stiff-jawed ringer for Michael Douglas, had managed, even as an impoverished resident, to wear an Armani suit and drive a used red Porsche. And once women's breasts became augmentable, Jay became one of the new breed of West Coast surgeons with incomes like movie stars. He married a sports commentator in the second round and was now on his third wife, the surviving child of a disaster-plagued movie family, maybe DeMille or Goldwyn—Ursula couldn't keep them straight. Recently he asked on the phone (Jay calls once a year, affecting interest in Ursula's *fulfillment;* but Ursula thinks he feels sorry for her), "Did you catch my appearance on Oprah?" When Ursula said no, Jay, with a choke in his actorish voice, replied, "I spoke nationwide about you. I told Oprah, 'My first wife is responsible for my understanding of women.' "

Ursula seduced Daniel Dorfman the day she met him, at his party for clients that night. The idea of having sex with her mother's money manager had excited her, made her feel securely herself, accountable to no one. His penthouse. Silent stars above and glass all around, and his wife's shrill laughter climbing the other end of the winding stair. Ursula knelt in the observatory on what had been identified, moments before, as if it had just flown in the window, as a fourteenth-century Dagestan rug, and unzipped his fly.

But now, with her mother sinking fast, she can't bring herself to say, "Daniel, I'm hurting. I need your help."

Daniel is very focused, which may account for his phenomenal success. He jumps hurdles like a horse wearing blinders, paying no more attention to inconsequentials, such as his wife's suicide threats, than he would to a fly in the ditch. The day after they became lovers, Ursula found a box from Bergdorf's in her hallway. She thought the crepe de chine nightgown in pink tissue paper was ridiculous (the tag said dry clean only), but also romantic. The hunger to please her is huge in Daniel. Why is she so afraid to ask him for what she wants?

That Friday, they squeeze into the hospital elevator among the jolly good sports who visit the sick and dying. In Ruth's room, Daniel, wearing his navy blue topcoat, glowing with vitality and money, positions himself at the foot of the bed. "What are you doing here, Ruth?" he calls over the maze of tubes and the capricious buzzing and clicking of the life-support system. "You look too healthy. Move over and make room for me in that bed!" Ruth lights up, either from excitement or fever.

"She looks terrific," he says when they're circling down the ramp in the parking garage. "Better than last time." Last time was in the parlor at Woodside Nursing Home. All Ursula remembers is leaving after ten minutes, as if they had a taxi waiting with the meter running.

◆

Blood is tested daily. X rays are routine. Ultrasound, a popular variation. Ruth is slid onto a plastic slab like a loaf of bread for baking, and hustled upstairs to radiology by a loose-limbed black man in Nike high-tops. Infectious disease teams are brought in. Pulmonary, geriatric, cardiac. Each new team orders new tests; sometimes the new team redoes the old tests. The chief resident is an intense, frizzy-haired young woman in bridal white, who swoops through like the queen bee with the male drones clustered around her and the same potent air of entitlement.

After three weeks of investigation, overnight there is a switch in management. Same white coats and green scrub suits but new name tags. The internal medicine honcho is a Dr. Jane—and since so many of the doctors are women, Ursula isn't terribly surprised to learn that a male doctor has a woman's name. Meanwhile, Ruth has contracted diarrhea with the Flaubertian title, C. Dificile.

At the end of a month with no diagnosis and no explanation other than a flat temperature for twenty-four hours, the tubes are removed and the teeth and hearing aid reinserted.

On the day of Ruth's discharge, Ursula discovers that she needs her mother alive. She still wants to be loved; she's still hoping for approval. She's afraid that if Ruth dies, she herself will collapse like a puppet with no one holding the strings.

Is Ruth well? Not exactly. But she is only a little more frail, a little more confused, a little less able to function than before she went to the hospital. Ursula believes that in the familiar surroundings of the nursing home, Ruth will improve. Instead, swaddled in silence, she closes her eyes and stops eating. That this downward slide is the beginning of the conclusion does not occur to Ursula.

One day Lucie, the RN, puts her arm around Ursula's waist. "You should get some help for yourself," Lucie says.

"For me? What for?"

"Your mother's deteriorating."

"Deteriorating?" The word stuns Ursula. Slays her! She can see what's happening, so why does she need to be told what it means? Once alerted, however, Ursula begins to make mental preparations, as if she, not Ruth, were soon to leave on a journey from which there'd be no return.

◆

That Friday, she tries out her suffering self on Daniel. He's sitting on the living room sectional, once Ruth's, which Ursula finds almost impossible to look at, with the leaf pattern of the embroidery threatening to reveal the fatal day, the hour. Eyes on the ceiling, Ursula blurts out, "My mother's dying."

"So are you and I," says Daniel gently. "Everybody's dying."

"But she's dying now," Ursula insists.

Daniel stares. At last he comes up with "I'll be satisfied if I make it to Ruth's age."

"I feel alone," Ursula tells him, forcing herself to speak plainly. "I need you."

Daniel assumes he understands; he reaches for her hand. "Come to bed. I'll make you feel better."

◆

Ruth's body swings, curled and boneless as a worm, between the aides' broad arms. Ursula embraces her mother and they sway as if dancing. Propped upright in her wheelchair Ruth's head sags, neckless, to her chest. Her legs hang like sticks; she breathes in huge, chest-raising breaths. Ursula wheels her into the parlor, kneels, and turns up Ruth's hearing aid. "It's me. If you can hear me, give me a sign. Please don't die." Ursula whispers urgently in Ruth's ear, shapely and yawning as a seashell: "I want to tell you I love you. I won't let them hurt you anymore. Please, Ma, speak to me!" For an answer, the tongue lolls to one side of the crooked mouth.

◆

With *A Very Easy Death* resting on her coffee cup, reading by memory, Ursula hears the phone ring. She continues reading: *. . . even when I was holding Maman's hand, I was not with her—I was lying to her. I was making myself an accomplice of that fate which was so misusing her. Yet at the same time in every cell of my body I joined in her refusal, her rebellion: and it was because of that that her defeat overwhelmed me.* Now the machine picks up: Daniel's voice, distant, hurried, says he won't be in town that Friday. He's up to his ass, has to work through the weekend; can't help himself. "See you next week."

Ursula crosses the kitchen and erases him. You will like hell!

Leaving her cup in the sink, she goes up the staircase, Brontë at her heels. Her house is a dark red Victorian, high and narrow, with row houses on either side. The second-floor living room is a shrine, furnished in choice 1950s furniture, inherited when Ruth moved to Woodside. The pricey brocade sectional fits as if made for the space under the bay window. A low table with a slab of marble for a top extends to the middle of the room. There's a Corbusier lounge. Ruth had uncommon taste.

Ursula's books cover three walls in bookcases constructed of unfinished pine. Standing and looking at them now, she decides in a flash what she'll need to survive her mother's death: a book room. She goes upstairs to take inventory, starting in her bedroom.

Books fill two high bookcases, spill across the pillows of the bed and sink into the valleys of the quilt. There are three Lucite shelves of paperbacks in the bathroom and a free-standing rack. Going downstairs again she notices that the newest books were carried from the mailbox and stacked, still wrapped, on Ruth's black walnut dining table or piled underneath. No chair seat is empty. Ursula comes across books in places she hadn't known she kept them. They are angled precariously on stacks in the hall; they spread messily on the sides of the cooking range, leaving free one burner where she heats soup. Opening the cabinet for the bottle of vodka, Ursula sees that books have taken over several shelves. Gray wadding from mailing envelopes has found its way into Ruth's bone-china cups.

◆

There's an air of unreality about Ruth's state. Here is her body, whole and smooth-skinned, fleshed hands with freckles arranged on the counterpane. She doesn't look sick or ravaged, just soundly asleep as if under a spell; but not peaceful, because of the misshapen limbs and strong stink of urine. Everything's falling earthward, sinking, trying to slide under.

On Friday Ursula doesn't feel strong enough to get out of bed, and she decides to stay home. Late afternoon, after the stock market's close, Daniel arrives and puts a dozen yellow roses in a vase on the chest of drawers. He sinks down on the bed, dislodging Bronte. He shuts Dylan Thomas on "Do not go gentle into that good night," and lifts the thin volume off Ursula's chest. He tells her in agonizing detail about the high-tech company he is taking public. She has no idea what he's talking about. He opens the wine, hangs up his Wall Street suit. Gets in.

◆

Now she enters the overheated room at all hours. She keeps vigil from the chair beside the bed. Sometimes she lowers the metal side and climbs in. She kisses the fevered cheek and uncovers her mother. She and Ruth breathe in unison. She drywashes the lightly waved hair, which has grown girlishly long. Ruth's legs turn in at the knees like a nutcracker. Ursula tries to straighten them, as if Ruth were her doll. There are open bedsores on the heels; she smooths lotion on the scaled skin. But Ruth seems damaged beyond repair; she keeps getting smaller and farther away. Ursula has to resist the temptation to fold Ruth in a blanket and carry her home, where she can cure her of dying. Knowing, of course, that Daniel will dissuade her, she calls him at the office on his private line.

Daniel is used to managing crises; a 100-point drop in the market is a challenge. He responds to catastrophe like the ticker tape to a merger, speeding up to take the overload. On the phone he offers medical advice. Impatiently, she cuts him off: "I want you to be with me more." This is a sign of madness, she thinks. An independent woman; from Ruth she has learned never to ask anything from anyone.

There's an awkward pause, both of them speechless for a charged moment. He recovers first, says what's necessary: "Come to New York."

"I can't."

"Why not?"

"My mother might die."

"Yes, she might," he grants. But Ursula's overreacting, carrying on as if Ruth were already dead. It's not normal, he points out. Something's going on that he thinks he understands. Will she listen? he asks. "Maybe I'm wrong," he says, "but hear me out." Ursula sits in stony silence while Daniel keeps talking, unaware of her crawling limbs and her swollen heart clogging her throat. He says that Ursula can't face Ruth's dying because her upbringing was a form of abandonment: she was sent to private schools, sent away to camp, left in the care of maids; the closest they had ever come to intimacy was going to the vault. Her needs were decided on by her mother. Her impulses were denied. "As a result," Daniel says, "you've insulated yourself against intimacy. Getting close to anyone scares the hell out of you; you're afraid of being left. You've developed a carapace of detatchment—"

"Please!" Ursula says, in tears.

"Sorry to be so brutal, darling. I love you. To me your impenetrability is a challenge, a turn-on. I wouldn't have you any other way." Ursula is silent. "Okay, I'm through."

Ursula can't believe what she has just heard; she feels unprotected, alone. Abandoned!

"Think about New York. Any day next week."

From this clue, Ursula guesses that Cissy will be at the fat farm; she goes with her sister. Twice a year she deflates herself like an inner tube somewhere in New Jersey and returns home devilishly seductive. Narrow, sloped shoulders, rounded bottom and wispy neck—shaped like a radish. In person, Ursula has seen Daniel's wife only once, the night she dismissed her as a rival. But she'd taken a good look. Cissy was Giacometti from the waist up, and below she was a Henry Moore cast in bronze. Now Ursula makes no comment, breathes deeply, decides not to be possessive.

It's only ten o'clock in the morning but she goes to bed. Lately she has had trouble staying awake. Her sleep, however, is not restorative. She dreams: That's her, at the door of a New York hotel suite; it's ajar, she pushes it open. Daniel is on the phone, he flashes a cramped smile—like a snowbank. Ursula is unaccustomed to seeing Daniel outside of Cambridge, her territory, where she visualizes him in lion skin. A few times she has visited his corporate lair, where he apparently breathes fire into the economy, making money out of leveraged paper. She feels shocked now by this new Daniel. How has he changed, she wonders, without her noticing, from an unassuming youth with a sweet smile and close-cut ringlets into a capitalist behemoth? Long-haired tufts barbered into voluptuous waves on his neck. Broad chest as impenetrable as a shield and emblazoned with a coat of arms. Stepping closer, Ursula identifies a radically bright tie.

Daniel, on this island, disrobes her before the eye of the television and carries her to the wide bed in another room. He flings her down, kneels above. The phone rings. Daniel jerks back on his heels. "Yes, yes, what is it?" He listens. "Okay, thanks." He hangs up, lifts his pants, cinches the belt—waist still narrow. "Sorry, darling," he says, "but we have to leave. Hurry, now, get dressed." He is pressing her underwear on her still languorous body. In her dream, Ursula begins slowly, ineptly to catch her bra around her waist, turn it around and raise the straps. "Please hurry," Daniel urges.

"Where are we going?"

"I have to get back to my office," he says, lifting her suitcase. "That was my secretary. Cissy's home and she's wild. She's looking for me."

Out in the hallway, Daniel opens the door marked IN CASE OF FIRE. Ursula starts down the metal stairs, shoes clattering. She can hear the phone still ringing. Now Cissy seems to be standing at the top, shrilly screaming down. Daniel climbs back up to reason. Their senseless voices echo like an opera in Italian. The phone continues to ring. Twelve rings. Ursula is counting. When she finally sits up and lifts the receiver to her ear, the soft voice says, "This is Laverne."

In Manhattan, Cecily Dorfman fishes up two Zo-
lofts from the vial on her night table and swallows them dry. She
kicks her French grammar off the bed; her curved red finger-
nail taps POWER on the remote. Donahue is egging on a trio of
women, whose connection, Cissy gathers, is having been raped
by the same psychiatrist. A wise-ass smirk flickers behind Phil's
nosy outrage. Cissy diminishes the volume, her eyes glaze over,
her thoughts roll: Dr. Fastbinder must be ninety and she can't
talk to him about sex. Alix, her body trainer, with whom she
sometimes talks sex—only talks—tells her that her blood pressure's high. At this moment she feels her head filling with
blood, which will inevitably burst a vessel and flood her brain.
She's familiar with Patricia Neal's ordeal. In the in-the-mind
movie, she substitutes Glenn Close for herself, and Daniel becomes Von Bulow. Mimi, her sister, has turned up on *Donahue*.
Legs crossed and skirt hiked to the middle of her thighs, she offers Phil this tearful description: "Cissy doesn't respond and is
unable to move. But her baby-blue eyes show me her brain is
still alive in there. Somewhere."

Later that morning, Cissy lies on a chaise in a patch of sunlight,
between two prickly shrubs in pots. She has plastic eye cups over
her eyes. She can make out a pulsing siren twenty-four stories
below; the weeping and howling of a rescue vehicle; the vulgar
burp of a bullhorn. This, along with the faint background

sound of faraway screaming: people having fun, she supposes. Cissy gets on her knees and peeps over the parapet that encloses the terrace. There's no movement that she can see. But there is no stillness, either. A muted uproar seems to agitate the air, as if all of the people in the city were being crushed, and their sounds were then fused technologically into one lingering cry for help, piped through giant speakers. An identifying signal. Meant for whom? How should she know? Cissy thinks, while touching the tips of her fingers to the pulse in her neck. Madly irregular. Flat on her back, she begins practicing relaxation response, starting with her feet. But she never gets farther than her buttocks; she's distracted by waves of air drifting over the parapet, threatening to wrap up the building like one of those cocoon sculptures. When Cissy stands up, she feels the force pouring through the hazy sky, inching her toward the parapet; she glances down. The park looks supernaturally green, moss-thick and tangled as rot weed.

A jungle, she thinks, pulling on the knob of the glass door to the bedroom. It fights her; maybe she's locked herself out; she'll miss class this afternoon. She looks around. On the roof above is an awning of TV antennas like umbrella spines. The couple below, both psychiatrists, have a David Smith sculpture that, Cissy thinks, however impressive, is too large for the space. Now the door suddenly gives, the knob jerked out of her hand. Cissy spills into the bedroom. Quiet, but for the howling hush of air, and something else. What now?

The buzzer, she realizes. Fuck it, she's not expecting anybody. Coming back to the bedroom from the kitchenette a few minutes later, she realizes that whoever it is, is determined. Could be Daniel's come home for a quickie, but that hasn't happened in years. And why wouldn't he use his key? Cissy has trouble balancing as she steps into her mules trimmed with pink feathers. She crosses the living room, pulling out curlers. Her yellow hair twists down to her shoulders, gossamer, almost white. In her satin nightgown, filled to bursting with her very fair skin, she floats across the pale carpet and presses the TALK button with the middle finger of the hand holding the glass of Chardonnay.

"Whoisit?" Cissy murmurs into the grille.

"Me. Mimi. I'm downstairs."

"Lordy, I thought you went on home."

"I did, but I came soon's I got your message. You goin' to let me in?"

"Come on right up," Cissy says into the intercom, her voice silkening, for all at once she is transported to the sleeping porch in Tennessee, whispering between the cots. She props open the door to the hall with a slipper, and hobbles, one foot, one slipper, into the bedroom.

Coming in, Mimi closes the door and puts down the slipper and her carry-on; the bag has SMOKING GRAPEVINE painted on the side in phosphorescence, and a likeness of five vested, bare-chested musicians. Mimi is younger than her sister, solid and fleshy with a pretty face that just misses being beautiful. She's heavily made up and wears a red jacket with big shoulders; about an inch of skirt shows below the jacket, and a lot of sheer leg on very high heels. She opens her arms as Cissy trots in.

Gripping Mimi's shoulder, Cissy steps into her slipper. "Follow me," she says. Then she winds unsteadily ahead of Mimi on the spiral staircase to the observatory. At the top, bathed in light, the brilliant sky spread around and above, she throws up an arm to shield her face and taps a button with her foot. A blind slides over the east window.

Planting herself solid as a brick outhouse in the middle of the extremely pricey carpet, Mimi asks, "What's up?"

Before answering, Cissy circles the room drawing close her pink robe. It's made of a satiny material that clings like new skin. The collar of pink blowing strings stirs; she seems, with her flying tendrils, about to launch. Across the room she turns and says, "Daniel's cheating!"

"You think it's the first time?"

"Not necessarily. But this time I've caught him." Cissy walks quickly toward Mimi. Minced steps, the beauty queen's hip-thrusting walk, one foot coming down precisely in front of the other. All that motion sends the squiggly filaments dancing. "He didn't come home last night."

"Could be somethin's happened to him."

When Cissy stands still, it takes a few seconds for the chicken feathers to settle. "Nothing happens to Daniel that he hasn't planned."

Hoisting her skirt higher, Mimi sits down on the sofa—it's purple and shaped vaguely like a baby grand. She fishes around in the dish on the low, laminated table and helps herself to a Godiva truffle. "Did y'all see if he showed up at work?" Mimi chews, looking thoughtfully at Cissy, appreciating the twist of the silkiness on Cissy's full, soft hips. Like sculpted drapery.

"I called the Boston bitch's number."

"Holy shit!"

"Nobody answers."

After a silence, Mimi asks, "Where'd you git it?"

Reaching down, Cissy yanks up the chocolates as Mimi's hand hovers. "Detective," she says, looking at Mimi. "I'm having them followed."

"What're you plannin' to do?" Mimi asks after a minute.

With sudden violence, Cissy hurls the candy dish; it strikes the window wall. Neither the glass dish nor two thicknesses of Thermopane break, but the truffles scatter. "I'm not sure," Cissy tells Mimi. "Maybe I'll kill her!"

"Why don't you just walk?"

"I can't; you know I can't."

"Why'n hell not?"

"You know why in hell not." She sinks to the floor, her chin on Mimi's knees. "I'm scared."

Mimi says, "Tell your kid sister what you're scared of."

Cissy whispers something.

"Huh?"

Cissy gulps. "Of loosin' my looks."

Mimi frowns.

"Ah can't help it," Cissy says sullenly. "That's just me." She raises her face, instantaneously wet-eyed, and realizes by Mim's expression—reverent, the way it was when Mim was little—that she's got her in thrall. "In high school, I slept with the first boy that said I love you. 'Member Rickie? After the junior prom," Cissy tells her sister, "we drove to the lake and parked his daddy's car. The night was still, the sand was silky under my bare feet. He kissed me and the top of my dress jess slipped off my shoulders and down past my waist." Cissy shivers, recalling the coolness of the moonlight on her hot breasts. She's recalling the two shimmering pearls in Ricky's black eyes as he came closer. Now, with a feeling close to disbelief, Cissy says, "Ah saw how powerful my beauty was. That night I knew I could have anything in the world I wanted."

"I love it!" hoots Mimi, a raucous sound like a crow.

"It was like being run over by a bus when he married someone else," Cissy declares, standing. Kicking off her slippers, she wades over to the bar. With the wineglass held a distance from her body, she crouches, her back to the sofa, and lowers herself. Spinning carefully, she swings her knees up. "And what I wanted next was Daniel Dorfman! Ah can't start lookin' for a new guy, Ah'm too old," she decides.

"You're not! And you're gorgeous besides."

"I was—not anymore. I'm nearly fifty." Cissy rolls her head side to side, feeling foggy and desperate. "Sometimes I think about leaving him, but each day that passes, the idea of being on my own seems crazier."

WOODSIDE NURSING HOME IS STILL AS DEATH. BLACK skins shine from white uniforms, but they don't approach Ursula, those two women conspiring behind the nurses' station. Their soft brown eyes touch her as she goes by like a prowler. Their silence is a dead giveaway.

As Ursula passes the sitting room that she has passed countless times, the phrase comes to her: last time ever. She glances in at the unchanging figures. The gaunt man in a wheelchair with a pole that has a bottle hanging. The woman on the couch, calling, "Help me, help me." Another who, without surcease, jerks all her limbs at once.

Ruth's roommate is over a hundred years old. Essie sits everlastingly guarding the entrance to the room. Her filmy eyes escort Ursula toward Ruth's bed. Ursula at first feels enormous relief: Ruth looks the same as always, eyes closed, lips vacantly apart as if for breath. Then the aide, Anita, says, "She's gone."

Ursula feels the life leave her body. Her brain cannot process what she already knew; her blood releases no oxygen; she ceases to think.

"Ruth!" Anita's voice penetrates the silence. She speaks almost chidingly, the way they do to the aged. "Close your mouth; your daughter here to see you." The black hand cups the jaw and clamps the lips firmly together. "She don't want to see you like that," Anita scolds as she rearranges the expression on the face. "She come to say good-bye." To Ursula, Anita says, "Sometime if they want to see you real bad before they go, they open their eyes." For an instant she can't be sure of, Ursula believes that Ruth's eyes do open, barely. She turns to the roommate, and this venerable witness nods. Ursula falls forward on the high bed, her head on Ruth's breasts.

"Mommy, Mommy, Mommy."

◆

Some days after the funeral—she can't seem to remember it; she thinks Lucie was there, and Daniel stood beside her—Ursula fights an absurd impulse to drive out to the cemetery and bring Ruth home, the way Ruth had conscientiously driven to the Catskills at the end of every camp season, although Ursula was always sure she'd be forgotten there. She turns off the ringer on the phone; she no longer has to worry about receiving the bad news. Sitting up in bed, she turns on the lamp and picks up the George Eliot, begins in the middle and reads through the night. But she can't concentrate, she can't even cry; she feels drained by the weight of her grief. Toward dawn, she lets the whimpering Brontë out; he does his business quickly on the untended front lawn. Coming upstairs, Ursula drags the coffee table out of the living room, scoring the pine floor.

The idea for the book room had formed itself, whole, during the night. What she needs to survive is not a room with books in it, but *a room built of books*. She begins building at once. She arranges the pony-skin chaise lounge in the center of the living room, with the floor lamp beside it and the extension wire trailing to the outlet. At random, she plucks an armful of books from one of the bookcases, starts laying them flat in a wide arc, spines facing in. The books she'll want first must be held aside so that they'll be at the top of the wall. When she finishes a book, she plans (as she slides around on her knees) to set it on the inside of the existing wall, and the next beside it, following the wall's outline. Thus, a new, smaller book room will be constructing itself inside the original room. Of course she'll want an opening: a propylaeum, Ursula mouths silently, thinking of Mycenaean palaces. When the inner wall is as high as her head, she will reach the outer wall of books (then very low) by going through the magnificent gate. And food and exercise. And walking Brontë.

Bending and straightening, Ursula scoops and sorts, aligning the books without consulting their titles, like a blind woman knowing by their thickness and heft, the feel of the spine what is written inside. Whole scenes come vividly to mind as she handles the outer boards. Word for word, she can hear them, see them; they affect her viscerally. She works in silence, in a near trance: Classics. Victorians. Feminists. Modernists. *"Duty! Duty!" The declamation of the councilor at the agricultural fair drifts through the open window, mingling with Rudolph's smooth-tongued, "Ah, but there are two moralities."* The galloping horses and Emma's shudder at the sight of the blind man rolling his greenish eyes and sticking out his tongue as she speeds from her assignation with Leon. Edna Pontellier in her voluminous matron's skirts wading to her death. Living scenes, more real to Ursula than her life; so it seems, as she crawls through the haze of dust among the scattered columns.

The books mount but Ursula is beginning to despair. The round wall is already knee high but she dismantles it. Using an orange marker she draws a larger circle around the perimeter of the floor. Then in fervid silence, a thermos of coffee her only distraction—sipped hot and black from the lip—she works until she can no longer stay awake. It isn't for days—maybe a week—that she remembers to listen to her answering machine. Beep-to-beep messages from Daniel. He wants to see her, he's worried; what's going on? Secluding herself is not healthy, at least let's talk. I love you, on and on.

The first day of May, Ursula looks in the bathroom mirror and sees the mother of her lonely childhood. She draws her hair back from her high forehead to reveal Ruth's widow's-peak hairline, glints of gray at the dark roots. Tears well but don't fall, making her eyes glassy like Ruth's. What is the day, the date or the hour? she wonders—her watch is gone from her wrist. How long ago was the funeral? She doesn't know; she's living in an altered world; she has no idea. Now she hears the doorbell. *Bing bing bing.* The bell chimes while Ursula stands at the sink, horrified, staring at Ruth's bloodless face. The mouth has opened again.

Going at last to the bottom of the steps, she cautiously pulls aside the curtain on the little window. For a moment she doesn't recognize him, the man on her front porch. "Open up!" he yells, and she slides the bolt. He seems to come crashing into the small vestibule, filling the air with the fresh male smell of his cologne. His scent is pleasurable to Ursula, it raises longing in her flesh. Seeing him, she feels relief, gratitude. "Goodness! What are you doing here?"

"It's Friday. Don't you listen to your machine?" Daniel is looking at her, thin-lipped, as if she were a stranger.

"It's Friday?" Trying to reorient herself, Ursula starts to climb the steps, conscious of Daniel's breathing, testing bulk behind her.

"Are you sorry I came?"

"Of course not!"

"Have you missed me?"

"Terribly." How has she now, she wonders, in this new life for her, slipped into the same rut of conversation? Shouldn't there be new words? Isn't she a new person by virtue of her mother-lessness? Shouldn't she now change her vocabulary, her very thought processes? At the top of the steps, Daniel spins her around and folds her body into his as if he intends to paste her shape on. His tongue wets her mouth inside. He pulls her hand down to his swollen, unyielding penis. "Feel this."

Ursula feels acutely separate and distinct.

Glancing into the living room as he passes, Daniel exclaims, "Good God! What's happened?"

"I'm cataloging my books," Ursula responds easily, from somewhere miles away in a new dimension. "I thought it would be a good project to keep my mind occupied."

"What's that supposed to be?"

"A grave circle."

Daniel shivers.

In bed, Ursula tries to inhabit the woman's body that had made her feel pleasure before; but deeper, graver images—the purity of Ruth's last face, a flowering, almost, enclosed in a wimple, and in its center the nunlike death mask—have come between her and her sensations. She hopes that Daniel doesn't sense her preoccupation, but he must, for when he leaves he advises her, "Ursula, try to snap out of it. Ruth lived a long and healthy life until the last couple of months. You were a good daughter to her and she knew that. What more do you want?"

She kisses him, feeling the first real tenderness. "Nothing. I just feel sad."

"That's natural, it'll pass."

"I know. Thanks, Daniel."

As soon as he is gone she reaches for the book next needed, stacking it on the miraculously balancing wall. All around her now there is a circle of books waist high. Building without mortar, Ursula imagines the books bonding by the cohesiveness of thoughts, as if the characters could magically sense the surrounding presences of like characters, and hands reaching out, holding each, cover to cover. Ursula, like a good host at her own party, has only to stand back and watch the assembled crowd being drawn to companions, lovers and friends.

When the book room has risen around her as high as her upstretched arm, Ursula lies down, exhausted, on the chaise. She can remember as a child dropping off to sleep hearing the murmuring voices of her mother and father, and she has that feeling now, of being safe among half-heard words.

More time passes. Daniel is becoming impatient; she talks vaguely to him of being emptied. Across this emptiness, she says, she cannot come to him. He speaks another language, he worships other gods. From the shore of the living, he speaks FAX. He offers the palliative of sex.

"I can't," she says.

"Why?"

"I'm dry inside. It hurts me to make love."

Days, Ursula hurries preoccupied along the sun-dappled, red-brick streets. She goes to the Square, to Sage's or the post office. Nights, Ursula reads. Under the cold light entering from high up, she imagines the intangible thread of her sanity clinging to fiction like a spider to its web. On a low, three-legged stool painted black she has put a framed photograph of Ruth; in this pit of books the picture gleams with relentless intensity, drawing air like a candle flame. Ruth must have been in her late sixties when it was taken; dilated blood vessels riddle the cheeks, rounded by a slight smile. For Ursula the picture defines Ruth's inviolability and austerity the way a single leaf on a tree is the tracing of all others. The aristocratic, slightly aquiline nose, a vertical crease above the bridge; high forehead; mischievous eyes. An almost feline quality, thinks Ursula. A definitive face, only a scant trace of femininity. Density in the Russian-Jewish bones. Yet it is an elusive face. For as many minutes at a time that she stares at it, she can never to her satisfaction pin down Ruth's expression. Ruth's attention seems elsewhere.

Picking up the picture Ursula presses her lips to the glass. How can she connect the powerful mother she remembers to the frail, old woman who went so unprotestingly to the grave? Reveal yourself, she silently pleads, moving Ruth's face to catch the light, wanting to see through the eyes into the dead woman's heart.

Just at that moment a volume plunges from the topmost row of books. It thuds to the chaise between Ursula's legs. Ursula lifts it and glances inattentively at the title, her mother's face still burnt into her eyes. Then, mystified, she looks up. Above her head she imagines she sees something filling the pale, glowing opening. A solid, black shape, descending flat out like a huge bat, outstretched wings brushing the books as it wafts slowly down. Ursula sits bolt upright. Brontë hasn't moved; she briefly meets his unsurprised gaze, then looks up again. Yellow eyes stare without blinking from a waxlike face. The feathery breast swells. Foul air, the terrible stench of rotting flesh sweeps over Ursula; and with each powerful burst of the bird's exhaled breath, Ursula is reminded of the C. Dificile, the smell of feces that came from Ruth's hospital bed.

She realizes she's hallucinating, but it hardly matters: She's terrified. She springs to her feet and gets a grip on the bird's body, squeezing with all her might. There's a sound of cracking but her arms remain empty! She's gone crazy, she thinks; she hopes it's a nightmare. Wake up! she has time to think. Then they grapple, she and the bird, until the thing slips free and, wheeling about, flies as if blind, swiping Ursula with its heavy wing and knocking her to the floor. Grabbing for the photograph of Ruth, Ursula hurls it. Wounded, possibly, or dazed, the thing sits back on its haunches like a griffin, monstrous wings pressed to its sides. After a little hesitation it shivers once violently, then collapses.

On the floor of the book room she seems to see a hawk or raven, some iridescent, greenish-black fowl. One wing is bent, but the other flutters weakly. The bird's chicken-bone legs appear useless, twisted unnaturally as if they've atrophied. Brontë's head is still down between his paws; he's watching Ursula quizzically. He doesn't see any bird, only she can see it; she's lost her mind, she tells herself. Just the same, she crouches, holding her breath, and puts her hand on the bird's chest. There is a scant beat. One eye opens a crack. Ursula rears back but is instantly overcome by another emotion, an emotion she had once felt when a bird flew into her windowpane with an awful smack, then slid to the ground in her yard. She had wanted to go outside and save the bird, but she couldn't because she was afraid to touch it; it seemed so tainted with death. Ursula had waited, watching from her high window. And in a little while, with no help from her, the bird shook its wings and flew away. Now Ursula's brain reels with total perception of Ruth's helpless terror as she lay in the hospital bed being mauled by so many hands. And Ursula had allowed it, insisted upon it. She had spared Ruth no indignity. Until the end, when judging Ruth irreparable, she had capitulated with death. *She had let her mother die.*

On her knees, Ursula slips both arms around the bird's middle and begins to inch the heavy thing along the floor toward the opening in the wall of books. The bird does not resist her embrace; as if to help, it awkwardly folds its wings around her hips. She thinks that if she can get it outside where there is more air, it will regain its strength and fly away.

But the doorway is too small and the body will not fit; instead it stiffens and stops breathing. Frantically Ursula stuffs the tail feathers into the space first, and pushes. Halfway through there is a shriek of pain. Ursula grabs the beak, forcing it shut. She is not prepared for the sudden, wild rearing of wings; the feathered sides pull free and begin to wave and jerk and beat against the books. From under the body one bent leg shoots out. Ursula, not quick enough, is caught around the ankle. Looking down she sees not her foot, but an odd growth like a forked three-toed claw, clinging to her leg. Desperately she tries to pull off the clinging bluish talons. The bird twists its head completely around on its neckless shoulders. Its pleading eyes stare at Ursula. As it starts to drag itself backward through the opening, the books begin to fall.

TWICE A WEEK CISSY DORFMAN GOES UPTOWN TO Columbia for Intermediate French. Before French, Cissy studied decoupage but the fumes made her spacy. This year's section is taught by a twenty-six-year-old instructor who comes in late, in shorts, and puts her feet in running shoes on the seminar table. The other students, young enough to be Cissy's children, dump on everyone, particularly their mothers.

After class that day, Cissy is standing inside the graffiti-sprayed bus shed on Broadway, when her teacher runs past, into rush-hour traffic, breastless in a pink sleeveless tank top. Then a black car blocks Cissy's view. The limo sent for her has paused at the curb, and the driver hops out and holds the door. Cissy doesn't get in.

One block south, she enters the subway. Descending vertically into the underworld below Manhattan, Cissy feels like Alice falling down the rabbit hole. How curious everything is! On the train platform a giant comes toward her, black muscles glistening, a throbbing black box supported on his shoulder by his splayed pink palm. Solid-faced and pearly eyed, he looms in Cissy's path. The last moment he skims by; she turns in a circle, unable to stop looking. In his wake there's a strange, earthy smell like a battleground, thinks Cissy. Women grotesques carrying shopping bags lean against the posts, their billowing buttocks nodding in blue jeans; unshaven men lie half under newspapers. Untended children lean over the tracks. Where do these people go when they get above ground? Cissy wonders. They're not the same as the brown girls who wait in the hall to clean until she and Daniel leave the apartment.

The knot of bodies is rammed through the train opening, and immediately Cissy is thrown off her feet. She falls on a solid bulk; it shoves her away, jealous of its space. Gripping a strap against the violent sway, Cissy murmurs, "Sorry." Her white arms and legs make her feel nude. But apparently she's transparent, and they look right through her as if she were disembodied. Along the sides of the moving train, people sit like painted statues in lifelike poses. On the plastic bench a young black woman has a white, life-sized mannequin of a real child on her lap. Its limbs are bent, the jointed arms flexed around the woman's neck; its blond wig rests against her dark hair. No one but Cissy seems to have noticed this incongruity. Cissy tries not to stare, but the woman looks up. Cissy quickly raises her blue eyes to the lurid graffiti on the walls, curving around her like the circling levels of art at the Guggenheim.

Coming up from the subway, the false end-of-the-day brightness on Central Park South assaults her.

◆

Ursula floats up to consciousness, forces her eyes to open. She sees a veiled moon in the living room window, almost obscured by a halo of dim light. She tries to get up. There's a mountain of books lying across her, reaching almost to the tear drops of Ruth's chandelier. Books on her legs, and spilled over her stomach and chest; crushing her, she thinks. She frees her arms and begins to toss the volumes, some torn, to the sides. She feels no pain, only numbness and shock; a little faint. But no pain; she thinks she's all right. After working awhile she blots her forehead with her forearm. The arm comes away bloody. It's not sweat. She's injured, she realizes. A lot of blood seems to be running from below one eye and in rivulets from her scalp, seemingly unstemmable blood. She jams her nightgown against it, keeping pressure on it, feeling around it gingerly. Her hair is all sticky. As Ursula continues to shove the books off her body with one hand, she's thinking of Forster's Leonard Bast, and the books he had wanted to digest killing him. She supposes she's lucky.

It occurs to her now that the house is too still. "Brontë!" Ursula shouts. There is no click of tapping nails or chains ringing, so she gets up on one elbow and begins frantically to burrow through the rubble. Finally, with a vicious kick she loosens the whole pile. The books scatter and the pine floor rumbles with a noise like tenpins crashing. Ursula looks around, her mouth dry, her heart beating fast. Not a feather; she has unsealed no predatory bird. All she has unsealed is a faint rancid odor that reminds her of Ruth's ebbing. Toward the end the musty, sod smell of an unearthed urn had attached itself to the dying woman's bare, clean skin.

Then she sees it, the body of her dog. Brontë lies on his side, at first sight, undamaged, but rib cage unstirring, muzzle bared and a deep, open wound between the stop and the skull. His head is crushed in, the yellow occiput covered with blood. The eye facing up is glassy. Unable to bear looking at him, Ursula falls upon the lifeless form. She weeps the way she had not been able to for Ruth. After a while she stands up, still unable to sort out whatever happened during the night. Hardly aware of what she's doing, she pulls a sheet off her bed and folds her dog into it. She slides the heavy body across the floor, leaving a smear of blood, to the top of the stairs. Gently, the shroud slips down. She bumps him over the threshold, bracing the door against her back. On the street a steady drizzle streaks the dark sky. As

Ursula drags Bronte around back and across the muddy yard, a part of her marvels at how well she seems to be managing in this crisis. At the same time three thoughts come into her mind: She's aware that it's too much for her, that this second loss is the end of something, that she is probably crazy.

In the backyard Ursula pitches her strength against the rain-sodden bulkhead doors to the cellar, and folds back the doors. She's functioning now in an orderly, sane way; that's reassuring. She carries up the coal shovel and starts to dig. Then just when she doesn't expect them, tears start to fall; plentiful and sound-less, they mix with rain. That's normal, she tells herself. She is behaving appropriately, calmly and rationally. She's very brave, she thinks. She doesn't feel anything as she digs in the yard be-hind the house with shocked, insensate determination, with blood all over her nightgown and on the raincoat she'd thrown over it. Impatiently, Ursula throws aside the shovel and hacks at the wet spring earth with her hands, clawing up rocks and con-scious of her sorrowing heart only as a distant throbbing thing of no account.

When she can do no more, she lies down on her stomach and rests her head on the body—in size it seems as big as Ruth's. But Brontë is still bleeding, his life's blood emptying. Blood comes from his muzzle, his nostrils, his ear, coloring the rain-soaked sheet—and suddenly, in a curious turn, flooding memory:

Do you like them? Daniel asked.

His eyes, shining with pleasure, had been on the little box he'd put on the table. The diamond earrings twinkled on a plush blue ground. They're beautiful, she said, but they're not me. He smiled and said that maybe they were somebody she would become. But she snapped the box shut and put it in his palm.

Know what I'd like?

Brontë was a trembling ball clinging to his mother's tit. Runt of the litter, the breeder apologized, all that's left. But a famous sire, the stud is what counts. The woman swung the pup up by its ears and dropped him in Ursula's waiting hands.

Daniel said, Happy Birthday, darling.

In the first light of a new day, Ursula bundles up the limp body in the bloodied shroud and nudges it into its grave. She begins to shovel. No descending coffin, no rolled-up turf, no cantorial singing. Just a shallow hole and a mound of mud, unmarked and almost obscured.

Rain is falling in heavy, cold drops. From Cambridge Street comes the swish of morning traffic. As Ursula is approaching the porch steps, she hears the thump, feels the jar of the folded *New York Times*. Looking around, she meets the startled face of the paper boy. He gapes at her bare feet, stained raincoat. "John," she says, "would you give me a hand, please? I'm hurt."

There's a moment's pause, but he lays down his bicycle, shrugs off his sack and helps Ursula to her car in the driveway.

The pink neon sign on Cambridge Street flashes: WALK-IN CLINIC. NO WAIT. The doctor wears a grayish lab coat of some synthetic fabric that looks unfresh, and a bow tie. He is old; he seems on duty alone, like a battle-fatigued soldier awaiting word of discharge. As his hands swab the blood, they shake. "Nasty gash," he drones. His cigarette breaths flicker over Ursula's face. "You'll be all right. Head wounds bleed a lot."

No history is taken. Just his fleeting, hurried touch, the thin pale freckled hands. What can he be thinking? Ursula wonders. That she's been beaten by a man? Battered woman, bruised, bloodied—the usual, none of his business. He avoids looking at the stained raincoat. His red, watery eyes seem to identify: another solitary drinker, one more fall. "I'll have to suture the eye," he tells her. "Come back in a week to have the stitches removed. You may have a scar." Ursula pays him: cash, the fifty-five dollars in her raincoat pocket.

Before Ursula mounts the steps at home, she slips the raincoat off her shoulders. She stuffs the bloodied Burberry in the crawl space under the porch. From the porch she looks both ways down the empty street. Hastily lifting her nightgown over her head, she leans over the railing and flings it behind the lattice with the coat. Naked, she limps into the house.

Upstairs, Ursula stands in front of the bathroom mirror and swallows the antibiotic the doctor gave her. One eye is already turning lurid purple, the skin below gathered by a neat row of stitches into a single railroad track with cross ties. The upper lid has swollen grotesquely. She looks Cyclopean, thinks Ursula. Her nose is puffed, covering half of everything she sees; and her dark hair, loosened from its knot, spills almost wantonly over her shoulders.

"It's not rational, how you're acting," Daniel says later on the phone. "I must have called twenty times. What's going on there?"

His insistence, his passion, his need to know offend Ursula. Like a poked snail, she retreats inside her shell of silence. She likes being in there alone; it feels safe.

"What have you been doing?" Daniel intrudes.

"Sleeping. I had the ring off."

"I don't like the way you sound. Are you all right?"

Ursula looks down the length of her body. She places the receiver on the bed and sits up slowly, testing her bones. Into the phone she says, "I'm all right. Is today Friday?"

"It's Monday. I'm sorry I couldn't make Friday. I'm calling from my club," Daniel is saying, saying because he assumes Ursula's wish to know, insatiable hunger to know that he is not at home. "Just came off the court. Won in three straight sets. I'll tell you about it when I see you." Ursula's face has screwed up with the effort of keeping her anguish inside. She covers the receiver with her hand, whispers, "Brontë." After a few beats of silence, Daniel says, "I'll grab the four-thirty shuttle and see you in a couple of hours."

Some part of Ursula, functioning like a stopped clock that will tick a few times if you vigorously shake it, senses that he won't need much dissuading. One more phone call. The posh wife summoned for cocktails and dinner. Daniel adds, "If you don't want me to come, say so."

"I don't," Ursula murmurs. Blood rushes to her face. What has she said? What is she doing? Has she totally lost her mind? Pressing the receiver against her breasts as if to suffocate its appalling message, her eyes smart with self-pity for what she is about to suffer. At last she lifts the receiver, thinking he must have hung up. "We don't have to have sex," Daniel's voice says. "I don't think you should be alone."

Alone. That does it. She hangs up.

The phone rings again right away, but Ursula doesn't answer. No reason to. It's over. She's decided. Life seems purely uncomplicated now. Yes, the thought tests itself, Daniel is as remote and part of the past as Ruth. As Brontë. Relieved of him, Ursula feels entirely freed. She had been bound to Daniel, she senses, by the entries in Ruth's ledgers, which she, Ursula, understood to be the universal law. Ruth had approved of Daniel, she'd given them her blessing. Ruth must have believed—hadn't Ruth's old-fashioned ideas forced her to believe? hadn't Ursula allowed her to believe?—that Daniel would one day divorce his wife and marry Ursula. But with Ruth dead there is no more need for deception. Ursula recognizes that she's lost more of herself than she ever thought possible, and that there is no way now she can sink any deeper into grief. Her heart, like a dredged pond, has reached the point of refusal.

Under the hot pouring water, she washes the blood and dirt of the grave down the drain, leaving her body clean and her mind oddly untroubled. With all obligations stripped away, she feels undividedly herself, alone and unreachable. When she comes out of the shower, she squints sidelong at her face in the mirror, as Ruth used to, judging. Her awful bulging eye is slitted like the hawk's elongated eye in moonlight. Tentatively she touches the yellow, puckered skin under the eye, feels no pain, no regret. Decides she will wear the scar, if there is one, proudly, as a remembrance of relinquished ties.

This, then, was the thought that had been waiting to emerge. At last it had floated up to the surface, complete, where it was perfectly visible.

That afternoon she's parked across the street from Woodside, motor running. Some of the residents have been put like mildewed clothing on the upper porch, to air in chalky sunlight. So many rags draped on webbed chairs. Lined up, Ursula thinks of them, like sitting ducks in death's viewfinder. Here now comes Essie's middle-aged grandson, crossing the parking lot carrying a freesia plant. Next the well-dressed husband of the shaking woman arrives, suffering her illness with dignity: until death do us part.

Putting the car in gear, Ursula realizes she will never again go to Woodside; thinking this, sorrow files like an arrow into her heart.

On the highway cars crawl like a funeral procession, drifting out of the city. She remembers the long-ago Sundays, going to Laurelton to visit her parents' friends Billie and Irv. Ursula sang pop-ular songs in the backseat; she must have been ten or twelve. Charlie would crank down the windows when they got off the Belt Parkway. Pipe down, honey, he'd say. He'd say he wanted to hear Irv's grand opera records. Ruth would tell him, shush; she never did know a joke when she heard one. Billie, Irv's wife, was a big-boned blonde from the West; she could rest her chin on Ruth's head. Ursula was fascinated by the way Billie's voice struck the consonants plainly and hard like a hammer, giving every-thing she said authenticity. Their son, Ronald, made balsa-wood airplane models that dangled from the attic ceiling. Ronnie, lit-tle, runty Ronnie—he could stand without stooping under the roof beams—suddenly shot a foot taller than Ursula and grew god-beautiful. Her heart still strains over the unutterable love she felt for Ronnie when they were fourteen. Once when she was in high school, Ursula had seen the shape of his small blond head in the light of the dashboard, and held his soft-skinned, swelling penis. Irv and Billie, Ursula muses now, like a popular song: dead. Ronnie died too, she heard from his sister, several years ago of throat cancer.

Leaving her car outside the gate of Memorial Park, she climbs the paved paths between groomed lawns. There are no grave-stones; a bronze plaque beside Charlie's would mark Ruth's grave. Ursula picks up a map in the office, but she doesn't think she'll need it. She senses Ruth's restless, powerful presence draw-ing her closer. However, when she gets there, the bronze marker bears a stranger's name; no sign of Charlie, either, and the grass grows thick and undisturbed. Ursula feels panicky; for an hour or more she wanders in the hot sun, the lines on the map squirm-ing, going from marker to marker, trying another hill and an-other. Oh, God, she cries, they have moved her! Turning round and round, Ursula screams, "Where have they put you, Ruth?"

Can't take any more today, it comes to her suddenly. Too big a knot in her throat. Can't breathe: obstruction. Still, she dreads going home, seeing Brontë's plastic bowl next to the refrigerator, hairs on the mat at the end of the hall.

◆

Squinting in the late streaming sun, Ursula sits against a tree on the riverbank in Cambridge, sparse grass and roots under her outstretched legs. Passing bodies blur, feet tamp the dusty earth, fragments of music fly behind runners like bits of colored ribbon. After a while, Ursula turns onto her stomach and lies down with her ear against the ground's hardness, listening; envisioning the buried dead bound to the living by a network of roots, little tubes passing out their ears and nostrils. The inside of Ruth is hollowed out, she forces herself to think. All of the memories of Ruth's life are gone. Behind Ursula's burning eyes, hot tears spring.

Before night falls her phone has been disconnected, the bills paid, refrigerator emptied. Methodically, Ursula strips her bed, latches the windows, pulls down the shades but leaves some lights on to discourage prowlers. She leaves her car in the driveway. And that same night she is eating half a submarine sandwich at the counter in an Inman Square deli. Her carry-on balanced on the next stool is stuffed with a pair of baggy chinos and two no-iron shirts. There is a change of underwear, toiletries. And eleven books in her backpack—*Tess*, Brontë's *Jane Eyre*, Atwood's *Bodily Harm*, Virginia Woolf's *To the Lighthouse* and *Jacob's Room*, *Women in Love*, *Herzog*, a Lessing and the new Updike, plus two slim volumes of poems, Sexton and Hardy. She'd wanted to take them all, but the others had to stay. Instinct had told her to make a complete break. Grimly, she ticks off her losses: Ruth's gone, Daddy's gone, Brontë is gone, Jay's gone, and Daniel, he's gone too. How many parts of yourself can you lose—she is turning the question over and over in her fuddled mind—and still be yourself?

Strangely, what rouses the most remorse in Ursula now is the image of Daniel's baffled, inconsolable face: Women didn't leave Daniel; he left them. She looks around, almost expecting to see him; they'd sometimes had coffee in the corner booth.

It's nothing you did, she'd explain, sitting across the table. Running away when things blow apart is what *I* do, she'd assure Daniel. I've done it before, don't you remember? she'd say to Daniel, self-critically, if he were here now. First, her role of doctor's wife had come to an end; she was not made for that, and Jay made it clear he had big plans. So with her mother's disapprobation echoing, Ursula had fled. She took a giant leap, as if tethered by a bungee cord, that dropped her like a refugee in London, where for six months she had carried a student visa, a bank statement, proof of divorce and a letter of acceptance to King's College, Waterloo Road; and then, like a teenager, she fell desperately and totally inappropriately in love. He was an actor. One week later she had married Tony Doyle, a tall Welshman with an undernourished body and a white thatch on his forehead like a horse's mane. She had never mentioned this to Daniel; what was the point? Daniel didn't know how vulnerable she was, how much she had been hurt. Ursula had bummed around the UK with Tony for three or four years, going to school, barely getting by on his charm, her freelance travel pieces and what was left of the twenty thousand she and Jay split. That was over ten years ago—she sees, flipping pages—until Ursula's money had dried up; and what he made wasn't enough, he'd grumbled. Did he have to ask her for half-a-crown? he said.

When he left her, she'd become a British subject, complete with a work permit. Not a clue to where he'd gone, just a mocking reference to her having loved him "not wisely but too well," scribbled on the poster boards outside the empty theater, under his picture as Iago.

Now checking her waist pack, Ursula opens the UK passport. She supposes it's all right; it's valid. For a moment she contemplates her own jaunty, slightly nervous face above the name Beatrice Doyle.

The name Bea had never suited her. She was named after Charlie's mother, a pious Jewish woman dead before Ursula was born. She didn't know she was Beatrice until the first day of first grade. Ruth had always called her Ursula, no doubt a literary pretension, and her daddy called her dollface. The second day of school, Ruth came with her. Ursula felt embarrassed and proud. Her mother made it clear that she had given her the name Ursula and didn't care what it said on her birth certificate. She was to be called Ursula Kornfield.

Then what had happened? A month after Tony deserted her, Ursula descended on Ruth, bringing with her the deep, buried, speechless love that she bore for her mother. Her plan was to buy an apartment in Cambridge, she told Ruth, and settle there. As if by magic the down payment was provided, the mortgage procured (without an eyeblink and in the name of Ursula Gant); the small fortune Ruth's genius had accumulated bubbled up as if Ursula had struck oil. No discussion about what Ursula had been doing, whom she had loved, why she had again failed. Her second marriage was never acknowledged—any more than Ruth acknowledged that Daniel, the man her daughter was rapturously fucking, was actually another woman's husband. These small aberrations were tolerated (tolerated but not condoned, that was made clear) like an occasional binge of junk food. Opening her passport now to the first perforated page, Ursula sees that the expiration date is only four months off. Under the wire, she sighs, zipping the worn blue book into her waist pack with the wad of money withdrawn from Bank Boston; it was easy, they knew her.

At Logan International terminal, with its handful of desultory travelers and successive announcements, Ursula studies the monitors, then approaches the TWA counter. "Is there a seat on the nine-o-five to Paris?"

"It's boarding now. I'm sorry, you're too late."

"When is the next flight after that? Anywhere," she adds, very irrationally.

The agent doesn't hesitate. He taps his keyboard. "There's space on the ten-twenty-eight flight to Ben-Gurion, change planes at Kennedy. One stop in Athens. Tourist or first?"

As Cissy unlocks the door to 2401, after class, she hears voices. But it's not until she's been standing for several minutes on the top step of the observatory that Daniel mutes the volume. CNN continues in pantomime. "You came from uptown on the subway?" he asks in an exasperated tone. "Didn't the car show up?"

"Yes, but I didn't get in." Cissy pries off her shoes and stocking-foots it to the bar. He shakes his head, staring at the glass in her hand.

"Where were you last night?" she asks, after she's poured her wine.

"Chicago," he answers promptly. "We had meetings all weekend, so I checked into the Palmer House. I took the first plane out this morning and went straight to the office." He stands up. "I'd like to shower before we go to dinner."

"Why didn't you call?" Cissy asks, following him down the steps.

"I thought you and Mimi had gone to New Jersey."

In the bedroom, he undresses methodically, emptying his pockets on the dresser tray and draping his suit on the velvet back of the chair. "Send it out," he mutters. "I slept in it."

The shower is running. Cissy bends over the dresser and her eyes fall on a single key, unattached to his key ring. She touches it and feels her skin prickle as if the key were electrified.

As Daniel sits down on the bed and draws on one high black sock, she says, "What is this the key to?"

"No idea."

"Where did you get it?"

"I must have carried it from the hotel." He holds out his hand.

Perversely, Cissy closes her fist. Daniel stands up, naked aside from a sock, and she turns away in fright, remembering once on the street someone suddenly gripping her arm and digging thumb and forefinger into the hinge of her elbow until she dropped her handbag. Now she goes quickly to the sealed window and fits the key into one of the rectangular openings in the air-conditioning vent on the sill. They stand listening as it clinks down and down twenty-four floors into obscurity.

In the cab on the way to the restaurant, Daniel begins to talk too much; his subject is Mimi, what she ought to do with her life: "Quit show business. She's wasting time baby-sitting a pack of teenaged crackheads. How will she meet a first-class guy that way? She's intelligent and not bad-looking. Five, ten pounds' weight reduction, she'll get a lawyer. I guarantee it. I want to talk to her, I'll straighten her out." Two weeks at La Costa for the two sisters, he'll pay. "How about it?"

"She likes her life."

He's atoning, Cissy understands before the expensive meal is over, and it has to do with the Boston Bitch. She begins to burp. " 'Scuse me," she says, sliding out of the velvet banquette.

Sitting on the toilet seat in static brightness, she's thinking; she'd always thought she loved Daniel, because he married her, but now she feels humiliated. Now she carries in her womb, like the child she never had, the defeated feeling that she has striven without success to please a man who is giving her ulcers, or worse. Twenty-five years in bed with a man who makes her feel bad about herself, will-less, inadequate, and who, beside that, is unfaithful.

On the way home, the unquenchable lights of New York City are collected in the puddles like so many silver coins. The phrase "sold his birthright for a mess of pottage," seems stuck in Cissy's head. She's very quiet. Daniel doesn't appear to notice. Daniel notices the wrong turn the driver makes. "Why didn't you take Fifty-ninth Street?" The driver, in a knit head covering, says, "Sorry, boss."

Who is she kidding, how could she leave him? Cissy is thinking. He'd never let her; his hold on her is permanent, like a built building. He has only to turn around and look for her to be there. She realizes that he's looking at her now. "What are you thinking?" he asks. "Wait, don't tell me. Let me guess." Actually, she's thinking that there's something fantastic about the way she materializes when he looks at her. And it's not even herself who materializes, she's thinking, but Daniel's perception of her. And if on occasion she does something uncalled-for, like riding the subway, the fault is hers, she knows that, for not following his instructions. Now he is probing her brain in the dark backseat; it feels like a laser beam. Shall she tell him that being wrong suits her, Cissy considers, that wrongness is for her the correct way? No, she won't say anything, because Daniel would rather guess.

As the uniformed doorman holds the door, and she hears the light tap of her heels on the marble floor, Cissy imagines a treasured bitch, treated well, who pees in the elevator right after being aired. All that is left to her discretion is her insistence on unacceptable behavior. In the dim hallway on the twenty-fourth floor Daniel smiles, exposing white even teeth. He has found her out—her perversity, her futile, weak self-assertion, her certain self-destruction. "Nothing!" he guesses, throwing the door open for her to run through. "You're not thinking anything!"

The shine of the city bathes the spacious living room in an eerie glow. Daniel crosses the pale carpeting between bleached furniture to the blond bedroom. He has just had an extraordinary evening; he dined with a dummy. Last thing Cissy said was "Excuse me." She has been mustering nerve for a major blowup. He recognizes the signs—not eating, burping; and she had no luck recalling ordinary speech. Lifting the phone, Daniel asks if there are any messages, meanwhile palming the TV remote and pressing POWER. He undresses to the news. The woman hired to straighten up has turned down the bed; he gets under the creamy comforter and rests his dark head against the pillows. Reaching over, he turns off the bed lamp.

After a long time in the bathroom, Cissy comes out still fully dressed. Wearing the little black dress she'd worn to dinner and the Fendi ermine fur piece around her shoulders. Looking good, he approves silently. Cissy totters down the river of light spilled from the open bathroom doorway. "I know about the woman in Boston, Daniel." His eyes slide from the television.

"Name, Ursula Gant. I've got pictures of the two of you together; she's mousy."

"She's a client," Daniel says. "She took over Ruth Kornfield's portfolio after her death. She's the daughter."

Cissy marches to the bed and gropes for the television remote in the folds of the comforter. Staring down at it, she presses buttons but the news complacently continues. Dropping the remote she pulls off one shoe and hurls it at the female face on the screen. Uninvited, Jay Leno abruptly flashes on. Little phosphorescent vertical bars advance across the bottom; the volume soars. Snatching off her other shoe she attacks Daniel, hammering with the heel like someone attempting to drive a nail into a solid wall. "Why don't you be honest with me for once in your life? Admit you've been committing adultery!" With all the loud voices in the room it seems that there's a crowd. She's listening for his denial, his excuse, his plea for forgiveness. In a mingling tone, Daniel's voice says: "I've been committing adultery."

Cissy's howl is like that of an animal being eviscerated. The sound seems to lodge in the cooled air, bounce back from the mirrored wall of closets, and hang from the high ceiling to compete with the cackling laughter of *Tonight*'s guest. While Cissy is throwing clothing into the suitcase she dragged off the closet shelf, Daniel is breathing moistly under the sheet pulled over his head. His hands cover his ears but he can hear Cissy's cry, continuing. He can hear it even after he hears the front door slam and the elevator descend in its shaft.

◆

She's overreacting, she knows. In the cab through the night streets, Cissy hears Mim's voice saying over and over, *You're a hot ticket. You didn't jess walk, y'all flew!*

Yes, she tells Mim smugly, *and what's more, Ah'm plannin' to jump out in a new place. Fuck the consequences!* She asks the cab to stop on the corner of Fifty-third and Second Avenue and goes into a phone booth.

"Sorry to be calling so late," Cissy says to the sleepy voice. "It's an emergency. May I speak to the detective?"

"He's in Boston," the woman says sleepily. "He's on a case."

"I know," says Cissy. "It's my case. This is Mrs. Dorfman."

"Whyn't you try his mobile number?" the voice grumbles, and hangs up.

In spite of all her efforts to remain rational, Cissy is pretty sure she's out of control. "Hurry!" she orders the taxi driver, pounding on the Plexiglas between them.

At Kennedy, she charges a ticket to Athens. Why Athens? The flight is boarding, her knees are shaking, and she sees, twenty paces away, just where her private investigator had said, the white, heart-shaped face of Ursula Gant. As Cissy waits at the end of the check-in line, her mind flashes on the last time she was at this airport. A year ago she'd opened a florist's bill for a dozen yellow roses. At dinner that night she slid it across the table. Vertical grooves had rooted between Daniel's eyes; perplexed, he managed to look even more sincere and reliable, and faithful. "Must be a mistake," he said, pocketing it. "Good thing you caught it." And Cissy's smile had hardened on her cheeks so she could hardly move her mouth. She'll never forget that feeling. Burning with humiliation, with no luggage and no ticket she'd sat for hours in a molded plastic chair at Kennedy airport like an unmarked parcel, unreturnable to her parents (in their nineties, what would they do with her?) and unforwardable to Daniel, who didn't want her. Finally a porter had leaned over and asked sympathetically if anything was wrong, and Cissy gratefully put five dollars and a slip of paper with her telephone number in his palm. Daniel seemed relieved when he came to claim her; he gave the porter ten dollars for turning her in.

With shock, Ursula recognizes the woman standing uncertainly at the entrance to the waiting area, looking around. The hothouse blonde in the little black dress, a cuddly body like a cloth doll stuffed with sawdust, yellow hair, gold jewelry circling the neck and at the wrists and ears. A shrug of white fur—ermine, she supposes—hugging her shoulders. Cissy, all right. The same woman as the silver-framed beauty queen on the desk in

Daniel's office, ribboned across the chest: 1967 Miss Tennessee. A chicken fattened with hormones for market. Looking older now, thinner, hardened, cared for. Ursula quickly lowers her head to the book she'd taken from her pack, thinking, What is Cissy doing here?

A ubiquitous voice is announcing boarding for first-class passengers. As she passes, Cissy stops for a moment in front of Ursula and a flicker of misgiving passes over her face. *Why is she leaving him?* she asks, then supplies Mim's answer: *She's not; the bitch is testing him. She wants him to leave you, give up everything to prove her importance.*

There's a kind of defiant resolve in Cissy's agitated step: the brazen aerialist on the wire, head high, goose-stepping. From now on, she is thinking, she'll not perform for Daniel or Mimi. Or snotty James, the doorman. By taking matters into her own hands, she tells herself, breathing hugely, she's ripped out the label she came with, the one that said DO NOT REMOVE. INSTRUCTIONS SEWN AT BIRTH. She has become anonymous, thinks Cissy, oblivious to the heads turning to watch her, because heads have always turned. No one knows her, she thinks, the color in her face deepening with pleasure, becoming the pink of a tea rose, attracting more attention. No one censures her. No one tells her what to do. Not Daniel, not Mimi, not hateful Ms. Rubin, at Columbia, whose nasty eyes slide past Cissy. She is impelled down the incline toward the cabin, heels knocking; she feels a collusive chill suddenly ripple through her body. But *she* knows who I am, Cissy is thinking. The woman whose eyes met mine. And I recognized her, Cissy says to herself, taking her seat. She is Ursula Gant, Daniel's mistress.

*   *   *

Inching down the aisle toward economy, Ursula has the sense of being buffeted by the ongoing barrage of the other woman's thoughts. So many surging, intercepting, overlapping thoughts. She pauses in the first-class cabin, looks down. And Daniel's wife, as if drawn by Ursula's stare, just then raises her eyes.

Cissy Dorfman sees a woman, not young, but younger than herself. But what has happened to her? How has she become so bruised? The dark glasses don't quite hide the inflamed stitching under the eye. Swelling on one side of the nose, a bruise on the high forehead. But still her face is pure and haunting, Cissy realizes, brown hair caught back, and the starkness revealing fine, classic bones, the enviable beauty. What can be behind it— her remoteness, her sadness? Cissy thinks, turning to look back as Daniel's woman passes by, drawing in her breath at the dark hair escaping from its knot, thick and sensual, at odds with the unpainted face. I was wrong, Cissy corrects herself. She's not mousy. She's beautiful. All the money in New York could never make me so effortlessly beautiful. No wonder Daniel loves her.

◆

What if he didn't listen, Ursula broods once New York disappears and the motors settle into a soothing drone. What if Daniel came to Cambridge as he said he would? She pulls the shade, reclines her seat, closes her eyes. Her thoughts take off, she considers the possibility; it seems quite real. There is sweet Daniel actually rushing from the airport and tearing up the porch steps because he's worried about her. Her remoteness, her unavailability. Things that irritated him, but also made him want her. Impatiently he jabs the door chime. Getting no answer, hearing no dog bark, he would fish for his key—usually in his pocket with loose change—but not tonight; tonight he lifts the corner of the mat (Ursula realizes she's left the key behind).

With *The New York Times* in its blue plastic sleeve clasped under one elbow, he'll swing the door open with his shoe and drop an overnight bag in the downstairs hall. Is he planning to stay overnight? Ursula's surprised heart beats faster. Seeing the overnight bag, she thinks, Has he had it out with Cissy at last? She can almost hear him now affectionately howling from the bottom of the stairs, "Ursula. Ursula. Ursula."

He climbs to the top calling her name. Then, beginning to feel annoyed, he stops abruptly at the archway to the living room with its bedlam of tumbled books. Here, he winces, for disorder offends Daniel. The creak of a loose board in the hallway floor further annoys him. From the bedroom doorway he stares at the unsheeted bed. He shouts no more. Going into the kitchen, Daniel automatically—his mind framing the confrontation they'll have when Ursula walks in—he automatically empties the half-drunk cup of coffee in the sink and scrubs the dark stain at the bottom of the cup. At last he thinks to lift the phone receiver; hearing no dial tone, he wiggles the DISCONNECT button. Nothing. He'll be troubled, Ursula thinks, but at bottom no more alarmed than if he'd thrown a ball straight up into the air. She had to return, smack into his hands. He'll wait.

What will he do when he realizes that she might be coming down in another place? As Ursula's mind gropes with alternatives that could occur to Daniel, she seems to hear the clatter of his footsteps in the uncarpeted hall. Hunting, Daniel will idly open the cabinet in the dining room where Ruth's table linens are stacked, unused. What on earth is he searching for? she wonders. A television set? If that's it, he finds none. What he finds are books even she's forgotten. She exposes Daniel's back, stiffened in anger, receding down the hall of her apartment. In the bedroom he hangs his suit coat on the chair back, slips off his loafers and stretches out on the bed.

She imagines that Daniel is feeling uneasy. Is it possible, it may occur to him, that both women would desert him at the same time? How could they? He needs them, he will insist, just before falling asleep—he needs them both, not for what they can do for him, but as repositories for the love he bears them. Daniel needs to give; it's fundamental for him. He needs to be needed, sent for, asked to do something.

Heat will sizzle from the radiators at 5 A.M. The apartment will be airless. (Has she forgotten to lower the thermostat?) Ursula can see him pulling at the neck of his shirt; Tuesday's dawn is fading through the shade. Sitting on the edge of the bed, he'll give his head a shake. Shirtsleeves rolled, leaning over the bathroom sink, he'll splash cold water on his face. Dripping hands, eyes squeezed, he'll grope—sorry, no towels, they're in the dryer. A short time later, she pictures Daniel, carrying his overnight bag, running down the steps and coming out to Farrar Street before the street lamps are turned off. On the sidewalk he sidesteps to avoid the paper boy on his bike and walks briskly toward Harvard Square, hoping to hail a cab. With luck (she thinks he's thinking), he'll be at his desk, showered and changed, when the stock market opens.

◆

Over Switzerland, Ursula's ears plug; a breath-stopping pain shoots through her head. Her nose starts to bleed. She becomes aware of a repeated tone and a calm, insistent voice telling her to fasten her seat belt: The plane is dropping. The sky is seemingly bottomless—down, down they fall, very swiftly. All of a sudden an overhead bin flaps open; bags tumble out. A woman screams; the scream is the first sign of something really wrong. But now there is no air. The yellow mask hangs down on a curly plastic tube, swinging into her face, and she remembers those countless, disregarded instructions.

To Cissy it seems that the spiraling descent and pulsing pressure is localized in her own head, but internalizing the threat, she curls in a ball, whimpering like a struck dog, thinking, In his demanding, sometimes hurtful and blindsided way, Daniel cared about me. He loved me as if I were delicate and incapable. His possessiveness made me feel as if I were valuable, still beautiful, still young, and not a fifty-year-old piece of shit.

As the plane bursts into flames, Ursula feels a rush of scalding air that she identifies as the updraft of death's wing spread. She fleetingly pictures the raven; on its black silken head it wears Ruth's death mask. Ursula doesn't have time to feel afraid. Still strapped in her seat, she tumbles against gravity into a trough of silent, searing emptiness. She slides sideways along the ceiling, pummeled on all sides by unseen flying bodies. Thick smoke fills the cabin. Shrieks and moans come from an indeterminate distance, somewhere outside the small shroud of safety that she believes enfolds her. Ursula's mind is clear and says the word: Mommy! Just at that moment a great gaping hole opens in the roof above her head, and with a whoosh she is sucked up into the asphyxiating cold.

ALONE IN HIS CONDO, DANIEL WATCHES THE SUN RISE from the high terrace overhanging the city. As he sips his coffee, black, Daniel listens to the sounds of his city the way the mighty emperor once listened to his personal nightingale: It is sweet to him, the blast of horns and squeal of brakes and the chilling howl of power. But—he can't account for it—this morning he feels uneasy. His instincts are good, he trusts them; what's wrong? Behind the glass door, on *Good Morning America,* Joan Lunden's lips move silently. The cell phone is in his bath robe pocket; he flips it open.

"Let me talk to Cissy."

"Cissy's not heah." Obviously he's woken Mimi; her voice is a rasp.

"She isn't with you?"

"Uh-uh."

"Well, she left here last night."

"Where'd she go?"

"I thought she'd gone to Nashville. Did she call you?"

"No," Mimi cackles in the accent necessary to her backwoods identity, "but y'all know Cissy. Wherever she is, she'll head on home swifter than a spooked bangtail."

Daniel closes the door to his office, swings back in his chair and asks his secretary to get American Express on the line. "Lost card." The last charge, they tell him, was made on TWA.

"Where to?"

"Athens, Greece."

"I'll accept that charge," he says. "But cancel the card."

Rotating in his chair, Daniel considers asking the wide-assed paralegal out to lunch—lately she seems to be making a move on him. Better not, he cautions himself, she's too young and he doesn't want to risk being nailed for sexual harassment. However, when he's on the way down for a lunch date, the same girl gets on the elevator. As they slide fourteen floors in each other's company, Gail softly asks if he'd like to have a drink after work.

The taxi drops Daniel at a warehouse in SoHo; there is no identifying sign on the dark, empty street. "You sure this is it?" The cabbie, a Muslim wearing a knitted skullcap and sitting on a seat cover made of large wooden beads, has turned off the meter at $15.30. Daniel hands him a twenty-dollar bill and gets out with barely time to slam the door before the man guns off.

Daniel steps up on the loading dock. The metal platform rises to floor level and opens on neon, noise, and Gail. She knows he's married, she shouts over a tequila sunrise, but views matrimony as an obsolete concept invented by men for the purpose of patriarchal inheritance. And if he has a problem with that, to let her know. He has a problem: Ursula. And drowning in the memory of their first lunch in an uptown, mahogany-paneled room, he tells Gail, with damp eyes, that he is in love.

That first lunch had been all business; he was being ingratiating and unflappable. Then on the way back to his office, where he had yet to settle Ruth Kornfield's account into Ursula Gant's pale-nailed hands, the taxi in front of theirs abruptly stopped in the middle of Seventy-fifth Street. The driver sprang out, leaving his door open. A heavyset man in a white shirt and suspenders, he took off after a lithe black kid who must have jumped the fare. Full speed the two threaded half a block between honking cars. Caught, the culprit was shoved back into the cab; as the driver got in the boy popped out the other side and began to run again. It was a New York distraction. No one living in the city would have done anything more than be annoyed. But Ursula Gant had stood in the street in her sensible low heels, amid the cacophony of horns, and paid the startled driver what the meter read, with a tip. Daniel thinks it was at this moment he began to love her. Then that night at his party came the totally unforeseeable denouement; the intriguing, unsuspected part of Ursula Gant: whore! And now, after two years, when he thought he knew her inside and out—everything about her—the biggest surprise of all: "She left me."

"Should we go back to your place?" Gail is offering sympathetically. "I'd ask you back to mine but my roommate may have company."

He hesitates. What if Cissy's there—face slick with wrinkle combat, eyes at half-mast and the Chardonnay bottle empty? "Sure," he answers.

◆

Gail seems to know the way: She disappears in the direction of the bedroom, and Daniel strips down to silk paisley briefs. As he enters the bedroom, fingers of his left hand threaded between the stems of two snifters, and a bottle of Courvoisier in the other hand, he sees a somber-faced Peter Jennings reflected without sound in the mirrored doors of the closet. Turning his eyes to the screen, Daniel lowers the bottle and glasses to the marble-topped night table, pumps up the volume, and sinks to the end of the bed to watch. A handheld camera seesaws over the twisted remains of a plane—scraps of metal, arbitrary, unrelatable; he has no more idea of what they signify than he'd have of an installation at the Whitney. But he stands up, moved to attention. Just then the phone begins ringing, a startling sound past midnight. Daniel reaches for it, eyes still on the screen, anticipating Cissy's tearful apology. He's clumsy—damn! His hand brushes one of the glasses, and as it strikes the marble, it shatters. The crash seems to segue into the TV commentator's solemn-voice, abruptly very loud "—over Mont Blanc, some hours before dawn. Names withheld pending notification of next of kin."

When Gail comes out of the bathroom in her panties, she is frightened by the sight of Daniel Dorfman doubled over on the edge of the bed. "Hey." She kneels down in front of him. "You want me to call nine-one-one?" She touches his thigh, and he screams. Startled, she jumps back. "You want me to go?"

As the door clicks Daniel sits up, his chest tight, barely breathing, listening for the elevator's groan. And after the cage descends into quiet, he lifts the receiver, taps the buttons. The automated voice says that Ursula's phone has been disconnected.

Where is she? He needs her.

"Bitch!"

B

ITCH IS 60-PERCENT DEAD; SHE CAN SMELL HER OWN
burned flesh. She can't move, she can't open her mouth. The
same male voice, strangely accented, repeats again and again,
"What's your name?"

She doesn't answer; anyway, she doesn't know.

They are working on her. Many-handed monsters. Shadowy
movements above her eyes. Hands manipulating, probing and
piercing, wrapping her body like a mummy's for burial, talking,
talking all around her as if she weren't there. Maybe she isn't,
she thinks, maybe she has been trundled away, and all that's left
is this kernel of thought embedded in her disembodied body.
This excessive handling is what the dead must experience, she
thinks, before burial. No pain. Just an inconsequential numbness makes its presence known; but it doesn't seem to belong to
her, any more than the insensible weight of the body being
lifted and shifted and prepared for—for what? Autopsy? I'd like
some privacy, she would say if she were able, so I can think. But
her throat must be severed; it makes no sound. Voices go on in
a frenzied foreign babble around her. She tries to tear away the
mask clamped on her face, but her hand doesn't move; a voice
says, she thinks it says, "Vivere."

The light's too bright, the survivor would like to tell them.
Would you mind lowering it? After a while the light goes out.

One eye opens a slit on the swiftly moving ceiling, acoustic
tile blurred by the speed of travel; jolting intermittently, she

counts the seams on the floor. Running feet on either side, sense of motion. She views objectively the gurney on which she moves, as if she were elsewhere. So she's not dead, she decides. Experimentally, she tries to flex her knee, lift her arm, but her limbs don't respond. What's happened to my body? she asks. No sound comes. She feels herself being tipped and spilled; a noise like garbage being unloaded into the pulverizing jaws at the back of the truck. A plate is slammed into place and she hears the *buzz-click*, repeatedly, of radiation. Above, she senses the glare of a giant reflecting pan, and pictures herself emerging as a flattened sheet of metal. Only her hearing seems unimpaired. Human voices are now, uninterruptedly, shouting. No one any longer addresses her. She stops trying to figure out what they are saying. Just as well, she thinks, relieved, dismissed, awash: I am in some fundamental way missing.

◆

They are keeping vigil. They view the survivor from behind a glass window as if it were a cut of meat in a showcase. Daniel flattens his forehead against the pane; his breaths fog the window. Mimi begins the same wordless whining, on one note, like a cat's howl, that Daniel first heard when they deplaned in Geneva and hired a driver with a Land Rover for the long, quiet drive to Locarno; this is their second day in Locarno, on the Italian border. Both days, they have come to Ospedale d'Acosta in the morning and left at dinnertime. The hospital is a square building with a flat shiny face of alternating white and green marble and tiers of high rounded windows, which curiously allow in almost no light. It sits on the rim of a bowllike piazza, across from a cathedral through which they could see, when they arrived, the distant hills, the driver had called to their notice a remembrance of Allied efforts in World War II.

"She doesn't move," Daniel says now. "You think she's conscious?"

Maybe it's the sight of the thing itself that numbs the mind and leaves it blank. So far the foreign doctor has circled them at a respectful distance. He approaches finally, diffidently, gripping in his hand what looks like a small mail sack. Hearing the rhythmic suck of his rubber-soled shoes on the wooden floor, Mimi abruptly becomes silent. Daniel sees the tall white-coated man reflected in the window. He turns.

"Dr. Berini," the man introduces himself.

Daniel shakes his hand; it's amazingly small. "Who is she?" he asks the doctor.

"We were hoping you could help us with that."

"Is there any way to identify her?"

"There's always the possibility that, once she recovers sufficiently, she'll be able to tell us."

"How long will that be?"

The doctor transfers the gray sack to the crook of his other arm, where it rests like a football. He hesitates, possibly translating from Italian in his head. "She's burned over sixty percent of her body," he says finally. "It's not likely she'll survive. There is a chance."

"I was told she may be my wife."

"All of the relatives of women on the manifest have been notified. This woman is the only survivor; none of the dead could be identified." The doctor speaks very slowly, obviously unaccustomed to English; still, each word carries its appropriate load of reserve and sympathy. "Your wife's name appears on the manifest. But there's something else, as well." He reaches inside his gray sack.

Daniel closes his eyes, fearing God knows what. Clutching Daniel's arm, Mimi resumes her whine, tiny and high.

"A white fur cape. Virtually intact," the doctor says, and draws out a white amorphous shape as a magician might a bunny. Suddenly, Daniel feels his knees buckle. Mimi and the doctor each grip an arm. "It lay over the body of the survivor," the doctor says, opening it to reveal the red satin lining with a logo of back-to-back F's.

Daniel stares. "It's Cissy's; I bought it at Fendi's; Christmas, last year." But now he is not looking at the doctor, not at the white thing, not at the survivor behind the glass. He has turned his dark head and is peering into Mimi's bloodshot, very blue eyes. "You say this woman has dark eyes?"

"Yes, eye color is all we can verify. Very dark, almost black. But still insensate."

The edges of Daniel's nostrils redden. "I don't know how she got Cissy's fur piece," he says. "This woman is not my wife."

In the downstairs pub at the inn, the bartender is watching a small, fuzzy black-and-white TV, volume inaudible. There's a soccer game on. The seats of the booths are unforgivingly upright. Someone has carved the universal message LIFE SUCKS behind Daniel's head. Daniel slides his glass of warm ale around the tacky table top. He hasn't said much since they left the Ospedale d'Acosta. Mimi, looking across at him—he's white-faced, sitting stiffly, eyes blinking as if to hold back tears—is inexplicably overcome by tenderness. Strange, she thinks, gazing over the rim of her tumbler of Wild Turkey, straight up, she'd never felt tender toward Daniel before. Daniel wasn't the kind of guy to elicit tenderness in women; in herself, he had roused, sometimes, wishfulness. Often lust. But now, Mimi thinks, sliding toward the end of her bench, Daniel looks shell-shocked, martyred, vulnerable. His narrow face is twisted into the brave grimace of a little boy who has suffered beyond his years. Getting up she goes around the table. "Move over, hon."

◆

The patient is rolled face to feet in bandages, lungs collapsed, kidneys in failure, scorched to the bone. After days—or a week (it may well be)—she feels absolutely fine. That she is alive is surely a major accomplishment. Why are they keeping her here?

Never before has one burned so badly lived so long. She exists. Greenish-white islands of putrid infection float on the body's surface. Massive doses of antibiotics are injected. For many weeks, then months she is attended night and day. When the vital signs finally stabilize, patch by patch the body is laminated: Artificial skin, paper-thin, grown from pig cells, is rolled over the bones like pie crust; shipments arrive by air from the U.S; there isn't enough pig's skin in all of Europe.

Some time later (and by then she is having plenty of pain) she understands that she is confined in the sterile unit for the desperately burned. The nurses and doctors are gowned and masked, the floor is mopped hourly, morphine is injected before she can be touched. But now there is not much handling, for she is not expected to survive—she hears them say this. The overwhelming danger is infection; that's discussed too. Whatever lives beneath the skin has been exposed. No covering lies between her inner organs and the outside world. (Goodness! What must she look like?) When this realization finally comes (how much later?), her mind shuts down. Her brain becomes inaccessible. The eyes in the crack of the bound head close. The body is inanimate, except for the heart. Astonishingly, it beats.

◆

Nine months later the swathing is removed from the face, which was less deeply burned than the body. Mostly smashed. By now a veneer of raw, smooth skin holds in the cheekbones. Reconstruction begins. Eyelids are sewn on. The nose invented. A jaw constructed and held together by steel wire. The hole that is the mouth retains a whisper—her vocal chords are like twisted fishing tackle, her voice like the wash of a wave.

At the Convent of Our Lady of Labassecour, where she has been transferred for rehabilitation, the crash victim can sometimes be seen being supported down the hall by two women in starched gray habits. "Damn it, let go of me," she says to them, hoarse words hardly audible. "I remember how to walk." At last they do, and she goes alone in the arms of a walker, balancing on the bones of her legs and the soles of new feet with toes gnarled like scrap metal. Only her mind refuses to heal: It remains stubbornly blank.

"Can't remember. Can't remember."

"Perhaps another day you'll remember," encourages Dr. Marchmont, the psychiatrist assigned to her.

Another day. The clawed hand flexes and dances on her chest. Dr. Marchmont leans over the bed and puts her ear beside the patient's mouth: "Some vital part of me has died," the patient tells her.

"At the moment of the crash?"

She doesn't know; it doesn't seem so. "Before," she says. "When the plane was falling, I didn't feel afraid. I felt ready, I felt already dead."

"What did that feel like?"

"It felt like ashes; I needed only to be scattered. I'd lost whatever there was that connects one to life. It didn't matter to me that the plane was going down. I couldn't go on living."

"Why?"

"I don't know."

"What happened after that? Do you remember?"

"I heard somebody talking to me, and I realized I wasn't dead."

"A rescue worker?"

"No, there was somebody there when I gained consciousness."

Dr. Marchmont says, "Perhaps when they brought you in?"

"I couldn't see her but I sensed her, I felt her hands."

"No more now. Rest."

But she can't rest, not until she knows who she is. She could be anyone. Right now, in a way, she's invisible. If she could only see her face, even distorted or damaged, she'd be somebody. Before this she hadn't wanted to, but now she's curious, and nobody can stop her from looking. She struggles up on her elbows so she can see into the mirror on the back of the door.

What she sees is an effigy of humanity. Staring, she lifts her hand off the blanket and touches her face. The hand rises; and seeing that hand resting on that face, which must, then, be hers, she cries out in alarm. Her body trembles as her mind grapples with the sight, refusing to accept the unfamiliar image across the room as her *self.* Surely the thing that is the self, she silently reasons, is fundamental, axiomatic; given to you at the moment of birth to deal with all experience. So how can the image in the mirror, which she doesn't recognize, be her *self*? She looks long and hard. It is menacingly unfamiliar.

She rocks back and forth to the edge of the mattress and dangles her legs off the high bed. Pitching forward, she plunges heavily to the floor. I feel nothing, she marvels, spread on the floor like a crushed crab. I have become immune to pain. On her hip she slides herself across the floor and, reaching up, grips the doorknob. She hauls herself upright, shifts the bolt and locks the door to the hall—expressly forbidden. Reluctant and terrified, she stares at her feet. The toes, allowed to heal without surgery—hadn't all the experts said she would never walk?—are fused. Each foot ends in a lump, a craggy, undefined confusion of bone knobs and mangled skin. Next she tears open the ties of her johnny and lets it fall over the offending feet. Her eyes move up. Muscle and fatty tissue have been burned away, and what she sees are the sticklike lower legs of a bird. But normal thighs, although they have strange bulges inside each knee, like tubers. At this point she realizes that she feels apart from what she sees. This object in the mirror. Objectively, then, she evaluates like a scientist the identity of some species of ossified bone and flesh, eaten away; a remnant of something that had lived. Found in a cave or in a desert, maybe. Is it human? Yes, it's female, she notes. The small breasts perfectly intact. The torso itself not critically damaged. Only here and there, raised purplish nodules on the stomach and hips that could be the backs of hippos hiding beneath the smooth surface of a river. A glance over her shoulder shows her an unaffected woman's buttocks, and a back composed of paving stones of varying shades. This much she knows about herself: She has a woman's body. Feeling grateful, even giddy, she recklessly lets go of the doorknob.

"Are you all right in there?" a voice calls, augmented by others, more frantic; "Open up!" Rattling, then pounding.

She reaches up, can't grasp the knob, and looks at her right hand. The bones are rigid, allowing apposition only between the third finger and thumb. The other fingers are permanently frozen in a claw.

◆

During the dark winter months of the second year of her life, the burned woman hibernates on the sun porch of the Convent of Our Lady of Labassecour, in Locarno, like a misshapen plant, a confused botanical experiment withering in the steady heat.

The porch, an awkward addition to the Renaissance monastery built at the end of the fifteenth century, juts from the east facade beneath the crown of the campanile. In winter the sky glares whitely through the slanted glass roof. The green linoleum floor is scarred with cigarette burns; a large sign says SMOKING PROHIBITED. The patient sits in the humped seat of a stiffened plastic lounge chair. From time to time people in bathrobes drift out of the convent's halls, glance in, disappear.

Almost daily the psychiatrist pulls up her chair and hooks her sensible heels in the rung. One day the patient looks up from the yellowed sheet of *The London Daily Telegraph,* and says, "Well, I've read seven years' worth of newspapers."

Dr. Marchmont smiles, indulging her.

"Nineteen eighty-four to nineteen ninety-one," the patient says. "What else have you got in English?"

"Have you read this?" Dr. Marchmont fishes out a small book with a dun-colored cover; she's brought it from the cottage she shares with another postulant.

The Mill on the Floss seems almost familiar to the patient; certain whole passages leap to mind before she encounters them. There are two more Eliots, courtesy of her English companion; the woman with whom she shares her life, Dr. Marchmont divulges, shining face reddened.

Thereafter, the psychiatrist sits opposite, catches her heels in the chair rung and they talk first about the book. Then Dr. Marchmont bends her cropped head close and asks the patient if she's remembered anything.

"I remember language. I remember how to brush my teeth, how to eat and how to shit."

The psychiatrist blushes. "Good start." Now Dr. Marchmont will read aloud the women's names from the passenger list. The patient tries to visualize these lucky women. "Even if they're dead, they're lucky: they have names." She expects a rise out of the psychiatrist. Getting none, she looks up. Dr. Marchmont's eyes are open but her eyeballs have rolled up, exposing empty sockets. It seems she has put herself to sleep, erect in her ladder-back chair.

Gradually the doctor's bulky loose-leaf notebook makes its way through the folds of her habit; it lands on the floor, crammed pages waving in the vent breeze. Without a moment's hesitation, the patient reaches down. The report is written in English, it turns out, for presentation at the London conference on trauma. *I have never seen a clinical case before,* the psychiatrist demurs on the first page. *Suppositions* is the heading that follows: *Most antithetical to eventual recovery, the patient has lost the fundamental reference of self necessary to memory.* God help me, the patient thinks; she pages forward. *The interruption of an originally integrated entity of functioning has driven her into retreat. The unidentified woman presents to the world a mature yet diminished consciousness. Most likely as a result of some previous interdiction (whose, we don't know) the patient appears to have entirely separated herself from the life force which seeks pleasure. At all hours I come upon her haunting the halls like an unassigned ghost, accepting without protest a life of homelessness and denial.* Hearing a movement, the subject of the paper looks up. Dr. Marchmont is beginning dangerously to list. The patient skims, glancing up frequently: *The prior consciousness appears unable to acknowledge the current state; the functioning brain finds her present identity neither mentally nor physically viable.* What is to happen to her? the patient wonders, suddenly terrified. As Dr. Marchmont unbalances, she hastily sets the notebook down. But not before she has seen the last entry: *She has blocked out any memory of the past. The patient's amnesia may be presently necessary to this woman's efforts to survive.*

The psychiatrist jolts upright. The notebook's on the floor. The subject of the report has closed her eyes and seems asleep.

WITH NO BODY TO BURY, THE COMMEMORATIVE SERvice, on a raw day in November, is a small one. After a lot of red tape Cissy's been declared legally dead, and Daniel's decided on an informal ceremony at the Ethical Culture Society on Central Park West; three front rows are filled with a few friends and some members of the brokerage firm. Gail is there. Mimi has on a dark mink coat.

Following the eulogy, Mimi stands and lifts the heavy black veil covering her face. The five young men on either side rise. The marble walls echo their shaky rendition of "The Tennessee Waltz."

◆

Two men are waiting in Daniel's office when he returns from Cissy's memorial service. A flush of anger goes through him as he shakes hands with the one who comes forward. "Yes?"

"Sit down, please, sir," the man instructs him. He has gray hair, dense and shaggy, and the eloquent features of a Shakespearean actor: the articulate nose, full lips, and eyebrows that are heavy and unnaturally dark.

He whips out a scratched silver badge with a crest on it. "I'm Detective Lucas, Third Precinct Police Headquarters, Boston."

"We'd like to ask you some questions," the other, unidentified man says when all three are seated. "You don't have to answer if you don't wish to." Daniel remains silent. "It's regarding the disappearance of a Cambridge, Massachusetts, woman named—" He slaps his coat pockets, flips several pages, runs his finger down.

"Ursula Gant?" Daniel gasps.

The first detective, Lucas, raises his eyebrows. "You know her?"

Daniel gets up and comes around the desk. "Yes, of course I know her. Knew her. She disappeared about six or seven months ago. I kept calling and trying to trace her; her phone had been disconnected. I questioned neighbors. Finally I assumed she'd gone away, although I thought she would have let me know."

"What was your relationship with Ursula Gant?"

"She was a client." A tremor goes through Daniel. "Why? Has something happened to her?"

"Well, we don't know that yet, Mr. Dorfman," the man says. "We're investigating. We were contacted three months ago. She was reported missing."

"Who reported her?"

"Her ex-husband."

Daniel turns away. He walks past the desk to the windows, stares without seeing at the view of midtown Manhattan as static as a photograph. "The first thing I did was check with the editors of several of the journals she wrote book reviews for; she hadn't contacted them. I considered hiring a detective. I actually went to her house—"

It isn't until he snaps his head around and sees the twitchy smile on Lucas's face that he realizes he's made a mistake.

THE MEDIA HAVE MOVED TO MORE RECENT CATASTRO-phes; no one visits. There is one paragraph at the bottom of page eight of the *International Herald Tribune* at the time of her release from the Convent of Our Lady of Labassecour, nearly two years later. The unidentified woman has a name. She leaves Italy, the only survivor of the bombed 747, like an item tagged in a markdown sale. Lucy Snowe, the ticket reads—a name she chose from the book *Villette*, a present from Dr. Marchmont. The survivor is made of all-new materials, hospital built. Her body is spare but strong from the hours of physical therapy. She wears specially built shoes, high laced with rounded toes. She has new bones secured by pins and not always dependable, skin smooth as plastic, and hair—sprouted from the burned scalp in dark, baby-fine clumps. She knows nothing about herself, less about the world. Like an embryo developed in a test tube, Lucy Snowe leaves Labassecour with no history; on a clear May morn-ing she sets forth from the only home she knows with nothing but her life. But she has been issued a passport by the Fedeval Witness Protection Program for practical purposes, to prove she exists, and money—the seemingly inexhaustible out-of-court settlement of three million dollars from TWA—deposited in a Swiss bank account.

At the airport, the moment before departure, she thinks to ask Dr. Marchmont, "How old am I?"

"What age would you like to be?"

"How old are you?"

"Forty-four," the nun says.

"Forty-four," Lucy Snowe decides. "A good age for a woman."

PART II

"LUCY. LUCY SNOWE," SHE KEEPS REPEATING. GIBBER-ish! She wonders, if someone asks her name, will she remember it? There's almost an hour's wait for the flight to Ben-Gurion; she walks along the concourse looking for a coffee shop. The airport restaurant is almost empty: just two elderly women, silently and resolutely chewing. Lucy Snowe fills a paper cup with coffee; the coffee is free, but she has to buy one of the three sizes of cups. Good luck, Dr. Marchmont had said before she left, then she'd folded Lucy Snowe in her arms as if she held no volume and was embracing air. Luck? How can she count on luck? Lucy asks herself, starting toward the gate. Hasn't she used hers up, hasn't her survival been luck, a bonus like the tenth life of a cat? Lucy guesses she is lucky, if she thinks about it. She puts her small suitcase on the moving belt and walks through. Why doesn't she feel lucky?

There's a loud buzzing. At the same time, the pins in her bones tingle distantly, like a tooth being drilled in a numbed jaw. Lucy has been dreading this: She's been singled out. A uniformed guard, a muscular woman with a gun in a holster hanging under full breasts, motions Lucy aside. *The pig's skin stands alone;* it flashes on Lucy Snowe while the guard strokes her body with the detector. The buzzing surges.

She's taken into a room where another woman stands at the counter helplessly watching an airline official poke through the underwear in her suitcase. But Lucy assumes she's unique; she's clutching her medical affidavit in her left hand. She surrenders it now, and she surrenders her new face for inspection. Taut and smoothly seamed, it passes. Still, with what reluctance they finally admit her: altered goods.

Rattling and slamming, the plane reaches the end of the runway and lurches up, leaving its shadow on the ground. Patches of earth and then gray ocean are replaced by clouds. Looking down, Lucy is surprised that she doesn't feel afraid; she discovers her fear nerves have been severed. So she sits back and closes her eyes, trying to remember something—anything. She thinks about what she may have left behind: other trips, other skies, other clouds, other last sights. But no matter how hard she tries, there is only emptiness and the illusory memory, which she supposes will always be with her, of death.

The white and blue-tailed jet crawls to a halt, and the passengers crowd into the aisle. Coming down the shaky stair, Lucy stands with the others on the tarmac while the luggage is handed out. So far, she's like everyone else, she thinks: She can remember how to function. And if the past's gone, at least she's become acutely aware of her present, observing everything. Lucy looks—that's how she functions. The straggling line goes toward a squat building like a barracks, painted green with a flat tin roof. Inside, with the wind gone, Lucy feels the intense heat; so she can feel something. The baggage is stacked on wire racks against the wall. When her name is called, Lucy tugs at her plaid pasteboard suitcase, as recent as she, and carries it into the cubicle.

The official is a tiny older woman, almost a midget, with iron-gray hair and a sparse growth on her chin. Raising the suitcase lid, she asks, "Did anyone give you anything to put in?"

"The fur cape with a Fendi label."

Slipping her hands inside, the inspector discovers the white soft fuzz, hidden like a bunny. "Who gave this to you?"

"Dr. Marchmont," says Lucy. Her probity seems assumed; after all, she hasn't learned to lie. "It was on my body. She gave me the book too. *Villette.*"

"Why have you come to here?" the guard asks perfunctorily, snapping the lid.

"I'm not tied down; there's no place I belong. As far as I know I have no job, no family, and for whatever reason, I seem to have been on my way here," Lucy tells her. "The plane was supposed to land at Ben-Gurion airport. It exploded over Switzerland."

"Why Israel?"

"I don't know." This seems suspect; Lucy offers, "I think of your country as my *Labassecour.*"

"Your what?"

"From *Vilette*—my place to risk personal growth."

Innocent. Flown here like a sparrow, reasons unknown. The inspector impassively takes in the grafted skin on the new-begotten face and then drops her eyes to the clenched fingers of the right hand. Apposition between the thumb and forefinger enables the traveler to grasp her suitcase handle. A sticker is slapped on the pressed-board tartan. Lucy is released among the unoffending others.

◆

Apparently she's expected. As she enters the Ben-Gurion terminal, a man in a dark suit approaches. "You are Lucy Snowe," he says, not as a question, and appropriates her passport. Briefly, Lucy wonders how he knows her name; it seems that strangers know more about her than she does.

Lucy is admitted to the country, and she reaches the center of the city in a car that was sent for her. She has no idea by whom, but she tells herself that when you're in the position of remembering nothing, you may as well take what comes. It feels safe; the car is a black Subaru, bulletproof, she is told by the dark-skinned driver. A soldier waves them through the gate at the Ministry of Justice.

Inside the building the officials of the government are middle-aged men in shirt sleeves, moderately paunched, and three heavyset women behind the counter in the cafeteria on the lowest level, where Lucy is admitted. From the winding marble staircase Lucy hears the racket of hammering and drilling. Her escort is a bearded man in a long black coat and thick-soled shoes; he directs her without comment to step over the buckets and boards and drippings. On the third floor the bustle abruptly ceases.

Sunny air floats through a skylight. Lucy, like a found cat, is deposited just inside an office. A discussion is in progress. The Minister of American Law, according to the lettering on the mottled glass of the flung-back door, is bickering with a frazzled woman standing in the doorway. They don't seem to notice that Lucy's there; in any case, she doesn't know the language.

Left on her own, Lucy tries to figure out why she's been picked up and is now being detained. A man came once to question her before she left the hospital, but that was soon after the crash. If they believe she's connected to some terrorist organization, where are the secrets, the evidence of clandestine plots? The smuggling and torture, the records of deportations, the names of terrorists? Aside from one computer with fuzzy white symbols on a small black screen, information appears to be stored in folders, thumbed-through pages in curling oaktag covers. These sit in the open bookcases, available to any eye.

"Sit down, please, Lucy Snowe." The minister rises and gives her his own chair, behind the desk. He is young, probably in his thirties, compact and thin; his appearance is unexcessive but for an unpruned thicket of hair. His face is pure, stripped down to bones so fine and eyes so dreamy as to make him almost beautiful, the way Jesus is shown to be. He speaks precise English.

After a very short time, when Lucy has told her brief life story, he regards her with the empathy of one who is no stranger to suffering; he seems to assume their kinship. Like his adopted child she is declared a tourist with an unrestricted visa, courtesy of his government and the United States Diplomatic Corps—the relationship between the two isn't clarified; Lucy doesn't inquire. For suddenly she feels beyond exhaustion and is finding it almost impossible to sustain on her spliced-together face the timorous smile of the purely harmless. A vacuity eases over her features.

In the lower depths, she is positioned under a hanging bulb among cardboard cartons piled to the ceiling pipes. Her picture is snapped with a Polaroid and affixed to a visa that the minister then embosses with an official stamp and illegible signature. Currency is counted from a tin box. In exchange for the plentitude of faded paper she writes a check, to be withdrawn against the three-million-dollar ransom at Credit Suisse, paid by TWA for her memory.

The minister asks, "Is there anything else I can do?"

Lucy doesn't know, it's all too new. Hesitantly, she requests a pass that will skirt the many security checks. "When I go through," she explains, "I send off sirens. Like an air raid."

He regrets. This is not possible; everyone submits to searches. "You will become accustomed," he adds.

Not likely, Lucy Snowe thinks. Once outside the high wall she looks down at the document in her hands. The picture shows a face produced from a mold, waxlike. Like a mannequin's. Unfinished, perhaps, for it's too regular; there's no expression, only a flashbulb reflected in each dark, wary eye.

◆

The gold plaque at the entrance of the hotel has an emblem of a crown and, below it, KD. In Lucy's room the ceiling is fifteen feet high; there's a pastoral scene painted on it. An ancient bellman throws open the French doors to the small balcony. Lucy steps out and feels the warm air leap up to lap her skin. On the other side of the street, the tallest building has a bronze dome. The sign says YMCA. Whatever that means. Above it is the solidly blue sky Matisse painted in Morocco, and beyond, the stationary palm fronds and eye-burning brightness. Odd, she thinks, to remember what Morocco looked like to Matisse when she can't remember the street she lived on. She goes back into her room and lies down on the bed. A large, foreign-looking insect drifts into the room. Leaving the shutters open, letting light pour in—and insects; after all, it's their country—Lucy falls asleep listening to the occasional muted sheep-baa of an automobile horn, reaching her ears, sweetly.

◆

Nine o'clock in the morning, the air is heated, the pavement sizzles. Lucy slips among the tourists stuck close to the hotel, as if for protection, and climbs into a taxi, a boxlike Mercedes, a relic, a warhorse, roomy and noisy.

"I'd like to visit the wall," she tells the driver. She hasn't the faintest idea what that is, only that the concierge said that's why people come.

"No problem."

They drive at a snail's pace past belowground tracts, fenced-in craters moonlike in their desolation. Lucy rolls down her window. It only opens halfway but she manages to put her head out into the dusty city. Up-to-date machinery of construction stands idle on the packed clay. Dark-skinned men, wire thin, wearing kerchiefs knotted at the corners, guard the slumbering giants.

"Not safe," the driver says, hanging his arm over the seat and cranking up her window. Lucy meets the dark eyes in the rearview mirror. Staring at her skin, she supposes, stretched like shrink-wrap over her bones. She slides across the seat to the other window.

"Building goes slowly," the driver informs the American woman in approximate English. "Manpower is plentiful, patience also." Formal, yet decidedly intrusive, he begins to lecture, unasked. Lucy is becoming annoyed; perhaps he thinks it's his job, there's no sense saying anything. Along the edge of the street, gowned men squat, heads swathed in white filmy stuff. Covered women slip by, private and mysterious in the heat of the day. The wall itself, of pockmarked gray stone, rises very suddenly. "Cannon shot," the driver says, apparently as part of the tour, "from the sixty-seven war."

They've pulled up. "Will you wait for me here?" Lucy asks.

"Why not?" He sits back, lights a cigarette.

◆

Lucy stands on the edge of a large plaza, sunlit and warm. The figures at the wall with their backs to her seem dwarfed by the absence of anything to measure them by. As seen from God's viewpoint, Lucy assumes, remaining at a respectful distance, feeling isolated from those whose territory this is; a stranger, unrecognized by any god, especially their God. In the stark brightness, bearded, black-gowned men sway back and forth, heads bowed. As Lucy moves forward, she hears mumbling, a low singsong. This, then, is their life's labor, she thinks.

Women have pulled chairs up to the rough surface of the wall. On the other side of the plaza, like flocked birds, they perch on their flattened shadows. Seeing a space, Lucy fits herself into it and impulsively rests the side of her face against the coarse stone, as if listening. She thinks she can hear heartbeats. Pressing closer, she is dizzied by the impossible sensation that the heartbeats are coming from the wall, which she is gripping now with all her strength. Turning her face she opens her mouth and tastes the sun-baked stone. She breathes in the neutral smell, almost undetectable, because she had once known it, she thinks, known it as well as her own. And now, by an unseen force, she is snatched from the verge of recognition. *A door slams. Blackness.* Lucy's knees buckle, her hands begin to slide, she loses her grip.

As she struggles to her feet, surrounding legs adjust slightly, allowing room for her to stand. No one seems to have noticed. She backs away from the wall, and the knot of dark, quiet shapes tightens to form an unbroken mass. Lucy starts across the plaza. When she's almost at the gate, two black-garbed men fly down like crows, startling her. Their twinship is unsettling; from Isaac Singer, it comes to her, in their white shirts, black vests and black knickers exposing shapely calves in white stockings. Their hats are made of fur, and curls hang beside their ears. "Would you like a prayer said for anyone?" one asks, and the other, "Any wishes, any remembrance?"

Lucy tries to think. But something is preventing her, her memory has closed. "No, thanks." She thrusts some coins into their willing hands. They press upon her three filaments of yarn, red as rivulets of blood.

The waiting cab is smoky and smells of something eaten. The driver tosses out his cigarette. "You enjoy?"

Lucy doesn't answer; she's thinking about what happened at the wall. Whatever it was, it's part of her background. She wonders if she's Jewish.

In the circular driveway of the hotel, Lucy holds several bills through the opening in the Plexiglas that separates her from the driver. There's no meter, and, anyway, she doesn't understand the currency. He ignores her; she finds this frightening. She reaches farther into the front seat, dropping more bills beside him, various denominations. "Here," she says, nudging his shoulder. "Please take what I owe you." His dark head, topped by a round, crotched doily fastened with a bobby pin, faces the front, tipping right and left, apparently debating with itself. Believing he has not understood, Lucy tries again. "How much?" she says loudly. The driver turns abruptly. Lucy feels a grip of fear in her stomach and starts pulling back her hand. Suddenly reaching through the safety shield, the driver grasps the damaged hand. He pulls it toward him and touches it delicately to his lips. "Uri," he says, extending his other hand through the opening.

Without thinking, she shakes it. "Lucy."

They are eating in front of a picture window in the dusty, streaming sun. "Later will be full," Uri predicts, gesturing toward the enormous, empty room. Lucy looks around for the waiter; she'd like a drink. Something tropical with rum in it. As it turns out the wilted card in the napkin holder says in Arabic and Hebrew that they don't serve liquor—Uri translates both that and the menu. The food when it comes is tasteless; Lucy believes they boiled the lamb. Uri grows talkative on his second pot of tea: He's a taxi driver with a Ph.D. Gesturing, palms up, he acknowledges the irony. "In anthropology." Uri further volunteers that he grew up on a collective farm, he is forty-six, married for the second time. "And you?" he asks. "What's your story?"

His question is one of the two Lucy's been dreading. He doesn't ask the other one. She'd like to look him in the eye and get it over with: "Don't you want to know what happened, how the hand you shook in your taxi became a claw?" He may, she decides, but he doesn't know her well enough to ask. Tactful— or maybe he's not really interested; how could he be? How could any man be? Uri's face is deeply tanned, wrinkles burned in, the lines white in the dark skin as if they're etched. He's looking at her now with sympathy, but that's not what Lucy wants. All she wants, she realizes, is to be by herself, to avoid the strain, for it seems now an impossible strain of being Lucy Snowe.

Uri laughs. "I'm too nosy. That's what my wife says." From his wallet, he removes a photo of himself with a woman, young, attractive, with dark skin and red hair. "We live on a kibbutz with our seven-year-old daughter, Lisa. But Hanna is not there now, now she goes for six months on assignment—to photograph behind the security zone." Lucy doesn't take the picture, she stares at it, silent. Uri puts the picture away. "Eat," he reminds her. "Take your time, but finish."

His ministrations make her uncomfortable. What is it he wants? He's too attentive; she's relieved to hear he has a wife. Maybe, she thinks, as he is scrupulously dividing the check, she's not being asked for anything at all, which is fine; but then why is he bothering? He chooses two bills from her hand and three small coins; it doesn't seem like much. Unasked, Uri says that he is improving his English for the tour-guiding business. Future plans.

After dinner, they climb the broad, high steps of an amphitheater. Searchlights beam up into the dark sky, and soldiers on the rooftop are almost theatrically illuminated: like sentries on the ramparts in *Hamlet*, thinks Lucy, her mind jumping with random, unrelated references; proving what, that she's had a liberal-arts education? Seeing her look up, Uri hastens to explain that soldiers are routine, not to worry; the flag, limp in the windless night sky, protects everybody. He spreads a white, clean handkerchief on the stone step. "Someone is sitting there since the fourth century," he tells her. "Now is your turn. Sit." She does; why make an issue? She has already decided that instructing the ignorant is part of the culture. It has something to do with human kindness, more to do with chauvinism. With me, he's on a rescue mission, thinks Lucy. At intermission, Uri brings her a Coke. "You enjoying?" Lucy doesn't know what to say to this. She has no subject matter for conversation; she feels excruciatingly blank, angry at herself for coming, fighting to stay conscious.

Outside, the alley streets are alive with the blooming young. They are a river flowing down the middle of the street, singing, waving flags. Dancing in circles, their arms on one another's shoulders. Patriotism? Camaraderie? What impulse inspires them? Maybe some part of her emotions was lost in the wreck. Small tables are set up in front of closed shops. After the marchers pass, music comes from mounted speakers. Young people sit in doorways, on steps and curbs, eating yogurt with fruit. The girls, dark and vibrant, secure in the wonder of their beauty, and the potency, just realized, of their sex; the boys, awkward and eager, awaiting the power promised. Under the curbside table, Lucy's deformed hand twitches uncontrollably, on a frequency that has nothing to do with her will. Getting up now, she says, "I'm sorry, I have to go. I'm really tired."

Seemingly oblivious to what's bothering her, Uri takes her

arm and leads her into the center of the street; he holds her, waiting for the music to begin. Lucy can feel the pressure of his hand on her back as she stands stiffly against him. His closeness, his solidity, the denseness of his body are painful to her. An unwillingness, a coldness, an incapability in herself makes her clumsy. After a few minutes she pulls away.

"What troubles you, Lucy Snowe?" She realizes he's not looking at her in the way she's come to expect, eyes sliding off when she catches them.

"Nothing," says Lucy. "I'm just tired."

Has he done something wrong? Uri wants to know. He bends over her, his face close. It's his fault, he insists, seeming to crave blame as he craves praise. Lucy shakes her head. Is there any way she can explain to this man her physical and mental diminution, her loss? "Do you think it's possible to lose your past?" she'd say. He'd look blank, astonished. Not to have a past would be inconceivable to Uri.

◆

In the hotel lobby, Lucy keeps her eyes on the reflection of the teapot on the low table with a mirrored top. At the sound of laughter, she turns her head to gaze at the women weighted with finery and the men who have appropriated them. She searches among them as they circle and spin out of the revolving door; surely there must be someone she'll recognize. And just at that moment a woman's face surfaces above the others, returns her probing stare, and then submerges with the rest, like a boatload of the drowned.

"Talk to me." Uri distracts her. He sits on the other couch, set at a right angle. "What are you thinking?"

"I'm wondering why I came here. I don't belong."

Uri considers. "You have a different religion; that's okay."

"I have no religion," Lucy says. "I have no past of any kind."

He shrugs, the essential native gesture. "I have primarily a past, but an uncertain future. At least for tonight we can supply what the other misses, no?"

Lucy looks at him with more interest. She's reluctant to acknowledge her interest, though surprisingly she feels it stir. "Sorry, no," she says quickly, standing. "Good night." Uri reaches for her hand. She knows what's stopping her, something from the past, some part of her, something lost with her memory, a voice inside her head, a voice that says, *Must not!* Why shouldn't she? the thought persists. She's damaged but she's not dead yet.

Lucy sits down again and reaches for the small table lamp, pulling it toward her. She puts her chin over the pleated paper shade so that Uri will be able to see the tracings, not always clearly visible, spidery-thin red lines of mending like the raised seams on the underside of a leaf, bisecting her forehead, nose and chin; and the outline of a mask around the edges of her face, following her hairline, the front of her ears, the underside of her chin. Lucy runs the fingers of her left hand over her skin. She knows the markings well; still, she bends her face over the mirrored tabletop to confirm what she already knows. Her tight mask mirrors what's inside: the felt truth. Shame, self-loathing, the sense of her worthlessness as a woman. The lamp glows through the transparency of Lucy's cheeks. Below, on her neck, the darker, coarser skin flushes a deep, almost blood red, as Lucy sees in her eyes a look of desire, as if the grafted skin can not contain the woman inside. She glances up. "Does my appearance horrify you?" she questions Uri.

"No," Uri says. "My daughter had a cloth doll once. This doll was made out of scraps of material, sewn together, and Lisa loved her best of all. She called her Dollface."

"Dollface?" The name resonates; Lucy feels confusion. She lifts up her arm, shielding her eyes from the light, which suddenly seems blinding.

"What's the matter?" Uri asks.

"My head hurts," Lucy gasps. Astonished by the force of the pain, she seizes her head in her hands and begins to rock. Uri's alarmed face is above her. "What's happening to me?" she asks him. "I feel torn!"

She leans back against the couch, face tipped up, eyes on the enormous, slow-moving ceiling fan. Uri, as from a great distance, is asking if she needs a doctor. Lucy becomes aware of a moaning, a sound like a violin threading through the noisy lobby. It's from her; she stops it. She shifts her body in various directions, trying to resettle her center of gravity. "I'm all right; sit down, Uri," she says.

Once she's adjusted herself, Lucy feels a laxness in her limbs. No longer tense, she actually feels light. Suddenly she's calm. She leans back languorously, arms draped across the top of the low settee, legs crossed at the knees and the top leg bouncing. She motions to the waiter who's passing, orders Absolut on ice, twist of lime, no tonic.

Then she laughs and demands, "Look at me, Uri, I feel different. Has my face changed?"

Uri considers her in silence; finally he says, "It has! I think it has! Something about your expression. Your face looks fuller, more truly a doll's face. It's not possible, but, yes, you have changed." He throws up his hands at the absurdity.

"Who am I?" Lucy challenges.

Teasingly, he says, "You tell me."

Lucy meets his eyes, blinks. "I have no idea." Moving toward him, she says, "I may not know who I am, but I know one thing. I like you."

Uri looks uncertain but pleased.

They ride up alone in the gilt-walled, slow-moving lift. Uri keeps his eyes on the half circle above the doors with an arrow pointing to the numbers. He's remaining neutral. Just as they pass the second floor, Lucy takes his hand and puts it on her breast. Smiling into his startled face, she says, "I want to be first with someone."

He catches on: "Tonight, you are first with me."

Maybe she's forgotten how, thinks Lucy, or maybe this is the foreign way: Uri strives toward the end, then comes, hugely happy to have it over with successfully. Still full of heat, Lucy tries to rouse him but he's heavily asleep, and at last she lies on top, rubbing herself to orgasm against his sleeping body.

◆

The first light fading through the shirred curtains wakes Lucy. She scrambles out of bed dragging the sheet to cover her body. "Get out of my room!" she says loudly. The sleeping taxi driver opens his eyes and throws his legs over the side. He's nude. His body, even his shoulders, is covered with black hair like a bear's, except for his sex, which is shining white. He pulls on his pants, which lie puddled on the floor, and hurries to the door carrying his shoes. As the door clicks, Lucy feels the draft waft over her bare, deformed feet. Bile rises to her mouth; she gags. In the bathroom, she leans over the toilet but nothing comes up. Standing, she turns on the shower, the water as hot as she can stand it. When she comes out, the bathroom is sweating—the faucets, the dripping walls and the wet curtain, hanging like a limp white sheet. Lucy wipes a clear swatch in the mirror with a bath towel and views the woman's body, skin a raging red from the shower: small-breasted and narrow like a wren, stomach concave between the pointed bones of her pelvis, and from what she can see over her shoulder, her back is in patches like farmland seen from an airplane. There's a magnifying mirror on an arm; Lucy pulls it out from the wall. Enlarged, her face is a tightly constructed mask, rigid and forbidding; seeing itself, it refuses to smile. I am you, the unwelcome image reminds her.

Outside in the hall a woman in a head scarf is industriously running a noisy vacuum; she says, "*Shalom.*" After Lucy passes her she wonders if there is any reason to go out. What are her options? She can walk back past the cleaning woman to her room and watch the shooting and rock throwing, which look staged and are broadcast, apparently routinely, all day on nationally sponsored television. By doing this she can put off for another hour or day living the only life she has. But what about after that, tomorrow, next week? Lucy keeps walking. Whoever raised her taught her to do what she ought to do. Not what she wants to do.

She spots Uri as soon as she gets off the elevator in the lobby. He is glowing with God knows what memories of the night before, dreams of the future. She turns quickly and starts walking in the other direction. With a tap on her shoulder, Uri says, "Good day, Lucy," and presents four hibiscus blooms, the stems in tinfoil. "Where shall we be going today?" he would like to know as he steps on her heels. Lucy doesn't answer; just because he asked a question doesn't mean she has to answer it. She walks the length of the lobby between the array of flags and into the morning sunlight. Uri opens the front passenger door of his polished car, the color of pewter. Not for the world will she speak to him, Lucy resolves, pitching herself into the dark backseat.

"Yesterday. My mistake." Uri humbles himself above the awakening gasp of the engine. He's sorry, mixed signals, he thought that's what she wanted. She shouldn't worry, he's not offended. He winks, puts the car into gear, starts driving. This is too absurd! thinks Lucy. He has become gallant, playful, romantic; at the wheel he hums, this thick-bodied, middle-aged man with a tea cosy covering his bald spot.

And later he gallops from the sea slicked with black mud. "Smear yourself," Uri advises. "It's beneficial, cures you of anything." Don't come near me, Lucy pleads, sitting huddled on the coarse sand, swathed in towels, wrapped in solitude, brooding over what in herself is incurable.

◆

On the kibbutz, Uri cavorts backward, gleeful in the fields that he says join his country with their enemy. The dirt path runs between rows of olive and fig trees, and bushes bloodred with raspberries. Lucy's decided by now that he's a clown. He has a nice face, a little ragged and leathery, and one eye droops, a result of a SCUD missle explosion, he patiently explains—he's worried he may appear sinister. No chance. His shape is square and solid; he wears army pants, stylelessly baggy. Stopping beside the river he points out the peacocks. "The males," says Uri, "are unaware that their tail fans have been shorn, so they can't fly away. They strut and pose, the old game." He demonstrates. "It's the same for all of us males, we must struggle for attention."

That night, as they pick their way down an unlit road, a child calls to them in Uri's language from the lighted doorway of a caravan. Lifting the little girl to his shoulders, Uri bumps down the path with her skinny legs wrapped around his neck. Her happy laugh floats back. When he sets her down, he says she's Lisa, and he's brought Lucy here to meet her. Then he speaks to the child, and Lisa reaches for Lucy's hand, adjusting her own small hand to its fixed shape. But the child's fragile bones in hers make Lucy nervous; what if she crushes her? She wonders if she has children of her own, children she abandoned. Wouldn't the doctors have known, wouldn't she know? A mother could never abandon her child, thinks Lucy; whatever else she has forgotten, she would not forget her child if she had a child. The heat of the child's hand comes through the rough palm; maybe Lisa minds that her skin feels like broken glass. Lucy lets the little hand slip from her viselike grip, and watches Lisa's dark body vanish in an instant, swallowed by the night.

There's a small stone building in a graveyard surrounded by a low iron fence; the graveyard looks crowded, a little messy. The door to the building is wood, worn bare in some places, a Star of David carved at eye level. Uri takes the key from under a stone. Lucy follows him into the yellow gloom under the low ceiling, past rows of plastic folding chairs. On one, somebody has left a fringed white shawl with blue stripes. Uri puts it on his shoulders, its width bunched at his neck, fringe reaching almost to his knees.

Lucy sees nothing she remembers, but there's a smell in the place . . . of what? Eternity, indestruction, survival? She comes to stand beside Uri at the pulpit, and watches the back-to-front turning of the Bible. Her eyes swim over the black characters; the paper is foxed by age, limp from handling. Uri mumbles by heart in a singsong, his voice disturbingly melodic, washing over the surface of Lucy's mind like a wave washing over a shore. Leaving marks.

They seem to be sharing a room—carefully, with consideration for each other's rights, like rooming strangers on an economy tour. Sometime that night Lucy wakes to find Uri standing over her bed.

"It's okay with you if I come in?" he says.

She says no, and that's the end of it.

◆

When they return to the city Lucy showers off the dust of the desert and goes to bed thinking she's found where she belongs. But at midnight, having lain sleepless for three hours, she calls downstairs to say she'll be checking out first thing in the morning. She'll need transportation to the airport. "Can you make a plane reservation for me?" She's not ready yet to go home. "I just want to be somewhere that's not the United States."

"Try Greece. Pick an island," the woman suggests, "they're all beautiful. My friend just came back from Crete and it was great fun. I've been to Rhodes myself; it depends what you're looking for." Lucy thanks the woman and chooses Rhodes; then she packs her belongings—there aren't many, all that's new is a tiny clay oil lamp from a dig that Uri gave her. In the morning she pays her bill and carries her suitcase to the street. Outside the hotel, wind and rain, and dawn not yet evident.

Standing on line at Olympic Airways, she feels a tap on her shoulder. Uri produces a bunch of violets from behind his back. "They're wilted," he himself notices.

"Thank you, anyway."

"Welcome."

As they shake hands good-bye, Lucy has to fight a sudden, disturbing wish to change her mind and hold on to this connection. Feeling her nose stuff, she sniffs. "Leave-takings are hard for me," she explains.

The plane is parked far out on the wet, windy field. From the doorway she turns to wave. A mistake, she discovers, because then it comes over her fully, the remembered firebrand of grief. Uri's sad, sweetly outmoded smile with his arm raised seems a small death.

DANIEL DORFMAN, SUMMONED ONE MORNING FROM HIS Park Avenue office, is sitting on a curved-back wooden bench on the ground floor of Central Police Station, in Cambridge, Massachusetts. He has been there three hours. Daniel doesn't wear a watch; he knows time with great accuracy, internally. Now he doesn't have to check the clock behind the chest-high police desk. As a rule, Daniel doesn't wait for anybody; somebody is waiting for him. He's having trouble breathing. The musty aridity of the air brings back grammar school, some forty years before, with its clapped erasers, floating chalk dust and withering heat; he feels helpless and overlooked. At John McCormack Elementary School, it comes back to him, after he'd skipped from grade three to five, he was never again overlooked. He'd graduated first at the high school for bright boys, and then Harvard, the law and business schools, had been child's play.

Daniel climbs the marble steps one lofty flight. The building shares with the Latin School the grand proportions of Depression-era construction. On the third floor are the courtrooms and judges' chambers. Harried, adversarial couples line the halls, whispering to their smooth-faced lawyers. A crying woman occupies the phone booth. Daniel raps on the glass, motioning her to come out; he paces until she leaves. His man on the floor of the Exchange runs down the closing list of stock quotations. Daniel returns between the warring parties, down the wide drafty staircase, to sit on the bench.

Still on the bench at four-thirty, Daniel hears himself making the sucking sound, pasting and unpasting his tongue from the roof of his mouth, repeatedly. "That's stress, Danny, baby," Gail had advised him. "Chill out." Between the buttons of his suit coat Daniel surreptitiously flattens his palm against his abdomen to determine if he's breathing correctly. All he finds is that his shirt is wet. *Hum-sah,* Daniel grunts, letting all the breath out. Just then his name is called. Loudly, just as it was called over the PA system when he was singled out by the headmaster for some special commendation. Daniel follows the uniformed back down the hallway and through the door marked HOMICIDE.

He's inside, the door shut behind him. The room is hot and messy. Papers everywhere: a stack precariously fluttering on the wide sill of the open window, exploding from the file cabinet, and a curled sheet in the platen of the relic typewriter. As Daniel's organized mind picks through the disorder, he feels angry. He had been expecting something institutional, organized, bureaucratic, something he could deal with rationally. Running his eyes once more around the room, he does see, behind the curtain of dust particles floating in sunlight, one gesture to civility: a small, graceful but poorly framed line drawing of a nude.

Hesitating only a moment, Daniel steps on the worn Bacarra carpet as if it might sink with his weight. In front of him, in the midst of the unimaginable chaos, he distinguishes the shape of a man, inseparable from the decor. The man is sprawled in one of those copious, melted-leather lounge chairs afforded by Fifth Avenue shrinks like Cissy's. The man leans forward, disengaging himself slightly from the background. "Hi! Sit down, Mr. Dorfman."

He points to the other chair, a mission-style dark wood with an upright back. "Remember me? Lieutenant Lucas; and you've met Detective Beck."

Daniel turns around, having missed completely the man standing in the corner like a coat tree. Disconcertingly, Detective Beck's shirt is the cream color of the wall above the molding, and his pants are the deeper beige of the wall below. Beck wears wire eyeglasses and has wire-terrier hair. His lips strain over dentures.

Daniel seats himself in the mission oak, resolved not to say a word. "Why am I here?" he says immediately.

Both men start talking at once. Lucas glares at Beck over Daniel's shoulder. "When was the last time you saw Ursula Gant?" Lucas asks.

"Again?" Daniel relaxes a little. "We've gone over that, Lieutenant. You guys questioned me almost two years ago, several months after my wife's death."

"These things take patience," Lucas says defensively. "We got lucky. We got a tip."

Daniel goes on, "At that time I told you everything I knew about Ursula Gant's disappearance—which was zip."

"Yes, indeed," Lucas agrees, fidgeting. "The woman had simply left everything behind and gone away."

"Has she turned up?"

"Nooooo," Lucas says indecisively.

Then he swings one leg over the other knee, so his tasseled Top-Sider moccasin is almost level with his head. His piercing blue eyes, in the opening behind the jackknifed knee, have a thoughtful expression. After a minute he tosses his shock of gray hair off his forehead with a jerk of his head. His handsome but dissipated face collapses in wrinkles. Daniel, annoyed by the histrionics, looks elsewhere: Beneath the old-fashioned window, several large plants, resting in a trough filled with gravel, cunningly extend their twining trunks and jungle-sized leaves toward him. As Daniel watches, fascinated and repelled, a striped orange and black cat bounds through the window and begins to groom itself on a daybed of Freudian extraction, covered by an Indian print.

Pulling his eyes away, Daniel volunteers, just to move things along, "I'm still trading her account. Until she notifies me to liquidate or take some other action, there's nothing else I can do."

"Of course," Lucas says respectfully. "Making money?"

"Yes," Daniel says. "Is there anything else?"

Lucas's baby-blue turtleneck jersey expands in the opening of his corduroy sport coat. Mail order from L.L. Bean, Daniel identifies. Leather patches on the elbows. Lucas's laced fingers rest now on his solid gut. Slowly he takes one hand off his stomach and, without taking his eyes off Daniel, feels around the table beside his voluptuous chair. He turns on the brass table lamp, shaped like a ship's wheel, and runs his eyes down the paper he has recovered.

"Oh, yes," mutters Lucas, as if reminded of something. He tosses the paper toward the table, but misses; it floats to the floor near Daniel's feet. "Take it," he offers. "I have a copy. It may interest you."

Daniel reaches for the paper. Across the top it says Admission Report. Ursula Gant is printed on the line for Patient's Name; her address and phone number are entered. As he reads, Daniel's mouth gets dry and his hands shake, shake so badly that he has to flatten the page on his lap in order to keep it from rattling. "Oh God!" Daniel exclaims. The doctor had written, above his illegible signature: *Laceration under left eye requiring suturing. Hematoma on scalp. Gross loss of blood. Question of severe beating. Patient appears extremely disoriented.* Daniel suddenly feels sweat pop out of his pores, and it occurs to him that he's going to faint. Just then the trembling page is snapped out of his hands. His forehead is roughly clapped and his head shoved forward, plunged between his knees. After a few minutes he is swung up; his tie is loosened and a deft hand unbuttons his shirt collar. Directly in front of his nose, Daniel focuses at last on Beck's glinting silver belt buckle shaped like a buffalo head. Dropping his eyes, Daniel sees—what else?—lizard-skin boots with pointed toes. Obligingly, Beck hikes his pants leg and turns his foot sideways to display the stacked heel.

When Beck steps out of the way, Daniel sees Lucas smoothing his coarse gray forelock with both palms, alternately. "I know how you must be feeling," Lucas murmurs sympathetically. "I was stunned myself." Daniel nods. He's not sure if he has moved his head himself or if Beck, whose closeness he senses, has moved it for him. "The doctor remembered Ms. Gant when we questioned him," Lucas says. "He said she wasn't the usual type of battered woman he sees at the clinic." After a histrionic pause, Lucas raises his eyebrows. "What do you make of it, Mr. Dorfman?"

Daniel, quietly dying, isn't able to speak.

"Nothing's been concluded," Lucas tells him reassuringly, "nothing even speculated. It's just that the circumstances bear looking into. You agree?"

Perhaps to keep Daniel from bolting, Beck's hot, heavy hand lands on his shoulder, straddling it like a saddle. The cat, apparently part of the choreography, at that moment slouches across the floor. It twines between Daniel's legs, purring, then suddenly springs into Daniel's lap. This moldy specimen of animal has fur corroded like a junkyard Plymouth. As Daniel instinctively arches away, Beck's hand (a gold ring with an opal on the pinky) scoops her up by her bloated midsection. Going to the window, he tosses her out, closing the window behind. Then he looks back and asks, "John, do you know Mr. Dorfman?"

Daniel turns; a boy is standing in the doorway. He has a long, tubelike torso; he is dark-haired with an incipient mustache under his man-sized nose. He could be fourteen or fifteen, Daniel guesses, staring at him.

"I can't say as I know him," John answers. "But like I told you when you showed me the pitcha, I seen him that mornin' comin' outa numbah two Farrar."

John's accent is Somerville, unmistakable in Daniel's ears. Ursula hadn't spoken that way; her voice was cultured, educated; if it had any accent, it was a trace of New York—the New York of Riverside Drive, where Ruth Kornfield lived before the nursing home, where Ursula had lived as a child.

"What time was that?" Lucas is softly asking John.

"I was comin' back from my papah rounds. That's around six-thirty."

Lucas's high brow creases, as if he is sincerely trying to make sense of this bit of information. Daniel watches, suddenly terribly frightened. "You, ah . . . did business with Ms. Gant in her home, at night, from time to time?" Lucas is asking. "Is that accurate, Mr. Dorfman?"

Daniel stands. "I believe I have the right to have my lawyer present."

"You do."

The knob is slippery in Daniel's hand, he can't get the door open. Beck lays his own hand on top, gently, and turns the knob. Daniel looks up at him. "I'm free to leave, I assume?"

Beck removes his hand.

THERE ARE TWELVE ROWS ON THE OLYMPIC AIRWAYS flight from Tel Aviv to Rhodes; it's about half full. Lucy stands alongside the second row consulting her stub. "Excuse me," she says to the blond, almost silver curls tumbling under the overhead beam. Without looking up, the woman switches her knees to the side and Lucy steps through. Seated, Lucy gropes for either of the two books in her carry-on, inhaling deeply, almost to insensibility the potent fragrance worn by her seatmate. The female scent that male peacocks prance for, she remembers, gazing sidewise at the woman. She, the seatmate, wears her slash of bright red lipstick like a banded bird, to identify the species; there's no mistaking her power.

Almost as if sensing Lucy's curiosity, the woman raises her head to look at her. She's not young, Lucy realizes, but extraordinarily beautiful, wrenching Lucy's heart toward a haunting she cannot grasp. Lucy looks away, out the window, disconcerted by the suggestion of pity she thought she saw in the other woman's clear blue eyes.

◆

Fifteen minutes after they land, the Rhodes airport is empty. When the conveyor at last stops revolving, with nothing on it but a trunk of considerable size plastered with stickers, Lucy reports her missing suitcase. The man behind the little window says through the hole that they'll forward it when she's found a place to stay. The only item of value, she writes on the form, is a white fur cape.

On the turning rack in the kiosk, brochures show narrow streets paved in sea stones, a sea too blue to be believed and whitewashed pensiones. Interchangeable, with pots of red flowers. The third place Lucy calls has a vacancy.

She pays for a week in advance and leaves her carry-on upstairs; the room is small but looks clean. She realizes she's hungry.

The dining room is crowded; there's a wordless volume of noise. Tables are covered with white starched cloths and the bud vase of each has one red flower. Lucy waits while a small table with legs that snap in place is borne upside down on the head of a waiter and hastily set for one. Fine, thinks Lucy, propping her guidebook against the water glass. She shuts it out, the French, the Greek, the German, just as her past has shut her out, and reads while she eats.

Suddenly a shriek of laughter isolates itself from the surrounding din, and Lucy looks up to see, she thinks she sees, almost certainly she sees, the blond woman who was on the plane. She sits with her back to Lucy at a table where they're speaking English; as if sensing Lucy's scrutiny, the woman turns. Their eyes lock and Lucy's mind wobbles on the brink of recognition. The woman pushes back her chair and starts for her.

Lucy gets right up. The last thing she wants is the where's home? conversation. Unzipping her waist pack, she releases a scatter of paper money on the table and stuffs the remaining handful back in the pouch.

In the lobby the music of the bouzouki, deep-toned and seductive, streams from the cocktail lounge. Surprised to find a cocktail lounge in a pensione, Lucy is tempted. There's a part of her that would like to climb on a bar stool and watch the world-famous belly dancer who's pictured on a poster that sits on an easel outside the door. However, looking in, she decides she can't. The last thing Lucy wants is to hear some man beside her say, Hi, there!—and, after taking a good look, turn away. The worst are those who stare from a distance and, when she catches them, look shamefaced. Or the ones who smile fixedly, gazing straight at her, as if to prove they see nothing wrong in having a plastic face; in fact, they may get one for themselves.

Lucy walks the length of the empty lobby, past the concierge, whose deadened eyes she imagines following her. She tries not to hurry; if she hurries, the length of her legs unmatch and she limps. Removing the damaged hand from her pants pocket, she punches the button for the lift. It scrapes down from above and thuds to a halt, continuing to rock in the shaft as the door is thrown open and people push out. Among them the blond woman—or perhaps it's only her scent. From the lift Lucy sees the blond head disappear in the dark of the cocktail lounge. Lucy gets out again, and walks across the lobby.

At the entrance to the lounge, she hesitates. But she's blocking the doorway, and people are turning as they go in or out to see what's wrong with her. Forcing herself, Lucy plunges into the dark, asserting her right, as she sees it, not only to go into the barroom—but her right to be on this earth.

The air is thick with smoke; she makes out silhouetted forms sitting at the small tables around the dance floor. In a funnel of pink-pouring haze the belly dancer, broad hips and bare stomach rotating and thrusting in a mounting frenzy, is spotlit, to the crowd's apparent indifference.

Stepping up to the bar, leaning forward with one foot on the brass rung to read the label on the bottle, Lucy tells the bartender, "Ouzo." The bartender's lips move. "No ice," Lucy tells him. "Straight up."

The taste of ouzo is sweet. She signals. "Another, please."

From behind the rows of bottles, doubled by the blue mirror, her marred and joyless face, a pastiche, gaunt and forbidding, stares at her. As soon as she has swallowed the second drink, Lucy turns her stool. She feels dizzy, she's had too much to drink too fast. She goes round again. Each time she rotates, she glances at herself in the mirror. Another rotation. Another Lucy.

There, among the many bottles and the massed cluster of heads, her dark sprouted hair sticks up, unruly. She pushes off the bar with her hand and goes round in the other direction, twice. As she slows, the ghastly face in the mirror breaks into a grin. She pushes off, the face streaks by; this time she could swear the hair is yellow and shines in the dark, almost white. Who are you? Lucy asks the blond woman as she passes her in the mirror, are you following me? Maybe she's been hired by the airlines, thinks Lucy, trying to make sense of it. Maybe they want to make sure the woman they gave all that money to is really injured. Catching the bar, Lucy stops her stool. Determined, dead serious about getting to the bottom of it, she sits gazing at the reflection directly opposite. The eyes meeting hers are decidedly not her own. Now, for the sake of demystification, Lucy raises the empty shot glass above her head into the blue-lit air. At the same time the other's arm rises up in the same gesture. Looking hard at her, the blond woman calls out, Go away, Lucy Snowe! You are living in the wrong body.

◆

Shortly after getting into bed Lucy's heart begins to race. She has isolated a sound: Someone is moving in the hall outside her door. She closes her book, snaps off the bed lamp. First there's a silence, then, *knock, knock, knock.* "What is it?" Lucy calls out in the dark. Abruptly, the knocking stops.

Lucy stands on bare feet looking down at the whisper of space between the door and the threshold. There is a flurry of movement in the hall. With a scraping noise, a paper slides into the room. Lucy picks up the torn flap of an envelope and carries it into the bathroom to read: *I found some money under your table. Ring room 23.*

Her waist pack is on the dresser; she fumbles through it. The Greek money, the rainbow of tissue-thin paper that had been slid into the tray at the money exchange, is gone.

Lucy sits on the edge of the bed debating with herself. What she'd like to do, late as it is, is to go downstairs to the front desk, where Bead-eyes, owner and concierge, sits in wait, and check out that night. Forget the money—she can cash another check. She could find another pensione, she thinks. But she's already called Olympic Airways with her address. Lucy picks up the phone and asks for room 23.

A woman's voice answers, in English. The voice is soft, almost a drawl: "Who's this?"

"I'm in room twenty-eight," Lucy says breathlessly. "You left me a note?"

"You bet," the woman says. "Ah have got your money."

"What money?"

"When you left the table, you dropped it; lucky I noticed. Come on over, I'm down at the end of the hall."

"I can't, I'm in bed," Lucy says immediately. She realizes that the woman is trying to be nice, but what if she asks Lucy to have lunch with her? "Could you leave the money downstairs at the mail desk?"

"Y'all want me to bring it on over?"

"No, thanks. Tomorrow would be fine."

"Sure thing. What'd you say your name was, hon?"

"Lucy. Lucy Snowe."

◆

In the morning the money is there, soft, pale notes. Lucy shakes them out of the envelope like fallen flower petals. "The guided tour of Lindos is leaving now," the clerk behind the desk alerts her. "We have a place for you, as arranged."

Lucy can't remember having arranged anything. "Can you tell me the name of the woman who left the money?" she asks. "I'd like to thank her; she's in room twenty-three." His eyes scan the register. "I have a Mr. Mario Mazzocco in twenty-three; he came in yesterday."

Under the portico the bus is filling. Lucy keeps going. She may not know who she is, but she knows she doesn't belong among them: women traveling in pairs, for the most part older than herself—or her own estimation of herself. Flat-heeled, cotton-skirted women comfortable in their full bodies, broad-brimmed hats clapped on. Spunky and mildly defiant—nothing to do with the blond woman who seems to be following her around. That one, Lucy's decided, is someone *temporarily* unattached. Like a flying acrobat, she's nowhere now, but she'll be on her feet when she lands. The key word is *temporarily*.

◆

Lucy walks to the north end of Ródhos, following the mimeographed map she'd picked up at the desk. She's looking for the Jewish Quarter, listed under "Churches" in the Blue Guide. It's hardly a Quarter, Lucy sees when she's found it, more of a single street of vacant lots growing sunflowers. As Lucy stands in front of a small concrete-block building reading the names carved on the memorial plaque, a woman peers out from the cracked-open doorway. "Is it possible to look inside the synagogue?" Lucy asks her.

The woman responds in Greek; Lucy catches only the word *Jew*.

"I don't know," Lucy says, as the woman steps aside, "whether I am a Jew."

She goes in after her, and isn't able to see the woman after the burning brightness. Lucy walks toward the small flame and only then sees the figure in black bent almost double, it seems to Lucy, with weariness and piousness. The woman speaks first in Greek, then Spanish; and when Lucy shakes her head, she says haltingly in Yiddish, which Lucy seems to get the drift of, "The town of Ródhos once had six thousand Jews, now there are six. I am the youngest."

"What has become of the others?"

"They were killed in the World War or went away."

"Why did you stay?"

She doesn't understand, Lucy sees. The eyes that seek Lucy's are lost in wrinkles and sunk in wells of deepest black, as if she has seen the dead where they live in darkness. She has stayed so that someone will remember, it occurs to Lucy. As the old Jew pulls the curtain on the little cabinet, Lucy, with her heart beating fast, mimics the woman's gesture, touching her fingers to her lips and then to the maroon velvet cover on one of the rolled scrolls.

At the door, the woman lifts her loose sleeve and shows Lucy the faint number tattooed on her forearm. In response, wordlessly, Lucy holds out her deformed hand to show that she too is a survivor.

She starts downhill, toward the harbor. She's not entirely sure where the harbor is, but she climbed up to find the Jewish Quarter, so she heads down the narrow, winding road. She walks on the shady side, hugging the stone wall. Rounding one of the switchbacks, she trips over a man's legs. He's sitting on the ground with a tray on his lap; he doesn't move. Lucy buys a post-card from him and a Fuji camera in a box, the film inside. She wants to help him, but more than that she wants to feel better about herself. Maybe she can keep a record; she'll remember where she's been. Stepping back, she asks, "Is it all right if I take your picture?" The man smiles; his teeth are broken. She takes the picture and drops a few coins in his tray. Then leaning on her guidebook, she addresses the postcard to Dr. Marchmont at the convent. But she doesn't write anything; she can't think of what to say.

Down some winding steps Lucy comes out to a small square where there are a few shops that have no fronts, just merchan-dise piled high along the edge of the narrow sidewalk and hung on ropes with clothespins. T-shirts with pictures of the Colossus, leather sandals, woven bags, beaded waist packs. Some ham-mered-metal necklaces. Farther down the street there are real stores. Lucy buys a blue canvas satchel with leather trim to re-place her lost suitcase. She doubts she'll ever see the fur cape again. She buys sunscreen, sunglasses, a straw hat with a brim. In another shop she buys a nylon rain poncho in a zipper case. Af-ter that she wanders around the *farmakio;* she has plenty of money but no idea what else to buy. The afternoon has turned warm; in her black turtleneck jersey and black pants she's too hot and feels a little faint. Not quite real, almost invisible, she thinks. Like someone's shadow. Well, she's tired of that; she wants to be seen. She looks for a clothing store. She'll pick out a short-sleeved shirt, denim, she's thinking, to look like every-one else. Or a print dress like the ones worn by the women on the street.

Suddenly Lucy feels buoyant; she lifts her knees high, she seems to be wading through layers of sunlight. She's boiling hot but isn't sweating. Burned flesh doesn't sweat, they'd told her. No pores.

She steps under an awning and presses her forehead against the store window. Bright colors glitter behind the amber scrim. Through the dark reflection of her own figure, the palm of her good hand spread on the glass, she sees, behind her, a woman winding an iron pole that raises the striped awning. Without turning, Lucy says, "I'll take the white dress in the window and the pair of black leather clogs as well."

"Come back. I'm closed until three-thirty."

"What if I don't try them on?"

"You don't want to try them on?"

Lucy says, "I don't have to. I'll take a chance."

"Final sale."

Lucy doesn't miss a beat: "Naturally."

The woman gives a last, warning look and says, "Come in." She climbs into the front window and pulls the dress over the dummy's head. Meanwhile Lucy's not thinking anymore of the seams and scars on her body, her ridged flesh; she's thinking of the beach she saw behind the pensione. Rummaging in the rack she finds a bathing suit; then, before she can decide against it, she opens her waist pack and tosses a handful of drachmas on the counter.

"It's on sale as well," the shopkeeper volunteers. The suit is yellow and very brief. It's cut high on the thighs; the front attaches to the back by laces, open a few inches to show the bare skin. The saleswoman hesitates. "If madam wishes," she offers, "I can take a few stitches to counter the décolletage."

"All right," says Lucy; and five minutes later, when she hands it to Lucy, Lucy asks, "Will it be all right if I quickly slip it on?"

A radio plays somewhere in the shop. Lucy undresses behind the wavy curtain. She doesn't make a sound for a long time. The song on the radio ends, followed by a commercial. The saleswoman calls out, "How does it look?"

Lucy laughs. "There's not much of it."

The curtain sways, a hand reaches inside holding a long terry-cloth robe with a hood. "Perhaps madam would like this as well?"

◆

The beach behind the pensione is not large. The sand is dark and grainy, mixed with gray, smooth oval stones. Lucy's new robe reaches her fused toes, where the skin is thickened and layered and leaves a print like a horse's hoof. She sinks deeply. Pebbles crunch and small stones shift. Lucy puts on her sunglasses and hat and walks over to one of the few empty beach slabs—narrow rectangles made of white plastic—randomly strewn around. An old man, mustached like a walrus, covers the slab for her with a thin striped mattress and waits politely for a tip. Lucy gives him some coins and lies down, still as death.

The sun is at three o'clock; under her robe Lucy's body feels on fire. Perspiration pops out of the living pores, behind her knees, between her breasts; after a while she feels it sliding down the sides of her body. At last Lucy decides to risk it; she's applied her number 40 sunscreen. She sits up and wiggles out of the robe.

Everywhere under the hot, pouring sun she sees half-nude women displaying themselves boldly, unaffectedly. Any shape—flattened breasts, hanging breasts, large and small breasts—all out in the open; and the men take no notice! The viewless view, Lucy notes to herself, because nobody watches. Nobody snaps a picture. Nobody talks or throws things in the air; they seem to have come here with one purpose, to burn as much of their bodies as they can before leaving. This, then, is the only activity.

These are the natives, not tourists, thinks Lucy, gazing around. All of them in partial undress, ignoring each other.

More than anything, Lucy wants to be one of them. Digging her fingers deeply in among the tiny pebbles, she lifts handfuls and lets them flow in a stream playfully up and down her legs and between her thighs. Heaviness spreads like warm honey through her veins. Shaking her shoulders, Lucy lets the top of her new bathing suit fall to her waist, exposing her small breasts. She looks to see if anyone's noticed.

To her left is the blond woman, lying on slab with her arms folded under her head. In each armpit is a patch of kinky, gold-streaked hair. Her breasts are full, spread bounteously across the width of her narrow brown body; the nipples, with large areoles, have a copper tinge. Her hair is oiled, sleek as an otter's. At her side is a gray-haired man wearing a skimpy, silken bikini that clings to his sex. His hair is long, his muscles long and graceful; he wears chains of gold on his chest. Now his midriff muscles suddenly tense, and he heaves himself up on one elbow. He is trying to read a curling paperback. It's no use; after a few minutes he tosses the book in the sand. He sits up and begins lovingly anointing himself with oil; he glistens. Lucy catches her breath, stirred, perhaps, by her own seminakedness. She rolls off the slab onto her stomach. The stones are hot against her belly and thighs, hard against her breasts. Finally she sits up on her knees and, with her back to the man, slowly brushes the sand off her body, letting her fingertips brush her nipples. Meanwhile she imagines that the man is watching her, but when she turns, she sees that the blond woman has seen her and started to rise. The arm of the man swings up and slaps across her body. Not hard, but hard enough to push her back on her slab. Intimacy. Ownership.

Lucy quickly gets up and walks toward the water. At the edge she stops and glances behind; the man is sitting up, embracing his knees, surveying the strewn bodies. The woman has put on large round sunglasses and is peering in Lucy's direction.

Lucy goes in deep, deeper, past the waders and the dippers. Past the screaming children. The icy water slips between her thighs; she feels it there, where the skin is whole. Since the crash she's thought this about sex: She is not a normal woman, but she has her life. Is pleasure too much to ask? It's not out of the question, physically, but who'd want her? Besides Uri, who was so good-natured he didn't mind. That's gone now, and she resolves not to think about it. But she can't help it. When she's waist deep in the soft, gentle water, Lucy eases her bathing suit down past her hips. Exposed, she floats on her back, eyes closed, fantasizing that when she opens them the man who is with the blond will be standing beside her. Now she moves her gnarled fingers between her thighs; their roughness excites her. When she is about to have an orgasm, she stops. *How bad, how shameful you are!* Thrashing about to gain her footing, Lucy scrambles toward shore. *Why can't you control these unacceptable urges? What is wrong with you?* Immediately, Lucy feels sickened by the thought of the evil that's in her, from before. That must be controlled. She remembers almost nothing, but one thing she's apparently retained is that she's got to be *decent*. She has been told that. "I'll try," Lucy promises in a soft, frightened, breathless, childlike voice. She tugs up her suit straps.

Under Lucy's feet the shallows are murky with seaweed. Slippery tendrils grasp at her ankles, and she drags them with her as she runs over the sharp rocks and broken shells at the edge of the sand.

Crossing the hotel lobby, Lucy clutches her flapping robe around her. People are sitting on chairs or couches, talking; she is aware of laughter. A voice calls, "Lucy, y'all get your money?"

There's the blond woman, silhouetted in the doorway against the outside glare. As she starts forward, her reflection in the shining floor follows a smear of blood, which Lucy looks down at now with mortification.

At that moment the elevator door opens and Lucy steps on. But not before the blond slips in behind. She's wearing a narrow, sheer shift through which you can see her bikini and the outline of her legs. The small enclosure is suddenly filled with the expensive smell of her perfume, body heat and oil. "Thank you for returning my money," Lucy says. "I'm sorry if I was rude."

"I've got something else of yours," says the woman, pushing the second floor button.

"Of mine?" Lucy asks, as the elevator starts ponderously up.

"What happened to your feet?" the blonde asks, looking down, wincing.

"Pardon?" She's taken by surprise; people usually avoid asking about her injuries.

"You've cut yourself." They've halted. The woman shakes her head and pushes open the door to the hall. "Looks nasty," she says, as she moves to the first door and puts her key in the lock. "Come on in, hon." Lucy stands in the doorway, trying not to stare. The room is not made up; there's a man's shoe in the middle of the carpet, a half-eaten salad on a tray, and tennis clothes draped over the chair back. The sheets are tangled and there's a big box on the bed. "It was left here by mistake," the woman says.

Lucy walks around the shoe and guardedly reaches the brown carton that's tied with thick yellow rope. LUCY SNOWE, PENSIONE AGHIA TRIADA, ROOM 28 is printed on top. FRAGILE is stamped everywhere in red.

"Maybe they thought it said twenty-three," the blonde offers.

"We're probably the only two American women traveling alone. Actually, I'm not registered. I'm staying with a friend."

Lucy doesn't respond. She looks at the box. "What's in it?"

The blonde thumps it with her knuckle. "Ah've no idea; maybe a present. Maybe a nineteen-inch TV." She kicks the shoe under the bed. "But I'll help y'all lug it to your room, if you want."

♦

The next day Lucy gets out of a taxi at the Amboise Gate and weaves between the tour buses. Sleeping behemoths, emanating waves of heat. Lucy hasn't bought a thing so far, she'd have no place to put it, and she refuses to be saddled with this box. Up the steep hill she goes, hugging the box, negotiating the shifting oval stones underfoot. Far ahead Lucy sees a burning white hole centered in the sky. The attached buildings on both sides of the street appear not so much to meet at the horizon as to be falling inward. The box in Lucy's arms is not particularly heavy, but it's bulky and awkward, and she can barely see around it. After ten or fifteen minutes, she's breathless. She sits down against the buildings on one side. Piano music is coming from an open window across the street; Lucy thinks she remembers that she too once played a halting "*Claire de Lune*." Suddenly a deluge of water (she hopes it's water) splashes down. Luckily it misses the box, but Lucy's drenched. Getting up, she hoists her burden by its yellow rope and starts walking again, feeling almost certain that she's lost. Approaching a gate between two houses she sees a man is sitting at a wrought-iron table in the garden, edged by trees so severely pruned the limbs are stumps. Lucy thinks they're mulberry trees. But there are so many things in the world Lucy has no name for. Instead of asking directions, when the man looks up, she walks on.

*   *   *

It's after noon. Lucy is resting on a stone bench under an enormous arch where there's shade. She is baked, dehydrated, ready to give up. She slides the box off her knees; it lands with a soft thud on the tile floor that glints with gold bits. A uniformed guard, who'd been obscured by a pillar, claps once sharply. He's about to tell her to move on. But then he looks at her, the hesitation a little too long for Lucy's comfort, and walks away. She gets up. Lucy's arms strain to circle the box. She has no idea where she is; hasn't she seen that empty lot with one intact Ionic column, standing unattached, its grooved sides partly eaten away?

Just then she sees it, the sign over the door: ATELIER PHIDIA, she checks the name on the box. A plaster Laocoön gathers dust in the sun-stricken window; the door's ajar. Lucy walks past cluttered shelves of pottery in various stages of completion, some glazed, some decorated, some fired. She looks through a doorway into the back room. Under a funnel of light a man in half-glasses is balancing an unpainted vessel on his fingertips. He glances up, brush poised. "What's wrong?" he says. "Is it broken?"

Lucy lowers the box to his table, declaring that she'd like to return it.

"For what reason?" the artist asks. He stares for a moment, his eyeglasses so covered with paint spots, she doubts he can see anything. "Just yesterday you bought it." He goes on to remind her that she stood right where she is standing now and praised his work to the skies.

Lucy looks around; she has no memory of ever being here before, but rather than dispute, she says, "I believe you." Then while she is insisting that she made a mistake, the artist scoots by and lifts a catalog from the top of the file cabinet. He blows off the dust, pushes his work aside so he can set it down, and shuffles through the shiny pages. Lifting his eyeglasses onto his forehead, he brings his nose close to the page. "The priceless original," he reads, triumphant, tapping a photograph of a long-necked vase, "from Attica, fifth century. Attic Lekythos, depicting Proxinos as she leaves for the afterlife, and Ellisso, her daughter, in attendance."

Lucy shakes her head. "It's beautiful. I'm really sorry, I can't keep it." All she knows is that she must rid herself of the vase; it reminds her of something in her past, something that frightens her. Seeing her distress, the artist seats her in his chair. Then, wetting his index finger, he flips through his receipt book. "Here, you see the proof."

Lucy stares at the thin page, smudged by a carbon. "I don't doubt you."

"You paid me thirty-six thousand drachmas, in cash," the man says emphatically.

"I know I did."

"I told you no refunds."

"I know you did."

He lets out a nervous laugh. "I recognize you. It was you, or your double." He hesitates and slides his eyeglasses to the bridge of his nose; they are bifocals with bull's-eyes that magnify his pupils. "Truthfully, you seemed a little different," he admits. "Your face was the same, but . . . I don't know how to say it, your style was different."

Lucy stands up and starts toward the door. He follows her and brings her the box. "However, if you don't like this one, I have others."

"I like it." She gathers the box against her breasts, when what she wants is to smash it to the floor. In the street the box in her arms suddenly weighs a ton, the hairy ropes cut into her. She's determined to leave this vase somewhere; she looks left and right. Something has been triggered in her brain, something dangerous, something she cannot allow herself to think of, or she may lose her precarious hold on sanity. She keeps on walking. Then, stealthily sidestepping until she's against the wall of a house, Lucy lowers the box to the doorstep, and backs away as if she's abandoning her baby, born out of wedlock. Running down the center of the cobbled hill, she comes very close to hurtling herself off the surface.

The trough of sky between buildings is painted purple, and the newly emerged moon casts a grotesque shadow, like Quasimodo's, on the ground. Every smashed and reconstructed bone in her body aches. At the bottom of the hill, where tourists milled, Lucy walks through an empty plaza like a stage set with a motionless fountain. Now, cold in the swiftly fallen dusk, she takes a taxi and limps into the pensione.

Packing, her knees shake. She throws everything into the blue satchel but the yellow bathing suit. This, she deposits in the elevator on the way down. Downstairs, voices come from the dining room. Lucy settles her bill. Passing through the gloom of the lobby, with its polished wood and leatherette chairs, she suddenly feels her arm gripped. She freezes.

A stranger stands behind her dangling a small, shapeless yellow thing. Expressing surprise and gratitude, Lucy reaches for it, meanwhile decrying her carelessness. Outside, she walks rapidly half a block and opens the door of a parked taxi. The driver shakes himself like a dog from a dream and turns the key in the ignition. "I'm in a hurry," Lucy prompts, looking out the rear window.

There's an hour's wait at the airport, but she catches the last flight to Crete.

THERE ARE NO TAXIS IN CRETE; IT'S ALMOST MIDNIGHT. While Lucy is fishing in her purse for the pay phone, a man spearing papers into a sack says it's out of order, but buses run all night. Lucy walks from the airport to the bus station, which isn't far.

About an hour later she disembarks arbitrarily in Iraklion. The street looks run down, with a row of dark, empty stores on one side. On the other side the lit marquee of the Galaxy Hotel advertises V C NCY. The Galaxy is a square brick building that has three floors of blank windows, as if it were a closed-down factory. Lucy crosses the street. An arrow points down to BAR; from the sounds, it's the only place awake.

The room she's assigned is at the end of the third floor. Along the corridor sconces leave fan shapes on the dark stucco walls. Lucy has trouble unlocking; the key is a bad fit, or maybe the lock's been picked. There's room enough for one body, she thinks looking in, her carry-on bag propped against the door. Then she turns on the dim overhead saucer. On the floor there's a mustard-colored shag carpet, brittle loops—a style from the fifties, something Lucy knows about, although she doesn't know why, just that it's familiar. The television's bolted to the wall. Lucy slings her satchel onto the foot of the single bed, and switches on the metal, bullet-shaped lamp above; the bulb's out. The place smells of mold and sweat, it needs airing.

Never mind, she says to herself, she'll move tomorrow. Tonight, Lucy strips the grimy cover off the bed and stretches out, fully dressed. She thinks about taking off her shoes but she doesn't. A few minutes later she gets up, throws the dead bolt on the door, and covers the pillow with the smaller of the two towels from the bathroom.

The buzz of the ashtray on the night table wakes her. Digits on the television say 3:09. The walls are vibrating, and the photo of the Parthenon over the bed has slid to one end of its wire, and hangs at a slant. Jumping out of bed, she moves to the heavily shuttered window. The metal blinds open vertically with a weighty clamor. She peers out. In the next building, across a narrow alley, men and women are dancing on a balcony outlined in pulsing blue neon. For all their movement they look strangely static and desolate, like an Edward Hopper painting; Lucy feels encouraged to remember this, but she doesn't want to see them. She promptly lets the blind crash shut, sealing herself in, and sits down on the edge of the bed. Now Lucy feels tears rise, and she finds herself fighting the loneliness and the resentment, and the blankness and bewilderment, and the deep-down certainty that she is living the life of the wrong woman, not herself.

Standing in the bathtub the next morning, extending the spray hose with its sputtering of tepid water, Lucy washes her exfoliated skin—not a hair grows on the grafts—with the tiny bar of hard soap. The elongated faucet handles with their protuberant knobs, the sinuously curved silver bracket that grips the shining snakelike hose like a snapped mouth, assume the shape, in Lucy's gaze, of a death mask. Clutching the side of the tub, she hauls herself out, unrinsed. As she pulls on the white dress, she hears a frightening noise. A death rattle coming from the tub drain.

Lucy stands in the hall waiting for the lift. When her floor number appears, she opens the door. At once she sees that the little moving box has shot past. Peering down into the gaping shaft, Lucy catches sight of the top of a woman's head with flying golden hair. Or maybe what she saw, she thinks a few minutes later, when she's walking down the stairs, was only the frayed ropes swaying.

♦

Outside there's a bus blocking traffic: Luxe Tours. Already peering faces in the windows. Beside the folded-back door, a gray haired man—nametag reading NIKOS—is shouting through a megaphone, in English: "Authentic Greek dinner in a quaint taverna on Mount Ida. Music, Greek dancing. Back here by midnight; like Cinderella, ladies. Forty thousand drachmas: twenty dollars, all included. And if you are interested," he says to Lucy, confidentially—does he pity her, being wounded, being alone?—"you'll be making a good choice to go with me as guide." Still deciding, Lucy unzips her waist pack, and Nikos, reaching forward, plucks several bills. "One of these, one of these," he says. "No tickets. You're all set; step up." Lucy shrinks back, then feeling her arm gripped, mounts the high step.

Going toward the rear she grips the seat backs hand over hand, shifting her weight for balance. She knows to steady herself when the bus lurches forward. Lucy really knows how to do these ordinary things. She understands the way the world works. She wasn't born yesterday in a hospital in the Pennine Alps.

On the outskirts of Herakleon the driver reins in the bus with a firm backward yank. Lucy, wedged between two wide, flowered laps, tries to extract herself, the thighs expand like blown balloons. She seems to be stuck. "Excuse me. I'd like to get off!" As she starts toward the door, Nikos comes back and tells her to get in her seat; he stops midsentence and stares wooden-faced at the hand that grips the pole, as if he can't figure out who had let it come on the bus.

Not a soul but Lucy pays any attention to the single lane winding around the mountain. On one side a blind cliff and, on the other, swiftly passing treetops in the green valley below, blazing Scotch broom in full flower. The driver keeps his head averted from the road, one arm insolently draped on top of the steering wheel, the other on the stick shift. He makes wide swings from mountain to cliff, wheels flirting with the drop-off. Nikos presses a microphone to his lips. "Turn your attention!" he addresses the busload of passengers. "If you survive an accident," his voice booms, "the tradition is to build a little altar on the spot." He adds with a laugh, "If you don't survive, it's up to your relatives." They are passing these memorials in alarming numbers. Massed at curves they flash by in Lucy's window, little dollhouses with burning candles inside. If she's killed, Lucy wonders, who will build her altar?

Nemea. The bus barely inches through the narrow street. Big-eyed, beak-nosed harpies in black call to them. There are tablecloths embroidered with flowers and birds displayed on tables. Withered men at outdoor tables, smoking and sipping thimbles of coffee. "Come this way," Nikos calls, herding them into the *taverna.* "This way, under the trellis."

Five costumed men, wearing black silks knotted low on their foreheads, begin the slow, sideways stepping to the plaintive sound of the lyra. As the tempo increases, tassels swing; the dancers slam down their hard shoes, cracking the wooden floor with sounds like gunshots. Their arms shoot up, hands crash. The thunder of drumming shoes comes through the floor, each boom makes Lucy's feet—poor, disfigured feet—jump. There's jostling inside her body; she imagines some part of her, improperly attached, snapping off. Like a leg at the knee. After a particularly violent jolt, Lucy loses her grip on her fork and it clinks down under the table.

Ducking down, Lucy crouches for a moment among the many legs.

In the dark, Lucy sees a child walking down a dirt road. The child is herself, sturdy legs in navy blue shorts and a camp shirt. Lucy knows she's imagining this, because she's a child again. There is a field ahead of her, a field where goldenrod beckons in the wind. The child sits down with her eyes on the road, so she'll see her mother when she comes for her. The sun gets lower until it is a burning orange ball that rolls behind the distant hill. Afraid and cold, the child begins to cry, and then she can't stop. She is thinking, What if she doesn't come? She prays to God and to her dead grandmother, and a miracle happens. There is her mother storming along the moon's silver path, and the child jumps up and runs to her. Her mother swings back her arm. Then the child feels terrible, stinging blows, and clasps her mother's legs, grateful to be wanted.

Under the table Lucy's damaged hand is mashed by a sandaled foot. Reflexively she slaps the black-haired, muscular calf. The foot is snatched away and an arm slick with black flat hair gropes down. Lucy does not see the hand, just the flurry of white napkin swatting around, and then it is gone. She comes out from under the table cloth and looks both ways at the line of heads turned toward the dance floor.

One of the men in the dance troop is edging along behind the row of chairs. He holds out his hands to Lucy; she shakes her head. But already people are rhythmically clapping, urging her participation. Lucy, close to panic, sidles as fast as she can in the other direction. But the dancer claims her. He puts his knuckles on her waist, and leads her to the center of the dance floor. There are grinning villagers she hadn't seen before crowded in the open windows.

Dancing, Lucy dares not look at anyone, but holds her back arched in a haughty pose, chin high and her head thrown back. Around and around she spins; the tempo quickens; she kicks off her shoes. She brushes past each table, singing in a high, nasal voice without words like a loon. She holds up the hem of her dress, twitching it, exposing the bones of her legs.

When she is getting on the bus, she feels her bottom patted in a most familiar and obnoxious way from below. Turning, she meets Nicos's eyes.

◆

Someone once must have taught Lucy that if you make a fool of yourself, you should take responsibility for it. In the coffee shop, early the next morning, she rests her satchel against the chair leg, and the viselike fingers of her right hand, gripping the pen ineptly, draw an irregular line on the map that's on the place-mat to Ayios Nicolaos, on the other coast of Crete.

It's three hours by bus. But at last Lucy is sitting at a metal table under a striped umbrella in the white sun of late morning, drinking espresso. She drinks four tiny cups. On the quay, farmers are hoisting leftover crates of onions and cucumbers into trucks. Big bulbs of fennel, turnips, parsnips, and carrots with bushy wilted tops. They cover the vegetables with tarpaulins. A few kerchiefed women, looking for a last bargain, rummage among leftovers, haggle, and reach down to toss small shining fish on a hanging scale. Fishermen in hip-high boots straddle the remaining still-wiggling bodies. A trio of men stand in sun-light, talking. Business as usual, thinks Lucy. Grateful to be here, she feels safe. She buys a string bag of oranges and then asks a priest in a black robe wound by a scarlet sash if he knows of a place she can stay for a while.

◆

The line of small whitewashed cottages runs along the edge of a cliff; on the land side there are wild green bushes dense with flowers that seem impossibly red and too large to be real. Lucy had called Olympic Airways from the lobby; her suitcase hadn't shown up, but she left the name of Hera's Palace. An arched stone gateway leads to number nine, and at the door there's a tangle of unabashedly blooming roses.

The rest of the day she dozes in the little courtyard. She wakes feeling rested, still wrapped in her robe, wearing her owl-eyed sunglasses and the wide-brimmed hat tipped over her face. The sun is gone; it has left a red stain on the horizon. Lucy heaves the light mattress back on the bed in the front room. There's a small table with a checkered oilcloth, and the two chairs have high backs with a decal of a flower on them. A draw-string sack hangs on the wall by its ties, and below that a fragment of multicolored kilim.

Lucy pulls aside the curtain in the archway and finds an ordinary and familiar white bathtub. The name Sears pops into her mind from nowhere. She likes the uncompromising bareness; the future stretches out before her, a blank, a space. Sufficient. Here's where she can stay, solitary and peaceful; she's seen enough unknown things. So thinking, Lucy gets under the thin wool blanket on the narrow bed and immediately falls asleep.

The phone wakes her with its foreign pealing, and she is told that dinner will be served for only ten minutes longer. Suddenly she's hungry. Lucy fits the heavy key like a jailor's into the round keyhole and goes down the unlit path toward the shining windows. Everything is very black, but as she passes other cottages, she hears voices. She can see the sparse lights of some town across the calm water. Misted air blows up over the cliff.

The dining room is almost empty inside; narrow wooden chairs are pushed under the tables, and the white tablecloths set for morning. Nobody comes forward. Seating herself next to the windows, Lucy puts her book on the table, sliding it under the little glowing lamp with a pleated shade. But there's not enough light to read by. She looks around. Across the room an older couple gaze determinedly elsewhere, as if any view would do as long as it's not at each other. Why that particular woman with that man and not some other? it occurs to Lucy. It's the combination that puzzles her, as there's nothing about either that suggests the other as a choice.

There are no menus. A fresh-faced waiter in a fisherman's jersey pulls the cork on a bottle and puts the bottle on her table. Lucy pours herself a glass of red wine. She watches the lamp shimmering in the black window.

◆

For breakfast there's a buffet of pressed meats, cheeses, stacked yogurt cartons and baby squid. Biscuits, muffins and something trapped in molded aspic. A group of Germans enter singing; they're tourists, like her, with canvas shoulder bags and peeling noses. They pile their plates and fill the window tables, where they make jolly guttural noises and spew tiny specks of food. "Bad tippers," the waiter, the same one as last night, confides, unfolding Lucy's napkin and placing it in her lap.

There's something insinuatingly familiar about his remark and his gesture; may be she's imagining it. She pours some condensed milk from a can into her coffee, and, looking up at the waiter as he saunters away, she misses the cup.

*   *   *

After breakfast, she starts down the newly paved road toward Ayios Nicolaos. From the top of the hill the harbor looks no bigger than a puddle with the reflection of a cruise ship on its surface. In town, Lucy walks past the ubiquitous MONEY EXCHANGE. At the end of the street there's a store with a live black cat in the window and, inside, hundreds of Zeuses and kores, goddesses with rocket-ship breasts small enough to take home in your suitcase. Going back, Lucy enters a shop with woven rugs and jewelry in the window, and aims herself down the narrow aisle to the rear, her eyes not yet adjusted. For a few minutes she pokes arbitrarily through folded scraps of cloth, flipping them back on one another. She doesn't see the proprietor until the woman speaks; "Is it for the wall or the floor?"

What wall, thinks Lucy, what floor? "If I choose one, can you send it?" asks Lucy, as if her luggage is too full for one more thing.

"We can send it, by all means," the owner assures her. "Where is it going?"

Ignoring that question, Lucy shakes out a small, heavy rectangle of colorful cotton and tosses it on the floor between the counters. She has the money, she's determined now to buy something. "Is this a rug?"

The door opens with the sound of a bell. A woman enters and leans over the counter, head bowed in contemplation. The blazing midday light blanches her hair into a gossamery shape, a halo of gold.

The saleswoman has left Lucy's side to remove the tray of jewelry, setting it within reach so the woman's practiced hand can swoop like a gull for a fish, pluck up an earring and slip it in an earlobe. "I like these," she states, turning her face side to side in the handheld mirror. "What y'all think?"

"*Me?*" Lucy feels her flesh prickle. She didn't think she could be seen.

"Yes, you, Lucy Snowe," says a soft Southern accent. "We met in Rhodes; I found your money, 'member me?"

Stumbling slightly, Lucy drags the woven piece by the knotted strings on the corner toward the shining light, like the light at the end of a tunnel. "I'm surprised to find you here," Lucy says; then feeling gutsy, "Are you following me?"

"Following you?" the blonde exclaims. "I thought you were following me."

"I can't believe that," says Lucy, and she can't. "Why would I?"

The blonde considers her for a moment: "When you're running away, it's natural to think someone's in pursuit."

"Are you talking about yourself?" Lucy questions her.

"Course I am! I thought you were a detective."

"Me? Come on."

The woman from Rhodes laughs, throwing her head back. In her ears are the elongated silver masks of Greek tragedy with downturned mouths and punched-out eyes. "Do you think they're a pair?" the bright red mouth in the small mirror questions Lucy.

Lucy believes that there were originally two pair, and someone had wanted both masks of comedy, so these are left. Before she can speak, the shopkeeper answers, saying yes, they are a pair.

The blonde bargains in Greek, then counts some bills from a black beaded bag, and with a wave she's gone. As Lucy sees her passing behind the window glass she holds out a crumpled handful of money. "Take what I owe you."

"If you want them," the saleswoman suggests with a sly smile, "the masks of comedy are available."

"What?" Lucy asks, thinking she's missed something.

"The other set of earrings."

Lucy says skeptically, "Why didn't you let her have the mixed pair?"

"I know that one, she doesn't want to spend," the saleswoman says. "She probably will resell them, to make some money. The smiling masks cost more because people want the luck."

Lucy goes out the door thrown open by the owner, and walks to the end of the street feeling the pinch of the new earrings and carrying a small rug, crudely woven, rolled up.

The road to Hera's Palace flutters in Lucy's sight like a kinky black thread. She feels the top of her head for her sunglasses and realizes they're gone, most likely in the rug store. She looks back, then ahead; she can't see anything but waves of heat rising and falling. Starting to walk, Lucy snatches up each clumsy foot, but the scarred, permeable skin feels on fire. She walks for half an hour. The sun burns malevolently down from the sky and radiates relentlessly up from the scorching blacktop, so hot it's almost melting. Lucy's face stings; why didn't she bring her hat? She quickens her pace, her watering eyes on the horizon. But the sensation she has is of walking in place like a mime on a stage. She slings the rug to one shoulder.

Lucy mops her face with the back of her arm, then heaves the rug to her other shoulder and puts her thumb in the air. A car slithers past, slapping the air and leaving a ghost of foul fumes. Another is coming, a black dot. Lucy quickly sets the rolled rug down on one end, thumb up. Without warning the cord snaps; the column of rug slumps to the ground. Watching helplessly, Lucy sees the runner plunging end over end down the long highway toward the harbor.

At the blast of a horn, she jumps. A man vaults out of a truck and runs as if balancing on a tightrope down the yellow line bisecting the road. Hopping lightly, he stops the rug's descent with the side of his boot and, beginning with the bottom fringe, swiftly winds it into a fat roll that fits under one arm.

"You're staying at Hera's Palace," he says to Lucy when he returns. "Climb in." When Lucy hesitates, he asks, "Don't you recognize me?" She does, vaguely. "I waited on you at breakfast, last night also." He tosses the rug in the open flatbed.

Lucy cranks the burning door handle. "I appreciate it," she says, after they've shot off.

"You smoke?" The pack under her nose has a brown cigarette jutting.

"No, thanks."

"Mind?" Lucy shakes her head, and he rubs his thumb on the wheel of a silver lighter. Moving only her eyes, Lucy observes him through the gauze of smoke. Quintessentially Greek: smooth olive skin, alabaster clear. Ringlets like bedsprings. His nose descending in a straight, elegant line from his brow, bridgeless. Lucy observes the way he smokes his cigarette, delicately balanced between the tips of thumb and index finger, scowling as if he'd learned how on reruns of Hollywood movies. The white shirt covering his chest balloons as he deeply inhales; tendrils like dragon fumes leak from his nose.

Lucy turns to look out the open window. A hot wind slaps her face. A postcard picture streaks by that she makes no effort to look at. Suddenly she's aware that the Greek man is looking at her, his conceit demanding attention. Turning, she asks what his name is.

"Minos."

"Minos," Lucy repeats. "After the myth?"

"No, after my father," he says, and laughs.

Lucy feels stupid. "Well, Minos," she says, "I'm grateful you stopped. I don't think I could have lasted another step." She realizes she's compounding the impression of stupidity; she sees him glance down at her feet, then up at the road again. "How could I drive by?" he's saying. Lucy's conscious not so much of what he's saying but of his teeth, in his reflection in the windshield: very white in his dark face. "You looked so . . . so . . ."

Pitiful? Is that the word his English vocabulary lacks? A freak, middle-aged and defective. "You could have driven by," Lucy says, startling herself by the stridency of her voice. Something too strong to dismiss is stirring in her brain and demands with a thwack of pain to come out. "Plenty of others drove by." No helping it, she thinks, smiling inanely. "You have a heart!"

Lucy regrets the words as soon as they're out. He'll think she's coming on to him; she ought to know better by now. What if he opens the door and throws her into the road like refuse? But instead he turns toward her with a puzzled look; she sees his dark eyes slide over her face, as if he's feeling for the curling flap of mask that will reveal her as a fake. Then the blur of his hand approaches, coming out of focus. "You get those here in Ayios Nicolaos?" Minos asks, touching her earlobe.

Lucy tips the rearview mirror. "I did," she says, not at all certain. "In the same store I bought the rug." There's another silence, and it comes to Lucy that what Minos is interested in is a hefty tip for rescuing the stupid tourist who was stunned in the midday sun. She relaxes a little. "What do you think, Minos, are they a pair?"

He doesn't answer immediately. With a surge upward, like a roller-coaster, the truck picks up speed. "I am not sure what to think," Minos says finally, aloof, satirical. "I am trying to figure you out." They are going higher and higher; Lucy's ears block. The motor strains; its steady snarling fills the cab, making talk difficult. She stops trying to think of anything to say. Each hump in the road vibrates through the floorboards. Her backbone feels rammed into her skull; his intent seems to be to loosen her flesh from the bone. Gripping the top of the window frame, she looks out the window. Her eyes burn. She sees a blur of green studded with stumpy trees and tumbling gray rocks that dance as if possessed. Downy sheep, and little goats with silken hair trotting one behind the other up the slope on the worn path. Cemetery, farm, golden field. Everything slides by like film slipped from the sprockets. The truck rises and dips; the little bull on the mirror swings wildly, flitting a constantly moving beam over Minos's arm, his sleeve, his chest, his face. Lucy tries not to look at him, she's beginning to feel the way she had felt on the beach at Ródos, every trace of decency gone, and in its stead some liquid in her bones.

"Look there!" says Minos, signaling her. Up ahead a village crowns the mountain. Shining white, coming swiftly toward them.

Minos drives slowly between the whitewashed boxes, all identical, except for the grand blue-domed basillica with its thrusting, glittering cross of gold. When the truck stops, the buildings shimmer for a moment, then settle. "Where are we?" She turns toward Minos; it strikes her anew how extraordinarily handsome he is.

"We've stopped for lunch."

The restaurant is open like a bird's nest to the burning blue sky. The legs of the tables appear to bend and lay flat on the cement floor; the chair seats are on fire. Minos sits opposite her, outlined by mind-numbing brightness. Black-and-white stripes slant across his face from the overhead trellis, and Lucy has to screw her eyes against the boldness of his chalk-white shirt.

The waiter comes, finally, emerging from a screened structure across the roof, throwing her shadow before her. She is more than six feet tall, Lucy gauges, when she stands above them with pale barbered hair gleaming as if oiled. She is broad hipped and deep voiced, her shoulders wide and waist narrow; yet her figure doesn't suggest an hour glass, but a costumed male.

A Campari and orange soda is set before Lucy; thirsty, she drinks it and instantly feels the wallop. Tiny impulses like silver fish swim down her legs. There was something else in the drink, she realizes. Paradoxically, her head feels clear now. Like an empty bottle. A second Campari and orange soda—or whatever it is—arrives. Another for Minos too, and she drinks her own and sips some of his as well. Just to have something to do while Minos talks with the waiter. The sound of their voices seems barely audible and Lucy is lulled by the words, which are meaningless to her. She closes her eyes and eases her head down into her arms on the table; after a while she murmurs, "Minos." The conversation stops; she hears him say, "What?" But no other words will come out of her, her mouth is terribly dry, her lips feel thick. Lucy can sense him leaning over her, but she remains as remote and aside as an anesthetized patient.

A very long time later, it seems, she feels someone touching her cheek. "Are you okay? Time to go home."

"I can't," she refuses, "because I can't raise my head." She giggles. "You'll have to carry me."

"What is your name?"

"Lucy Snowe," she says into her folded arms, realizing as she says it that it isn't her name; she's a fraud. She turns her head and puts her finger on her lips, saying, "Shhhhhh." She's not supposed to say what her real name is, that's the rule. You must never say, her mother had told her. To say would cause difficulties. Difficulties are what you avoid. Lucy visualizes the closet. *A*

little smear of light came under the door, not very much. But is was bet-
ter than the pitch-black dark. The door wasn't locked, she could have
reached up and opened the door any time she wanted to. But she never
did. While she was closed in with the dim bulky shapes smelling of moth-
balls, she waited quietly. The door would open when she was come for,
and she never knew when that would be; there was no turn of a key, be-
cause of course there was no key. Just the suddenly blinding light. Now
Lucy sees a flash that she thinks is the door opening. But when
she lifts her head to see who is there, a shining bolt tears free
and stabs her brain. Again. And again. Lucy almost screams,
turning rigid, not wanting to look again and see the silver light
and feel the stabbing.

"Lucy," a voice sings. "Lucy Snowe, time to go."

Lucy raises her head, dazed, trying to determine where she
is. After a few seconds she sees something on the table moving a
little; then fingers, shapely as gloves in a box, point at Lucy's
scarred hand. "What happened to you?"

Lucy recognizes Minos. He is the waiter who gave her the
ride. She says, "Fire. The plane crashed."

"Yeah?"

Minos turns his eyes away, looks at the sky. His face wears a
crooked half-smile, as if he suspects himself of missing the joke.
Lucy asks him if he'll take her back to the hotel now. Minos
seems undecided, he slowly shakes his head. "You have not
taught me English yet," he says finally. For the first time Lucy
feels a little stab of fear, she wonders what he really wants. "Your
English is fine," she assures him. "But the best way to learn," she
adds, when he acts as if he hasn't understood, "is by conversation. Ask me something."

However, Minos seems less interested in conversation than
in his own irresistibility—the smoothness of his skin, the inso-
lent fullness of his lips. Now his lips turn down mockingly, his

skin flushes red in the opening of his shirt. He poses, he ducks, he feints.

"What's the matter?" Lucy asks, suddenly stone sober and angry. Taking hold of his averted face, she forces it around. His mouth is arranged in a tight smile. "Can't you bear to look at me?" He seems to be deciding. After a minute's silence, Minos lifts his hands one at a time to Lucy's shoulders. His hands are hot, and apparently of their own weight they slip down, easing off the top of her dress. The soft cotton gathers at her waist and Lucy feels the warm sun on her breasts. She shivers, a current goes through her body. "Look at me," she pleads now. "Please." *Lucy wants to be looked at, she wants to be touched; she wants it so bad, her body aches with the need. Anyone will do, just to relieve the loneliness.* But Minos's eyes wander away, he is looking past her; Lucy turns around. The woman who waited on them, her stark hair shining in the brilliant sunlight, floats as if borne on a wave across the rooftop.

And then she feels herself lifted. She feels the heated wood of the table under her back and the warm hands and the heated breaths of her lovers.

This is it, Lucy thinks, trying not to panic. *It's not decent. But get it over.*

◆

Reluctantly, Lucy heaves her body from unconsciousness; someone's knocking. She's in her cottage at Hera's Palace. The clock says ten o'clock—morning or night? There's brightness in the window above her bed. She snaps the shade onto its roller; outside, another faultlessly clear day. "Just a minute," Lucy calls. But it's hard getting up, she's groggy. She sits for a minute or two on the edge of the mattress looking down at the woven runner on the floor. Which day was it she went to the harbor? She stands and sees on the sheet a bloody stain, and her body feels bruised; between her legs she's raw. The knock sounds again. "Coming," Lucy says, pulling on her robe and going to the mirror. She lifts the matted hair from her face, sees the earrings and again is aware of the pain, which feels very deep inside.

The receptionist wants to know if anything's wrong. Lucy didn't come to dinner the night before or breakfast that morning. "I'm hurt," Lucy says, terribly ashamed, looking at the young woman as if for denial. "I've been raped."

◆

The shingle reads, OTTO WERNER, M.D. Below the bell there's a small sign in Greek. The gray stone building, windowless to the street, stands by itself on a flat lot. Around it are broken sections of walls, coils of barbed wire, refuse, weeds, discarded boxes. Lucy looks around; the taxi has left. She steps on the upended cement block and rings, then goes inside.

Women sheathed in black are jammed against the four walls like a thick hedge, some with passive children in their laps or folded into the bunched cloth between their knees. Their head coverings are wound low on their foreheads. A row of dark watchful eyes survey Lucy. She stands uneasily beside the entrance; there are no vacant chairs.

Suddenly a man ducks through the archway on the other side of the room. His figure in a long white coat straightens up, attenuates and stretches tautly to a withered neck that looks wrung like a turkey's. His knob of a head hangs forward and down, as if connected by a thread to the tragically humped back. He has a shock of yellow-gray hair and a rock face. A nose like a crag. His pale eyes sweep over the penned women. As he begins to prance past them his bony wrist darts out to poke, as if testing the women for doneness. Some cry out softly in protest, most are silent, enduring. Lucy wonders if it's possible that a man so unusual-looking and repulsive could be so blind as to fancy himself a ladies' man. Dr. Werner crooks his finger. "Come, scrawny bird," he says, beckoning. His nurse in the archway, a large woman in a white uniform with massive arms folded over her breasts, laughs and comes for Lucy.

She undresses in an area curtained off by a curved rod, and puts on a gown that smells of bodies. When she comes out the doctor says genially, "So, you are not feeling well." He speaks English with a German accent. Unfamiliar instruments hang from hooks on the wall. In the corner there's a bulbous machine with a dangling arm, something like an outsized dentist's drill. Calling Lucy's attention back from the equipment, the doctor indicates that she should get up on the table. "What could be worse on a vacation? Where are you from, my dear?"

"I'm an American."

"Of course," Dr. Werner says. Addressing his nurse, he adds an aside; "Who else but Jews from America have money to travel?"

"Yah."

"They get away with murder," the doctor continues, ignoring Lucy, "giving Palestine money and deducting it as a tax write-off. What happened to you?" he abruptly asks, in one motion pulling down and switching on the bright lamp suspended from the ceiling; it oscillates, back and forth, over Lucy's body.

"I was burned in an air crash—but that's not why I'm here."

"Quiet! I'll find out soon enough why you're here. Lie down."

Lucy feels the heat of the examining lamp on her skin. "Raise your arm straight into the air," the doctor directs. He begins to place little packets, weighted and sweet smelling, one at a time on her stomach. She has no chance to look at them.

"Hold your arm up! If you have a weakness in your system, I'll detect it. Hold!" the doctor repeats with each new substance, and tries to force her arm down. "Resist, don't let me!" he directs. Lucy closes her eyes, lets him. "Sit up," he shouts rudely, pinching her thigh. "You're wasting my time. There is nothing the matter with you, it's your imagination. You're not fooling anybody."

"I believe I was drugged and raped," Lucy insists.

"Symptoms?"

"When I woke this morning there were bruises on my body. My vagina feels dreadfully irritated, and I have a pain in my lower abdomen. Here."

Dr. Werner turns to the nurse. "They all say the same thing."

The nurse finds this funny.

"They ask for it and when they get it they yell rape."

Lucy says indignantly, "Look, I don't know what others say. I don't think I would do anything to encourage it."

"What do you mean, you *don't think you would?*" the doctor cuts her off. "Don't you know?"

Lucy suddenly feels helplessly to blame. "There are things I don't remember," she admits.

"Ah-ha!" says Dr. Werner. "Two aspects of a personality undergoing a profound separation."

Yes! thinks Lucy, feeling relieved to be found out.

"Nonsense!" Dr. Werner's voice startles her. "You'll get no sympathy from me, hot pants! But all right, lie down." His hand on her chest forces her back on the table. "They get what they deserve," he says to the nurse. The doctor's long fingers caress a large shiny silver instrument; he opens the hinge to spread the two halves apart. "Be still. Spread your legs. Both of you." He laughs. "You are a neurotic, dissatisfied American Jew bitch. Accept your life, no matter how limited, that's my advice. That is the secret to a woman's health. Stop wandering around, go back to your husband."

The cold metal enters her. Lucy gasps with pain. Her knees jerk, her eyes suddenly open wide and she feels tears running. She holds her breath, trying not to cry out. Abruptly it comes into her head that something is seriously wrong with her. In this moment of pain and humiliation, the thought isolates itself, separating from the general feeling of despair that she accepts as her lot: She can no longer count on her mind to control her behavior. *When something too awful occurs, her brain shuts down. By forgetting.* On her arm now she feels the grip of the brutally strong nurse, who as she yanks Lucy up from the table is making a winding motion of craziness; this while pushing Lucy with her clothing in her arms into the waiting room. Walking through Lucy feels the censure of the hollow-eyed women; it's involuntary, like a sneeze, and ill-wishing. Lucy knows about that. With her back to them, she dresses.

◆

Time to move on, thinks Lucy, packing everything but the rug. When something happens too awful to be believed, a misfortune, a tragedy, an untenable humiliation, you pick up the damaged goods and relocate. It gets easier and easier; clear out the medicine cabinet, skip breakfast, pay what she's charged. Checking her out, the receptionist looks as if she's holding back a smile. She wonders what Minos told her.

◆

On the hydrofoil, Lucy sits with her satchel between her feet. When anybody passes, she sits up straighter and pulls in her feet. Her sneakers aren't pretty; the peaked joints of her toes bulge through the canvas tops. She bought the sneakers from a street vendor; they're a pair of men's Converse in a double-E width that must have been rejects from the States. Still, they look better than the laced black overshoes that were the original issue, Lucy thinks; and now she wears a T-shirt: a Minoan woman with one large oval eye, black curly hair and red lips. How's that for fitting in?

A flock of traveling children, stooped double under backpacks and bed rolls, tramp past, following one another like the goats on the hill. Either they don't notice her, which is one effect she has on people—invisibility. Or they'd rather not look, the second reaction. The children step outside to the deck, banging the heavy door on the high sill. The cabin is hot; Lucy hadn't realized how hot until she felt the draft. She unwraps her scarf and runs her hand over her head. Her hair grows diversely, the texture is prickly. Nearby is a young woman who repeatedly handles her long silken hair, running her fingers through, lifting and letting it fall. This one couldn't care less who watches, thinks Lucy. This one sits at a wooden table covered with paper cartons and leftover food. This one is being watched by, along with Lucy, the man sitting opposite her. Lucy turns her sick, envious eyes elsewhere. A slight, boy's-height Asian prowls the cabin in shiny, skintight bicycling shorts, glancing side to side, a sneer of reproach on his lips. He seems to see everything. But his eyes swing past Lucy as if she were transparent, while inside, she cries, *I exist!*

Thinking about yesterday, Lucy realizes that she gets into these mortifying situations, from which she has to quietly escape, not because of how she looks but how she feels. Plainly, she acknowledges to herself at last, she hurts. She hurts from wanting and not having love. Not even love, Lucy amends immediately, fearful of asking more than is possible—maybe love is more than she wants. All she wants is someone to like her. A man in a red jumpsuit with the company name embroidered on the pocket looks her way now. Not directly, but out of the corner of his eye. Lucy gets up right away, and weaves toward the door leading to the deck.

Teetering, she makes it to the stern and grips the railing. She's alone there. She feels a persistent vibration, the monster growling of the motors reverberating in the metal pins that hold her together. She hopes they hold her together.

Now hearing tapping behind, Lucy turns to see a woman with a dark, bloodless face zigzagging across the deck, cane wildly swinging, feet thudding in hikers' boots. Her face is skeletal, expressionless; she has wrinkled pouches under open eyes. She's heading toward Lucy. The tag pinned on her sweater says she's part of a tour group: Jewels of the Aegean. Seeing the purple lips move, Lucy puts her ear close. There's a low-toned rumbling, not like a human voice at all, like a machine running down. "That's Nea Kamene up ahead," Lucy says, fastening the blind woman's hands around the railing. "It's a barren, empty island." The woman looks, but in the wrong direction. The blind woman is the only person who knows she exists thinks Lucy, briefly, and she can't see her. This thought leads to the next: Lucy Snowe could simply disappear before she gets to Santorini. She is essentially nonexistent; whoever she was died in the crash. So with the blind woman as witness, Lucy decides to end this unreal life. She climbs up on the railing and lets her legs dangle. She lets go for a moment and balances, saved from falling by the force of the wind. How easy it would be to slip forward and drop into the sea, thinks Lucy. "What happened to her?" she imagines they'll ask the blind woman. *But who would ask?*

◆

She's late for dinner at the hotel, and waits in the doorway of the dining room to be seated. There is a whispered consultation about where; she gathers it has to do with whether or not she's with a tour, on the American plan. Around the corner where Lucy can't see it, there's a balcony in the large room that resonates with women's voices; they have a different menu, it seems. The staff is not yet organized, a voice behind her explains. Indeed, waiters rush in behind a screen of Greek deities and out again as if the location of the kitchen is uncertain. After ten minutes the maître d' says Lucy can go in now. "Sit anywhere." Someone touches her arm. "Hi!" Lucy turns. "We seem to be the only people waiting, all right if I join you?"

As soon as they're seated the waiter sets down a cup of clear broth with four half-submerged croutons. "I'll skip the soup," says the dinner partner. Lucy hardly knows her; she looks different every time. Under the recessed ceiling beam her hair shines, almost metallic, the silver of newly minted money. She wears it parted on the side and held by a barrette. Like a little girl, thinks Lucy. Like a farm girl with milky skin. But with the cheekbones of a model. She's not wearing any makeup, and Lucy feels somewhat staggered by how beautiful she actually is up close. Not beauty you can reproduce at home for the price of an *Elle*, beauty too mercurial to be captured. Yet there's a down-home sweetness in her. She's authentic, like the girl you knew as Norma Jean before she took off her braces. Now as she looks up her lips—so full, especially the lower, protuberant and tremulous, suggesting a pout—release a smile.

Then before Lucy's fascinated eyes, she almost transforms; the corners of her mouth crumble, small folds appear, there are creases on her upper lip. She's older than she thought, Lucy concludes. But not less spectacular—just slightly gone-by like last night's orchid. Lucy's memory is stirred, seeing the way she holds her head thrown back on her neck, imperious, self-absorbed. Her eyes are startlingly blue, liquid. She holds out her hand. "I don't think I've ever introduced myself. I'm Cecily Dorfman. Call me Cissy."

PART III

LUCY SUPPOSES SHE OUGHT TO GO, SINCE CECILY Dorfman—the only person in the world who seems remotely interested in her—asked her to come along. It's a promotion run by the Santorini Palace, Cissy had said, handing Lucy a free voucher at dinner. Lucy's not sure what the deal is, but she has the idea that Cissy is running the promotion. She's employed by various hotels, she told Lucy, in Israel and the Greek islands; her meals seem paid for. Maybe she's a travel agent or arranges conventions, thinks Lucy.

There's one other passenger on the tour bus, the blind woman.

"Is Jewels of the Aegean your tour?" Lucy asks Cissy, when she sits down after leading the blind woman to a seat.

"One of them," says Cissy enigmatically. "I advertise under a variety of names."

"Who else is on this tour?" asks Lucy.

Cissy turns to her. "You," she says, smiling, then alluding to the other passenger, "She's American, from Toledo, Ohio."

"Really? What's she doing on Santorini?"

"Alice is very plucky," Cissy says after a minute, as if she's just figured it out. "She told me she wants to see the world."

"You're kidding."

"That's what she says."

Lucy starts up the steep, dusty path to Ancient Thera, behind Cissy. A fixed dry heat bakes through the intense whiteness of the sky. The wind is fierce; in no time Lucy's face feels taut as the sail of one of those little boats. In the distance the ocean is dotted with small craft and little riffs of white foam; Lucy keeps in mind that they're really giant waves. She clings to the wall of the switchback faint with fear, her eyes on the spot that she has to next put her foot. The view is spectacular and she's trying not to look. It's too hot to be doing this; she's an idiot for getting herself into it. Cissy climbs swiftly, showing the magnificent shape of her legs. Not a ripple there, thinks Lucy, resentfully. And when at last they get to Ancient Thera, what, after all, is at the top? Six inconceivably surviving columns, scoured by sun, smoothed by time. It's hard to believe they survived, Cissy explains their attraction. But why am *I* here? thinks Lucy. I'm here because, inconceivably, I survived; that's what it's all about: survival.

Two hours later, with a slither of loose stones they're back in the parking lot. The descent was steep. Lucy can feel it in her knees as she gets on the bus. She's damaged. She wonders if there's a point when you're damaged that you stop surviving and start living. Now the bus driver lights a new cigarette and shakes his head, and Cissy gets off again. "We can't leave," she tells Lucy. "Alice hasn't come down."

"Are you sure she went up? We didn't see her," Lucy asks when they're outside walking across the parking lot to the base of the mountain.

"She went. The bus driver says he saw her."

After they've walked half a mile or so, Cissy crouches under the oblique roof of a crevasse. "Hello-o!" she shouts. *Hello-o*, her own voice comes back.

"Why would she go in here?" Lucy ducks into the narrow, V-shaped cave; it's dark, the walls and ceiling are brown and ochre. The temperature is about twenty degrees lower than outside. Between floor and ceiling there isn't space to stand upright.

"Probably to get out of the sun." Cissy has moved ahead and is nowhere in sight.

Going ahead blindly, Lucy suddenly bumps into Cissy. Whatever lives in caves scuttles over her feet. She stands still. "Sorry." As her eyes adjust, she almost jumps out of her skin. "Oh God!" The blind woman is lying on the ground, slumped against the wall, her straw hat is still tied under her chin, but dangling now almost jauntily over one ear. In the near-total blackness the woman's bald, exposed, shining head holds some faint light. She doesn't look like a woman, the thought occurs to Lucy, but like a large fly, or something else harmless. Dead where it was swatted. As they crouch on either side of her, the woman starts. She fumbles her wig into place and tugs down her bunched skirt. Cissy picks up the cane. Lucy picks up her pocketbook. Between them they grip her bony arms and go down the hill.

On the bus, they sit beside each other, silent. Lucy has withdrawn. She knows she's shared something with Cecily Dorfman, something intensely personal that can't really be talked about, something unmentionable, maybe shameful: the sight of a woman who is really not a woman but a discredit, sexually, to the order of things. The experience has drained her, she feels too close to it; somehow, she feels profoundly affected by the sadness of this woman's condition. "Shit," Cissy mutters. "I should have kept an eye on her. Now I'll probably get canned."

Lucy turns toward Cissy slowly, refocusing. "She doesn't seem any the worse."

The rescued woman sits four seats behind them, asleep, face flattened against the sealed window.

"This is the best job I've had," Cissy says, glancing back. "In fact, it's the first real paying job I've ever had."

Restlessly, she gets up and walks to the front to speak to the driver. Then she comes back and sits next to Lucy. The flare of sun flashing on and off through the window is brutal to Cissy.

Lucy turns her eyes away. Her mind flashes to the man Cissy was sharing a room with in Rhodes. She imagines Cissy bouncing like the metal ball in a pinball machine from one uncertainty to another, flashing light and color. A lot of action, but no idea where she'll land next. That's the way she lives. It isn't *decent*.

After a while she realizes that Cissy is leaning toward her, her eyes converging, her breath like cosmetics. She tells Lucy she's broke. Her voice is hushed, with a hint of the South that makes it uncomfortably intimate. Until a few years ago, she was living on the top of the world, Cissy softly characterizes her former position. She pauses and looks at Lucy to determine whether Lucy appreciates the value of where she was. In comparison with where she is. "You know why I left?"

Lucy shakes her head.

"I didn't trust my sister and my husband's a shit."

There is a pause. "Did you have to come to Greece?" asks Lucy, feeling obtuse. "Couldn't you just get divorced?"

"I came to kill somebody but she never showed up," Cissy says, smiling wickedly. "She disappeared in thin air."

"Your husband's lover?"

Cissy nods. "He loved *her* but he needed *me*. I was weak and couldn't do anything right. I was his justification for cheating."

Lucy is shocked by this description. She thinks Cissy should have more self-respect. "Are you going back?"

"I may have to," Cissy says, watching Lucy, "when I'm not able to attract men anymore, and women like you stop finding me."

"Like me?"

"I mean with money to spare," Cisssy says, insultingly. "Then again," Cissy asserts—her Southern accent is so broad now, Lucy has trouble making out the words—"maybe Ah'll tike off for somewhere new." Cissy's too-blue eyes suddenly brim, as if a violent sea were contained in two saucers. "It wasn't so much his unfaithfulness," Cissy sobs; she's picking on the net seat pouch on the back of the seat, pulling it out, letting it snap. "I could have overlooked that." They've stopped at a traffic light. With a glance out the window, Cissy abruptly stands up. Pulling Lucy with her, she jumps off the bus.

"This is Fira," says Cissy, as she watches the rescued woman's sleeping face slide by. Lucy is watching Cissy. She thinks she is beginning to see the cracks and she's afraid the whole structure might collapse at any moment before her unwilling eyes. Drawing Lucy into the covered entrance of a *trapeza*, a bank, with a sign OPEN AT 4:00, Cissy sags against the door, closing her eyes, trying to compose herself. But the pain of what she is about to reveal has permeated the air: "He loved her." Cissy is burning like a candle down to nothing; Lucy is afraid to breathe. Not until now does she understand how volatile Cissy is; and her volatility, which is quite thrilling to witness, can't be separated from Cissy, Lucy realizes, any more than the scent can be separated from a peony. Thinking she should be compassionate, Lucy places her good hand on Cissy's shoulder. "Listen, I'm sure he wants you back, if things don't work out here," she says.

"Why should he?"

Lucy doesn't know how to answer. "Well, for one thing, you're exquisite-looking," she offers, paying Cissy the homage due her beauty—the classic brow and wide-boned cheeks, the hair, wild from the wind on Mount Thera and thick as an animal's. Curiously, Cissy isn't comforted; in fact, she throws Lucy an annoyed look as if her beauty bored her. "This one wasn't the first," she declares, walking out into the sunlight. "And he's got Mimi waiting in the wings."

"What are you saying?" Lucy asks, following her. "You don't think he'll come after you?"

"No," says Cissy, "he won't, because there's no point to it." She adds slyly, "I died!"

"You mean, he *thinks* you died?"

"I mean *everyone* thinks I died." She says in a heated whisper, "Lucy Snowe, can I trust you?"

Lucy doesn't want to know what's coming, but she nods.

"You are the only person in the world who knows I'm alive!"

It's the middle of the day; in the town of Fira the stores are all closed, windows gated. Everything's bleached, colors faded. Cissy belongs here, it occurs to Lucy, her paleness part of the setting. "Ah've seen this film a thousand times," Cissy's saying theatrically. She stops walking and she glances at Lucy to make sure she's attentive. "Whether I'm alone or with a man. Doesn't matter if I'm drunk or sober. I do both parts. Of course I know the words, they've already been spoken. But details keep popping out new. I don't know," Cissy says, staring into space, "am I adding these things or were they there to begin with and I just remembered them? Like suddenly I'll see ten twenty-three on the bedroom clock. Or I'll pick up a single key that looks like the key to the woman's apartment, and feel the heat of it like a live coal in the palm of my hand." Cissy gestures: a multiplicity of rings and the points of purple fingernails curving from the ends. "Nights, Ah can't git his words outah mah head: I'm committing adultery."

By now Lucy has tuned out. She doesn't want to see this film. She's wondering how she'll get back to the hotel. In some way that's unclear to her, Lucy feels numbed by the other's lived life, if that's what it is, and she feels overburdened, like the crammed pages of a diary. All that beauty, thinks Lucy, alive and demanding. As Lucy is looking around for a phone booth, she realizes that Cissy's stopped talking. She is scrutinizing Lucy, as if she had been turning the pages in a photo album and had come across a snapshot of someone she once knew.

"Why are you looking at me like that?"

Cissy stares for a few seconds longer. "It's not you," she assures her. "It's the 'other woman.' I saw her in the airport waiting room. We didn't speak but she's stuck in my memory, haunting me like pictures you see of inmates in a concentration camp." Cissy adds theatrically: "Already dead, forever memorialized."

A taxi drives slowly into the street and parks at the end of the block. Lucy gets in. Cissy scrambles in after Lucy and sits frowning and fiddling with the clasp of her ridiculous little black purse covered with shiny beads; it hangs on a knit string from her shoulder. Rummaging inside, she takes out a lipstick, a key, and a revolver with a pearl handle.

Lucy says quickly, "I'll pay for the cab."

"Oh, thanks, that's nice of you," Cissy agrees, putting everything back.

"Can I drop you, or do you live at the Santorini Palace?"

"No, in Iya. My food's covered by the hotel if I eat there; otherwise I'm on my own." She gives the driver instructions and sits back. "I arrived in Greece with nothing but the clothes I was wearing."

Lucy thinks she understands Cissy's interest in her. "How do you manage?" she questions guardedly.

"Mooching," Cissy admits frankly. "Living cheaply. I do promotional work." She stops but decides to go on: "Meeting men," she says after a moment. "Most men want me. But not Daniel."

"Daniel?"

"DANNY?" HE STANDS JUST INSIDE HIS APARTMENT, breathing as if he had run up the twenty-four flights from Central Park South. He hears from the bedroom: "Ah'm so glad you're home!" She comes in wearing Cissy's robe with the collar of floating strings, filling it with more authority, less vulnerability, less possessiveness, less appeal. "Juss got here mahself." Several little islands of moisture, one on her breast and a soft oval stuck to the roundness of her belly, inform Daniel that she's come from the bath. With her dark hair turbaned in a towel, she shocks him, looking so much like Cissy.

Mimi must have been out of town, traveling with the band; he never knew when he'd come home and find her. This thought and all of the images that almost two years ago, in Italy, had set afloat like a paper boat in a puddle their shaky arrangement, come to him: the steamer trunk shipped from Nashville, the nights her tears for Cissy wet his chest while his brooding vigils were for Ursula, the months they had drifted, clinging to each other until both sorrows were swept under; until, it seemed to him, anyway, the two women had been lost together: Cissy and Ursula. And today, just when he was beginning to feel safe (if not happy), Daniel was suddenly thrown into the moving current. He puts out his hand for rescue. Taking it, Mim says, "You look awful, hon. What's happened? You get mugged in the park?"

"I've been in Cambridge, Massachusetts, all day. At the police station." Daniel crosses the room stripping off his suit coat, dragging the noose of his tie over his head, unbuttoning his shirt and flinging everything into a pile next to the door; he's wet through and through, the way he's been since he got on the six-thirty Delta Shuttle that night in Boston. He adds to the pile his trousers and jockey shorts. Nude, Daniel hangs his belt on the belt rack in the closet and arranges his shoes side by side on the floor. Mimi has come into the bedroom. "What happened?"

"I'll tell you later. Be nice and mix me a drink."

She hands it to him when he gets out of the shower. He takes a long sip and goes dripping, a towel thrown over his head, to sit on the edge of the bed. He has come to the surface by now, and he has plans to save himself. Picking up the phone, he says, "Boston. I'd like the number of Crane, Bucknell and Simmering." Tipping his head back he lets the towel slide. This is more like it, he thinks, reaching behind for the towel and mopping his face; the water is evaporating off the rest of him. He can feel Mim's eyes. "What's up?" she's asking. Daniel puts his finger on his lips, and with his other hand motions for her to sit down, patting the bed. "Marty, pick up your goddamn phone, it's Daniel Dorfman," he says into the ringing phone. Mimi, beside him, thigh to thigh, drops her head to his lap. "It's Danny!" He makes his voice buoyant: "I just thought of you and I knew you'd be working late, even though we haven't spoken for a hundred years. Listen, I need the best criminal lawyer in Boston, and I need her tonight." He pauses, laughs, looks at his watch. "Sounds good to me. I'll be on the nine-thirty shuttle, and we'll grab a bite afterwards. Thanks, Marty." Daniel sits motionless outside, churning inside. As he puts the phone in its cradle, he flops back, momentarily exhausted; the muscles in his thighs twitch. But then there is a gathering of strength, a call to battle. Everywhere he stiffens, even his sex.

Mimi pulls the towel off her head and leans over, tangle-haired. She kisses his lips, his chin, neck, chest, belly button.

Daniel sits up. "Not now, Mim, I've got to go back to Boston tonight. I'll be all right."

LUCY LIES AWAKE, LISTENING TO THE HOWLING SANtorini wind, a hollow sound like an oboe, banging about the plastic gypsy-sold chairs on the patio. The shutters slam, swollen with damp and not quite fitting. The hotel had been completed a week ago, and just opened, Cecily Dorfman told her at dinner. They ate tonight in a restaurant (Lucy treated) at an outdoor table under an awning; when the wind rose and the awning began to snap and billow, the proprietor moved them inside. A whitewashed hollow lit by candles.

Several times in the last hour Lucy has had to get up and rehook the shutters. But she can't shut out the wind that whistles through cracks in the recently poured cement, cold to the touch; it whips the curtains into a frenzy. Lucy takes the new blanket from a plastic bag on the closet shelf; she throws it over the bed, then gets under. She crawls out once more and puts on her sweatshirt. All these preparations, and still she can't sleep. Cissy Dorfman's face, licked by candlelight, keeps repeating in her mind like Warhol's "Marilyn." Lucy gropes, wondering if Cissy is someone she'd once known, someone she ought to recognize.

Just before dawn Lucy drifts off to the soft patter of rain. She dreams. In her dream the rain becomes earth pitting the soil. She feels her bones jolt, and perceives that she's hearing the sound from inside a coffin, lurching down. *It's me! You've made a mistake,* she cries out. Someone else has died! But it's no use, she can't be heard. Forcing her eyes open, gasping for air and terribly confused, Lucy weaves to the mirror, the blanket over her shoulders, carrying the night-table lamp like a candle, extending it to the end of its cord. In the eerie wash of light she is amazed by the changes in her face: the scar that had outlined the pallid mask is almost completely blended now and hidden by hair. Her hair is thick and dark with a few fine white strands, as if she'd broken through a spider's web. Lucy turns off the lamp; but it's still early, so she returns to bed and covers herself to the shoulders. Under the blanket her left hand pulls at the bent fingers of her right hand. Her fingertips search for the missing nails on her ossified fingers. On the cold, rigid claw.

When the sun warms the room, Lucy gets up and unhooks the shutter on the square little window, framed like a painting. Standing on tiptoes, she looks out. During the night the wind seemed to have tamed the sky; brushed across the horizon is a solid band of pristine blue. The Aegean has shrunk to an angular swimming pool. The scene looks so much like a David Hockney painting, Lucy almost reaches out to touch it.

◆

"I live up there." Cissy points to a low stone archway; behind it there's a doorway like a keyhole in the high wall. On the hillside above the plaza, Lucy sees a jumble of white square houses with semicircular roofs in the smoothest of stone, tumbling from the mountainside like fallen sugar cubes. "Lots of expatriated artists live here," Cissy says, starting up. "In the decorative arts. Jewelry makers, ceramists. They work out of their houses. They're in Iya because they can't go back home, and living's cheap." They walk up the steep, winding ribbon of cobblestones. "I can get you a good rate of exchange. Anything special you're looking for?"

Lucy can't figure out why Cissy has been so insistent on being helpful; if she's not careful she'll be saddled with her, and they have nothing in common. "What do I owe you for your help?" Lucy asks her. "I mean, whatever it is, tell me. It's all right, you've earned it."

"You don't owe me anything," Cissy says. "It's on the house."

"What's in it for you?"

"Plainly, I have to support myself," says Cissy.

"Is there a fee? Will I find it on my hotel bill?"

"No."

From this exchange, Lucy gathers it's appropriate to tip.

Every house has its own small courtyard: in most, there are jars of brilliant red and pink flowers; Lucy reaches in to touch a petal to see if it's real. When she looks up, Cissy has stopped to talk with a man who has gems, agate and moonstone and turquoise arrayed on a table. Lucy keeps walking, resolved to explore on her own. Ahead, some boys are playing soccer in the street. They look about ten to Lucy, long-legged in brief shorts and knee-high socks. But they may be older, she realizes when she gets closer. They suddenly begin to dispute in their own language; and then the ball is loose, and they rush toward Lucy; not very large boys but rough and sturdy. As they dash by jostling each other, Lucy is crowded against the wall. The boys pass, the ball is retrieved; presumably it could have rolled down into the harbor. But when Lucy steps into the street again, there is a tear in the sleeve of her black jersey. She carefully folds the sleeve back to examine the emaciated arm bone. Now the boys have come back and surround her. When they see her bloodied arm they draw aside, form a circle around her, staring, poking each other. And then the circle opens for Cissy to walk through. The boys are suddenly shy, cooing like pigeons. Cissy hands one of them a cellophane bag filled with unwrapped baklava and they turn away and crouch in a knot. "God!" says Cissy. "Are you all right?"

"Yes, I'm okay. I fell against the wall."

"Is there anything I can do?"

"No, it happens all the time. My skin is thin, it damages easily."

"How'd it get that way?"

"It's grafted. I was in a fire," Lucy says. She feels uncovered; Cissy is the first person who's ever asked directly. "Maybe you read about me," she says. "I was in a plane crash over the Alps almost two years ago. A bomb exploded. I was the only one to survive." When Cissy says nothing, Lucy feels her face redden; most likely she looks pitiful. Lucy doesn't want anyone's pity.

But then Lucy sees profound emotion fly into Cissy's eyes like a blinding; so swiftly that even before she has finished explaining, Cissy's eyes redden and she has tears on her cheeks. Lucy, who has seen many reactions to her injuries—aversion, discomfort, reproach—thinks that she has never before seen anybody so extraordinarily affected.

But why should she care so much? Lucy wonders.

As Lucy puzzles over this, Cissy is staring at her burned hand, hardly a human hand, twitching at the end of the torn sleeve. Lucy tries to cover it, mortified at having revealed an object so hideous, so shameful, so unsightly: the hand that held the flaming seat back; it is her secret, guarded from scrutiny, never deliberately left in the open. Then an unprecedented thing happens. Instead of glancing away out of decency—or fastidiousness, or distaste—Cissy lifts up Lucy's hand and peers at it with her close, focused eyes, gripping it in her two hands like a found treasure.

You are the one, you made it, Cissy is thinking. *My God, I can't believe it. I've seen myself a thousand times stumbling through freezing emptiness. White on white. The air too cold to breathe; the air so awfully cold it must have held me in a living death: the blood stilled, heart stopped, miraculously fixed by a numbness like death. This was the operating theater, they were giving me a heart transplant. I can see everything, clear and sharp. I am up in the sky somewhere, my body is lying there where you lay, in my Henri Bendel dress, slowly being covered by snow. I kept walking; I walked knowing I mustn't lie down. Days and days—or maybe a week; the silence so loud it drowned out reason. When the sheepherder found me I was still upright. Frosted alive. I wasn't hungry anymore; I told him, thanks anyway, I was doing fine. I had stepped over the bodies. All the pieces of bodies and bones and bits of metal indistinguishable from one another. My single feeling then had been one of joy. I am alive! I am alive, kept surging through my mind. And when I'd seen faint movement in a figure burned almost to ash, the skin curled away from the bones, how wonderful and astonishing was my only thought, that I am alive and whole and dressed for dinner in my little fur shrug! The next week I laughed at the sight of myself in the shepherd's tin mirror; that's when I woke up wearing my diamond and ruby necklace and both earrings, with my eyebrows gone and my hair singed bare to the middle of my skull. But at the time of the crash I had taken off my fur cape, and with not one bit of compassion, only wanting Daniel to know he'd done a terrible thing telling me he loved Ursula Gant, I lay it across the dying woman. Then I knelt down, I held my breath and averted my face and reached into the inner pocket for my passport and return air ticket. But Daniel would identify the Fendi cape—he'd bought it—and blame himself for my death. He'd have good reason to. Serves him right.*

When at last Cissy releases her hand, Lucy feels somehow impelled, as if for further proof, to move toward the steps leading to the house and, sitting down, roll the bottoms of her pants to her knees, exposing red skin, mottled, corrugated, thickened and fissured, covering bones like a bird's. And as Cissy looks up now at Lucy Snowe's uncomprehending face, her surprised heart is wrung and wrung again.

*   *   *

Above them, just then, the door to the house opens and two men stumble out. They leap over the heads of the two women, down the steps, into the courtyard. Scrambling up, they begin punching. At this point a woman runs out, pushing between Lucy and Cissy. She's in the courtyard now, screaming. One of the men grabs her and yanks her toward himself. The other man swiftly bends, and with great force, butting from below, lifts his large, square, shaven head. The man holding the woman ducks, and suddenly she lies still on the paving stones: white faced, the waves of her hair flowing out from her head as if she were drowned. Stepping over her, the man who had held her kicks open the door to the house, rushes in and reappears brandishing a chisel, a glistening wedge-shaped tool. In the courtyard the other man lifts a chair over his head, swiping the trellis roof. The two men circle, their flapping, voluminous white shirts casting shadows over the still figure of the woman. The woman's eyes open briefly and she seems to look right at Lucy, imploring. Her broad, handsome face is very pale; there is no blood. As Lucy stands stricken, paralyzed with dread, there is a shattering noise. At first she thinks it's in her head. But Cissy grabs her arm and pulls her into the street, just as the wood strips of the trellis one by one start collapsing; and then the entire roof crashes down. Splinters of wood, shards of glass, blood.

♦

It's some days later. They're wandering in this massive structure. This is the antiseptic underworld of Acrotiri, without shadows—the destroyed city, released from burial by archaeologists spoon by careful spoonful. Light seeps through the crevices, filtered, strained; air the color of weak tea. Cissy points at the stoppered jugs left undisturbed through the long night; artfully decorated, they stand perfect as the day they were fired. She puts her lips to Lucy's ear: If one day New York were buried by a volcano, says Cissy, what do you think they'd find when they dug up the Big Apple, where millions lived? Indestructible parts—microwaves, televisions and computer hardware; closest to human might be one foot of the statue of Verrazano in Battery Park. Lucy mounts a narrow stair, collapsed, the two halves folded toward each other like a half-open book. It wouldn't matter, Cissy goes on soundlessly, at her heels, what people individually were doing. Not one of them would survive. Not the woman who had fifth-row matinee tickets that afternoon for the latest Andrew Lloyd Webber, or couples who'd booked twelve months ahead for a cruise down the Nile. What good would it do you to have a house with a view of the water in the Hamptons, or a twelve-room co-op on the park?

She stops; shouts: "Stand up, Lucy!"

Lucy is sitting on a low wooden chair, the upright back elaborately carved. In an instant a guard appears and begins to berate Lucy in words she can't hear and if she could, couldn't understand. Lucy looks up, confused, frightened. "Essie?" At full height the woman is no taller than Lucy is seated; her head is set with no neck on her chest. The old face is enveloped in a shawl like a shroud, her skin is the ashen color of the cave. For a moment Lucy thinks she recognizes this old woman with filmy eyes; she was sitting at the entrance to the room. What room, whose room? She doesn't remember. On impulse, Lucy leans forward and grips the guard's shoulders. "I don't know what she's told you about me," she says loudly. There seems a hundred years of judgment in the other's eyes, the dim, unfriendly eyes with gray, bushy brows above. "You're right in some ways, Essie," Lucy struggles on, starting to cry. "At the end I did let her die. But that's what she wanted, she made it clear." Anguish rising, Lucy shakes the guard's shoulders a little, fearing that she's not being understood. "What else could I have done?"

"Didn't you see the sign?" Cissy asks her, steering Lucy outside into blinding sunlight. "The chair was from fourteen hundred B.C. From the throne room at Knossos."

Lucy pulls away, shouting back, "She's with me more now than when she was alive. Here—" Lucy touches her own heart.

"C'mon, hon. It's time for the boat to Nea Kamene. Somethin' you might want to take in."

◆

A cable car carries them wildly swaying down the mountainside. The boat's hull is rust spotted; gray metal sheets with prominent rivets; war salvage, so she's told, from the Balkan wars. Cissy has tickets—Lucy is beginning to understand that her job comes with lots of perks, if not much money, and Lucy is her current work. Tours at eleven and three, this is the early one; and they're barely on the pier when the fat rope is thrown on the deck in a coil. A man grips Lucy's arm, and she's hoisted over floating debris to the rocking boat as the foghorn blasts. The rigging creaks and there is an impatient throbbing below.

The two rows of wooden benches bolted to the open deck are quite full. The boat moves and Lucy lurches toward the nearest bench. There's room for one; a man is sitting on the end. As she steps past his knees, he asks, "Didn't I see you on the hydrofoil coming over to Santorini?"

Lucy says no and sits down. She feels self-conscious about her face, a face like a stocking mask. She can feel her hair being swept back from the seams by the wind; she reaches into her drawstring sack and claps the new cap on her head. It's a little round beanie with a brim like a duck bill. She reaches across the man to the bench on the opposite side of the narrow aisle, and

Cissy holds out a tube of sunblock. Lucy slavers it on her face. She can feel the man watching her. Why is he interested? Lucy wonders. Maybe he has a thing for old dolls with mended faces. She twists her almost lipless mouth into a smile and turns toward him. "What's your problem?"

He laughs. "What's *your* problem?"

After an hour of pitching and thrashing in the waves, the motor is cut and the anchor splashes down. A hush falls. Waves slosh, breaking against the sides of the boat. Then a voice: "This is your captain speaking. We will wait for twenty minutes in this harbor. You may swim from here to the sulfur pools, which take away the poison in your body and restore health."

Several people laugh, but Lucy slips off her clogs. "I'm going to try it." Why not? she's thinking. She's a prime candidate, she wants to be cured, she wants to remember something; anything. Cissy's mirrored sunglasses glint up noncommittally; Lucy steps up on the bench, gripping the back. "It's not a great idea, Lucy," Cissy says now. "Unless you're a real good swimmer." Lucy raises her arms over her head, places a clubbed foot on the rail and dives overboard in all her clothes.

The *Helena* slaps and rocks in the hot sun a quarter of a mile offshore. On the barren island a peak of black jagged rock spews smoke. Cissy goes to the railing and peers toward the pool where steam rises, using her hand as a visor. A long time passes. The captain comes above deck and raises his bullhorn. "We must be off, miss," booms out. "Please come directly on board."

Cissy beckons. Turning over, Lucy floats. The heavy sea pours into her ears, saturates her clothing, drags her down. The foghorn echoes, and from far away Lucy can feel the motor's grumble, magnified as it travels through the water.

As the shore begins to move, Cissy holds her nose and jumps in. She swims on her side, churning in the direction of the sulfurous steam. After a while she tries to stand, but sinks. She keeps looking back at the boat, like a toy being pulled toward the horizon. Finally, Cissy is able to wade into the pool of slick yellow water. She emerges slowly, walking across the oozing, muddy bottom that closes as you stand on it. The water is thick and uncomfortably warm. The air reeks. "The creep wouldn't wait," she calls. "But he said he'd be back for you when he'd taken on more passengers, before nightfall." Squinting against the glittering sun reflected on the water's surface, Cissy looks around. The blinding ripples go on and on without a break, as if they're solid; her voice rises hysterically, "Damnit, where are you, Lucy?"

What looks like a giant cormorant, its head under its wing, squats on the volcanic rock at the undulating edge of land, its black shadow floating on the water. As Cissy screams, Lucy raises her head. Cissy is coming toward her, pushing through the water. Lucy needs no mirror. In Cissy's round blue eyes she sees herself: her dark hair, slicked back behind her ears, glistens with sulfurous gel, and her face is no longer a doll face, it's boiled and bloated. "I don't know why I did that," says Lucy, who now feels foolish. "But thanks for coming after me. I think I'm cremated."

Cissy takes hold of her hands. "Come over here, Lucy."

The rocks are jagged; as Lucy steps on them she leaves shreds of skin, fresh blood. At the edge, the fine black sand lies in silken ripples. "Sit down," Cissy instructs her. "Let's look at your feet."

Lucy feels embarrassed. "I'm sorry."

"Are you in pain?"

Yes, she is in pain, Lucy wants to say. But it's not her feet; it's the pain of believing that there is something fundamentally wrong with her mind, something incurable. She wonders how much pain she can take before she lets herself remember whatever it is that's too painful. "I know now what upset me," she says finally, looking down at her feet, which are gradually coloring the shallow water red. "It was at Acrotiri. The guard's lined face with filmed eyes and her tiny bowed body."

"What about her?"

"She reminded me of someone," Lucy says to Cissy. "She knew what had happened."

"What had happened?" Cissy asks, and Lucy's mind balks.

"I don't know," says Lucy "If I remembered, I'd go mad."

In a sudden panic she gags, doubling over. Cissy claps her hand on Lucy's forehead and with her other hand thrusts Lucy's head between her drawn-up knees. Lucy's body convulses but releases nothing. She is sealed.

DANIEL DORFMAN HAS BEEN STANDING IN THE DIM corridor for only about half a minute, his knuckles poised to rap, when a shadow comes up behind the frosted glass. Marty Simmering opens the corporate door herself. He thinks, first seeing her after twenty-five years, that she looks middle-aged. But after she has led him, both of them wordless, through the labyrinth of hallways into her office, and is fearlessly seated in the glow of her desk lamp, and he is better able to study her plain, freckled face, Daniel decides that Marty looks not very different than she had in graduate school: pale face, brown hair hacked off at the chin, eyes too close together. She still dresses unbecomingly, a long, loose, greenish-brown dress. Walking behind, Daniel had noticed her gaping pumps, and he'd looked away, glancing through the open doorways: large, venerable offices, bare wood floors, books and minimum technology.

Now, standing before her, he is suddenly a ghost of a boy.

There is something truly magnificent about Marty Simmering, swiveling in her chair of scarred oak. Something, Daniel thinks, that doesn't show off but knows its power.

"Start at the beginning," Marty Simmering says, no small talk. "Don't leave anything out. You've got all night."

Daniel sits down. He feels the support of the black lacquer chair with the Harvard Law School crest; it fortifies him, promises preferential treatment, safety. "All I need is fifteen minutes," he says. "I don't know if you heard, but my wife died in a plane crash more than two years ago, in May. We held a memorial service for Cissy in November. On the same day two detectives showed up in my office, totally coincidentally. They asked if I knew where Ursula Gant was. I said I didn't—she was the daughter of a client. That was it. They thanked me and left."

Marty listens expressionlessly but with so much super-charged intelligence that Daniel feels himself almost hypno-tized. Nothing can remain secret, or personal. Everything said is sucked into her brain, a brain like a vortex. Daniel smiles, he thinks he looks calm. "This morning, a Detective Lucas called and asked me to come to the Cambridge Police Headquarters at my convenience. He suggested today at one o'clock. I asked him what it was about, and he said that he thought I might be able to help him regarding Ursula Gant's disappearance." Daniel pauses, thinking Marty might want to ask a question. When Marty says nothing, he goes on, "I was anxious to cooperate. I knew she'd been very, very upset, actually distraught, after her mother's death. She was unnaturally close to the old lady, dom-inated by her until Ruth became senile. Ruth had been a bril-liant woman—she'd made a killing in the stock and bond markets. Nothing risky, good solid investments. But she was a cold mother. And for all her independence Ursula had never stopped struggling for her mother's approval. It was a peculiar relationship—from what I gathered. After Ruth died, Ursula was acting . . . well, not herself." Daniel remembers, and goes on without wanting to, putting into words for the first time what he had sensed. "She completely lost it. It was as if the walls of her life had fallen away. She was all at once released, but incapaci-tated. When I called, she didn't answer the phone. I was afraid she'd committed suicide." He pauses. "Instead, she'd taken off." The lawyer's silence makes him add, "I was curious as to why she hadn't been in touch with me. None of the income generated in her account had been touched. I reinvested as it accrued." Daniel's mouth feels dry. "But what was she living on?"

After a short silence, Marty says, "I told you not to leave anything out. If you want my help, that's the deal."

"Have you got anything to drink?"

"Sure." She comes back with a paper cone of water. He takes a swallow. "Not strong," he says. "But wet."

When they were both at the law school, Marty had once invited him to dinner in her Medford apartment, he remembers. They ate cold lo mein noodles out of the carton with chopsticks, standing up. She owned no chairs, and the floors weren't safe. Her dog, a yappy sheltie, wasn't house-trained. Afterward he had sat on her bed with her unshockable face opposite his. She'd been intense, absolutely motionless, looking not much different than she did now across the desk. He had spent the night talking. About himself. "What I left out," Daniel says now, "because I didn't think it was any of their damn business, was that Ursula and I were lovers. I couldn't believe it when she left me without a word. I missed her terribly. I still miss her." His voice catches in his throat. "It was the real thing, Marty. I loved her better than I'd ever loved a woman before. If Cissy hadn't been such a sorry case, I'd have divorced her and married Ursula." Marty's lips purse, a slim gesture, as if to remind herself to keep still a little longer; Daniel adds, "I'm not sure Ursula would have married me." He is afraid of sounding pathetic, so he shuts up. Below on the Fitzgerald Expressway, a siren screams, and the night, so cold and clear, seems to amplify both the sound and the silence surrounding it, sits black in the blindless window.

"Did they say if they found her?" Marty asks.

Daniel feels frightened by the question, more frightened than he's ever felt in his life. "Detective Lucas showed me an admission record from a local clinic. Apparently she'd walked in there with a serious scalp wound and a cut eye." Daniel's hand around the paper cone squeezes; water is leaking out of his shaking hand. "Some bastard beat her up," he manages to say.

"Anything else?"

"A newspaper boy saw me come out of her house the day she disappeared."

S HE'S ALONE. CISSY SAID SHE'D WAIT OUTSIDE: BEEN there, done that. Lucy opens her *Ekdotike Illustrated Guide.* There's just enough light to read, coming from the small opening far above; through it, she can see that hot sky. When someone died, she reads, the Beehive Tomb was reopened and the crushed bones were overlaid on those already rotted there; the new dead would not be kept out. The living buried them. The dead were said to welcome them. Taking off her clogs, Lucy pads on toughened soles, like hide, her head tipped back looking up. The irregular rows of black-stained stones form a cylinder. The stones are rough to the touch. A trapped bird circles the ceiling, wings wildly flapping, and suddenly with no warning the bird swoops toward her, a black-winged crow. Lucy drops her guide book and throws up her arms. In the cage of her arms she imagines the beak, hard and cold on her face, where it had struck. *It was the black-winged vulture that she had wanted to kill; that suddenly descending thing that made her feel shame and guilt for being alive.* But then as it grew older, it was *her,* the tiny helpless woman whose lipless mouth cried silently for compassion. Lucy's legs feel weak, she squats down. Squatting on the earth floor, She raises her eyes fearfully to the opening in the roof of the beehive just as the bird, only seeking freedom, flies directly into the light, becoming smaller and smaller until it is gone. Behind her, Lucy sees the shadow of the child's humped shape against the closet wall.

◆

Sky clear, waves flat, wind still. A day without shade. Nine in the morning and the heat is already intense. At the bottom of the undulating stone walk is a small village. Through the ripples of fiery air, between the houses white as oyster shells, Lucy glimpses Oia, stacked, one dazzlingly white box atop another, rectangular shapes with rounded tops. Like a sea of gravestones.

She has paused now to look at a dog sprawled across a rounded rooftop, inert as a rug. He's a large, short-haired yellow dog. As Lucy extends the zoom on her camera, he lifts his head and the front half of his body twists around; on his back there is a ridge of upstanding hair. Deep inside he tunes an uninspired growl. "You're a good boy," Lucy says. The dog's tail traces one arc like a windshield wiper. Lucy focuses; he suffers this intrusion with steady forbearance, then closes his eyes and lowers his head once again to the warm space between his paws.

Cissy's head rises, barely visible below the next switchback; she comes gradually into view. "I thought you were right behind me," she says. "Why'd you stop?"

Lucy doesn't feel like telling Cissy about the dog. She doesn't want to tell Cissy anything else; she feels too closely watched. For someone Cissy's just met, who's been an unrelieved nuisance, Cissy has been too understanding. Lucy knows she should be thankful, but she's not; she's irritated. What's in it for Cissy? Where are her other clients?

The town is crowded; it's market day. Women in black selling strange little cakes on greasy paper. Rows of long hanging sausages, tied together. Mopeds for hire, fender to fender, gleaming like mirrors. Wooden-handled clasp knives, huge rubbery plants. "Don't buy anything here," Cissy advises. "This is for tourists; I'll take you somewhere else." But then Cissy stops in front of a rack of tablecloths hung over dowels and extends one to examine the stitching.

"Let me buy it for you," Lucy suggests, beside her. Cissy shakes her head; today she wears a thick braid like a pull rope down her back, wound with green and pink ribbons. Cissy says she doesn't want the cloth, it reminds her of her husband, the way he'd looked at the other end of the table, head inclined, the way he had of drawing people, especially women, into his magnetic field. His eyes would meet the captivated woman's and he'd lean toward her, ingenuously, shiningly. "I know the moves," says Cissy, "I saw them for too many years." She heads across the *platia*. On the other side there are fewer tourists; around the edges are square tables and in the center is a whole lamb, hair and all, roasting on a spit. A local *estiatorio*, a restaurant; Cissy is glancing around, seeing who's there. Two swaybacked, bejeweled donkeys stand nestled together; they wear silver medallions on their stops and beaded tassels. One street farther down, the scene abruptly changes to a line of upper-class boutiques. There's a man sitting outside a store with a transistor radio pressed to his ear. He follows them inside.

Lucy looks around; it's mostly carvings in freestanding glass cases or under glass on the countertops, everything very old, very authentic-looking. Very expensive. A few of the female figurines hold one hand over their mouths, and Cissy, who knows the owner, explains to Lucy: to prevent their souls from escaping after they die. She says something more in Greek and the owner goes into a back room. When he returns he unlocks a square wooden case and takes out a little purple velvet pouch.

Lucy holds out her good hand; he puts the pouch in her palm. She can feel the shape inside, and pulling the silken drawstring she removes a carved figurine made of terra-cotta. The embodiment of a real person, with a calm, sloped forehead and arms folded over the breast; its heft and shape fit her palm exactly. "Is it a man or woman?" she asks Cissy, bringing it into the light, turning it back to front. Cissy is scanning a tray of rings. "I don't know," she says. "How can one tell?" says Lucy. "It looks genderless." She touches the lids of the eyes, swollen as if with tears. And when she tries to set it down on the velvet tray, she finds that the idol cannot stand, but must lie forever on its back, straight and sturdy, neither old nor young, male nor female, simply smug and complete. Cissy, behind her now, says, "It's nice, it's Cycladic. Should I price it?"

"Please," says Lucy. "I'd like to buy it."

"Poso kani?" There's some haggling that sounds authentic enough, and finally the man winds the tiny thing in strips of newspaper like a mummy. "Keep it with you," Cissy warns, after Lucy signs twelve hundred dollars in traveler's checks. "It's museum quality. You got a bargain."

Lucy slips the little idol into her waist pack. They walk uphill in the direction of the blue domed cathedral with its golden cross bitten into the blue sky. When they reach the church, Cissy says she'll be back for her, and Lucy pushes open the heavy, carved wooden door.

The sanctuary is empty. There's a table just inside the door with a slotted box and a few postcards beside it. There's a stone basin for purification. To one side the icon of the Virgin is hung with votive offerings on little spikes. Hearts, legs, arms and feet in shiny metal; a hanging face with no eyes. The floor of the aisle looks carpeted, but as Lucy starts down she realizes it's made of minuscule tiles wound into an elaborate scroll of vine leaves. Halfway, she sits down in a pew and unravels the paper around her treasure. She slides it out of its case. How helpless, yet so solid, thinks Lucy, cradling the naked idol like a child with a doll in her cupped palms. The stone is warm, clean, smooth; it is hers to do with as she likes. Holding it up, she lets the myriad colors of the stained-glass windows play upon it. She can imagine the swollen lids rising and the eyes looking into hers; she presses her lips to the expressionless face.

Then suddenly hearing footsteps—or not so much hearing as sensing their soundless approach—Lucy quickly slips the amulet into her pocket, where, she thinks, she can feel it's stone heart beating against her thigh. When she looks up she meets the sidelong glance of a gowned priest, who slides by. At the front he goes into the confessional; the curtain stirs, then settles.

Standing, she can feel the almost sensuous weight tugging at the fabric of her pants, nodding against her. She closes the figurine in her hand and walks toward the confessional. Inside the dark booth a giggle bursts out of her before she can suppress it. An imposter, she doesn't belong; she presses her lips together. A voice speaks in Greek. Lucy brings her burning face close to the screen and peers through the zigzag mesh at the outline of a huge head, like Oz's. Incomplete, bodiless, supernatural. A breath smelling of sen-sen. Rhythmically, Lucy strokes the idol in her pocket. What is she doing here? It's forbidden, and that makes it even more exhilarating. *Must not!* a voice warns.

"Mommy," she says in a low voice. "I know you are close."

The voice behind the screen is silent, instilling guilt.

"I'm guilty," Lucy confesses immediately. "It isn't decent to sleep around. I do it anyway."

But now the oversweet fumes inside the tiny booth are affecting Lucy; she feels her heart pounding, like that of someone approaching a cliff from which there's no way off but down. "Help me," whispers Lucy, opening and closing her lips against the scratchy screen. "Help me to remember so I can forget."

Hearing the rustle now of someone coming, she cries out, "Is that you, Mommy?" But her cry is smothered by a hand placed from behind over her mouth.

Lucy lies on a bier of stone; there's a smell of decay, mustiness and dilapidation. On the ceiling is a painted goddess attended by a procession carrying vessels and basins. Lucy thinks she remembers seeing this, but how could she have? A piece of the fresco lets go suddenly; it plunges, just missing her. But she continues to lie as she is, limp boned on the narrow sarcophagus, in a little room with a curve of smoke from an oil lamp dancing like a genie on the wall. On the cracked wall there's another fresco, of an animal trussed on a table, blood from its neck dripping into a bowl on the floor. The strength and terror of the animal can be seen in its face. Its almost human face.

Sitting up, Lucy dangles her legs, feeling for the floor, thinking she'll get out quickly. Hearing a sound, she becomes aware she's not alone. It takes a moment to make sense of the swaying black shape. It's the priest, he's struggling into his cossack. Lucy glimpses the flash of his flesh, his bare back and naked shining buttocks. The gown slips down and his dark head turns.

The flowing gown hangs in loose folds from his shoulders. The round black hat of orthodoxy covers his head, which is frighteningly large and wooden-looking, like a carved puppet's. His face is partly hidden by his hands; they cover his eyes, as if he has been blinded by the sight of Lucy. "Shameless woman," the priest hisses, "let us pray for your soul." He falls to his knees in front of the crucifix and reaches for a lighted taper.

Jumping down and plunging through the velvet hanging, Lucy runs down the center aisle. "Hey, Lucy." The voice is damped but carries. "Ah came lookin' foh you. Where'd y'all go?"

Lucy rushes from the cool gloom into harsh brightness and

stands on the dry, sparse-grassed earth, gasping for air. She reaches into her pocket, fearing her amulet is gone. She encloses it in her hand.

"I didn't see you in the church, where were you?" says Cissy, coming out after her.

"In the priest's sanctum," says Lucy, going toward the low wall, keeping to the narrow grassy strip between the flat, upright gravestones.

"You were?" says Cissy, catching up. "What for?"

"I wanted to do what wasn't permitted," Lucy says, standing still and looking boldly at Cissy. "We fucked."

Cissy stares, "Why, for God's sake?"

"I don't know. Anyway, it didn't work; I still don't remember anything."

"You mean the horny bastard raped you?"

A harsh laugh bursts out of Lucy. "You don't think," she sneers, "that a woman has to wait for a man to initiate sex?"

Cissy's jaw drops. Finally she says, "With a priest?"

"Any man." As Lucy says this she's aware that she's saying it, but not saying it. It's someone else's opinion. She tries to remember whose voice this strident voice is. "It was up to him to say no if he wasn't interested," the bold voice says. Who are you? Who's speaking? She grasps the sides of her head; she's got a splitting headache. She runs toward the low stone wall, avoiding the tiny sunken mounds; most have no identity, time has rubbed the gravestones smooth. As she is about to step over the wall she glances back. She screams.

Cissy steps forward and throws her arms around Lucy, supporting her. "What is it, Lucy? What do you see?" Lucy's eyes are fixed.

"There!" she says.

Cissy asks, "Where?"

"Can't you see him?"

There, in a thick clump of trees, Lucy sees the massive figure of the priest, a clay-colored effigy! *Is she really seeing him? Or is he a trick of her mind to make her feel guilty for what she's done, when she doesn't? She tells herself she doesn't.*

◆

Heavy fog rolls in from the sea midway through dinner. The wind flaps the striped awning on its metal staves, making a snapping sound. Without consultation the waiter picks up their dishes and moves them from an outdoor table overlooking the ocean into the inner room carved out of rock. Since it's late, or because the prices are high, they're the only ones there. Cissy gobbles lamb pie and drinks most of the bottle of red wine. Her blue eyes, over the flame of one stubby candle—set in a piece of paper folded into a flower—are glassy. In them, Lucy can see reflected, tiny and distant, what looks like a shrunken head.

"What are you looking at, Cissy?" she demands irritably. "Am I such a freak?" Lucy can't get her mind off the priest. She realizes that what she thinks happened must have been an hallucination, but keeps expecting him to walk through the beaded curtain.

"Y'all are far from a freak," Cissy drawls; her Southern accent has ripened with the wine. "When you git rid of that rigid, introverted snit, you act almost *depraved!* Like there's another side to you."

Lucy doesn't know whether to laugh or cry, but Cissy is so obviously serious that she's moved to explain: "There is a part of me I keep hidden," she says, after more bleary-eyed staring from Cissy. "You've noticed?"

"Your burns?"

"No. That's the first thing everybody sees." She looks down

at her hand on the table, the scaly claw with knuckles like chicken's feet jerking in agitation. Cissy reaches past the empty bottle in its woven straw holder, startling her, and stills Lucy's hand with her own. "You mean somethin' in your past? You talk about it as if you weren't there."

"That's because I don't remember anything."

"How weird," says Cissy. Lucy can see that she doesn't know whether to believe her.

"Something happened to me." Lucy leans close. "To remember would be unbearable."

"Speaking of unbearable," Cissy says, changing the subject after five minutes of complete silence. Evidently her confession has made Lucy less interesting; maybe it's made her seem crazy. Cissy goes on: "Ah was faithful to my husband for twenty-five years." She has her own confession. "Y'all know what that is? It's a life sentence. C'n you believe it? My kid sister, Mim, all she wanted was a good time and some laughs. She made out with the brats in the band, includin' the female singer. Times Ah could have sworn she was comin' on to Daniel; she's the one tole me to 'walk.' Ah'd wanted to, but I was afraid." Here Cissy confides, "But that's only half of it." She eyes Lucy to see if she's ready for it. "The main thing's what happened the day I left." Cissy takes a deep breath and hunkers down.

"Mah body trainer's a doll no taller 'n me, maybe forty-five years old with a chest like a barrel, and hips so narrow he needs suspenders to hold up his shorts. Alix is Russian but now he lives on Houston Street. Ah've been workin' out with Alix for three years, and Ah'd always felt he wouldn't mind a little on the side, you know? Well, when I came out of the Verticle Club that Monday mornin', Alix is outside straddling his motorcycle, smoke fuming. We start to talk and he asks would I like a ride. I'd never been on one before but I perch my butt on the little seat and grab him around. I'm kind of shaken up when we get to his place.

"We sit on his futon and he gives me some carrot juice and we pop a few vitamins. We talk about his career; he's made a video; that's where the future is, Alix says. So far he doesn't hit on me. What's the matter, I'm thinking, you're always saying what great shape I'm in. Alix, I say finally, I've enjoyed spending some personal tahm with you, but I have a French class uptown at two. Alix hums like he does to think up the English; finally he gets out: Would you like it to come into my training room, and go ahead and have a mini workout? Sure, I say. He puts on some music with a strong beat and stretches me out on the bench. He counts me through two sets of eight for my quads, two sets for my hamstrings, and then rolls me over and admires my tightening glutes. Then I get up so he can demonstrate a few. Well, I'm ready to cut French, watching his pecs contract. But Alix has his own agenda; I haven't figured out what that is. I'm sorry, I grunt between sit ups. I think we have a communication problem. Then coming right out with it, I say, I don't think you invited me up here for ab crunches; do you find me attractive? And Alix, he says, Yes, he does, very attractive. He's always been attracted to older women. *Older women!* First time Ah'd been called an *older woman!*

Thanks for the demonstration, I tell him, you have great equipment. At the door, Alix asks me, as if it just occurred to him, how would I like to have his new exercise video? I say sure, and he tells me forty-nine dollars includes the tax. Which I have to agree is a bargain. Private sessions usually go for ninety-five dollars.

"Uptown, one of the kids tells me that the French teacher had looked in and said she had a date, and class dismissed. At Columbia they treat me like a senior citizen; they *ignore* me. I go home on the IRT to spite Daniel; he doesn't trust me uptown alone. When I walk in he looks at me like he's forgotten who I am. During dinner I think about walkin'. Only I've got the willies. Befoh we go to bed, Daniel tells me he loves the Boston bitch." Cissy picks up her knife, balancing it in her upturned palm like a switchblade, saying, "That night Ah set out after her. Ah'd of killed her if ah'd found her."

Lucy doesn't know what to say; she finally asks, "You never found her?"

"I did," says Cissy.

Lucy feels uneasy; she may have asked the wrong question, one she doesn't want the answer to.

"Only I don't feel threatened by her." Cissy puts down the knife. "I'm someone else and she's someone else."

Suddenly she's crying. She's not crying the way ordinary people do, their features all contorted. Cissy's face is like a close-up in the movies. Glycerin tears. Two swollen orbs rounding the perfect crests of her cheeks.

Lucy protests, "No need to feel sorry for me."

"Ah don't feel sorry for you," Cissy declares. "Ah feel sorry for mahself. For being an *older woman.*" She reaches back to un-hook her beaded bag where it hangs by its string on the chair back. Releasing the delicate clasp, she upturns it. Along with her room key, the gun with a mother-of-pearl handle thuds to the table.

Lucy looks at it. "Where did you get the gun?"

"Ah bought it. To kill the Boston bitch." Cissy tosses the key back in and wobbles, gun waving, to the arched doorway. "But Ah don't need it anymore." As she goes through, a bitter blast of wind blows into the little cave, rattling the beaded hanging, making the air suddenly chill and extinguishing the candle's flame.

Quickly, Lucy goes after her. She makes out Cissy's figure

through the fog. Cissy stands with her feet in water. With an awkward windup she throws the gun into the ocean.

◆

Lucy opens the door. Her room is dark although she knows she left a lamp on. The electricity has gone off; she inserts her key in the wall switch. When the light comes on, the first thing she sees is a battered suitcase tied with rope. It stands lopsidedly; the corner's bashed in and one cardboard side dented. Kneeling and grasping it on both ends—there doesn't seem to be a handle—Lucy lays it flat. The blue and white Olympic Airways tag reads LUCY SNOWE and it has been everywhere she's been, following after her. One lock is smashed but the other shoots out at her touch. And, oh! there it is. Lucy clasps the white fur to her breasts, burying her face in its softness. A faintly familiar perfume still clings.

◆

In the morning Lucy rings the room she put Cissy to bed in. Last night, Lucy had taken Cissy to the Santorini Palace and lain her down beside the sleeping man on the large bed, then left her.

It takes a long time for the phone to be fumbled up. "May I speak to Cissy?" Lucy asks the voice that says *yasou*.

Another long pause. "It's Lucy."

"Lucy?" As if she's never heard the name. "Wha' tahms it?"

Lucy looks. "It's only a little after seven, I'm sorry to wake you. But I couldn't leave without saying good-bye. My flight's at nine-thirty."

"Your flight?"

"I'm going to Athens."

"Why y'all goin' there?" Cissy asks, alert now.

"My suitcase showed up full of tags; I'm retracing my steps."

"But you can't just take off," Cissy objects. She sounds furious, as if Lucy's betrayed her. "I won't let you!"

Surprised, Lucy doesn't know what to say. Is she obligated to Cissy for showing her around? She doesn't feel obligated. What she feels, grudgingly, is alarmingly attached to Cissy. She's afraid that Cissy's too soft a touch, too accessible to take care of herself. Lucy vacillates, "I'm not leaving for the States until ten tonight."

"Where'll you be at?"

"Hotel Electra. I've taken a room so I can shower before I leave."

"I'll meet you," says Cissy. "In the lobby. We'll have a last drink."

"Seven o'clock?"

"See y'all then."

◆

Lucy has the whole day in Athens, and the dead are everywhere. No shortage, they left so much of themselves behind. She stands in the doorway of Gallery One in the National Museum, running her eyes over the gleaming sarcophagi lined up along the walls like a clearance sale of small bathtubs. A crowd of schoolgirls pushes in, about fifteen of them in dark pleated skirts reaching below their knees and navy-blue blazers. They throng to the center of the room and bunch up against the showcases of daggers, precious stones, double axes and a clay disc from Phaistos. Lucy edges past them and makes her way slowly around the walls, inspecting the painted friezes on the sides of sarcophagi: bulls' heads, argonauts, birds, fish and trees. Inside one coffin there's a curled-up skeleton with a bronze ring on its finger. Dead bodies still warm, she hears a tour guide say, were arranged in a hunched position, tucked in with arms and legs bent double. As Lucy stares down at a polished wooden tub from the New Palace period, sized as for a child, she realizes that a memory is trying to insert itself through the murmur of foreign voices.

Lucy sees the child being led into the dimly lit parlor. Lips clamped, she is afraid to breathe the sweet, stale smell that she supposes is the smell of death. But what was death? She didn't know; her mother said that it descended suddenly. Listening to her parents' talk, she imagined a fierce black-winged raven with wings outspread and talons to carry you off. Maybe it was like being closed in the closet forever. For you were never seen again. Death had made her mother cry. Now her mother and the man walk to another box. Neither touches it; they talk a long time. Her mother says a decent burial. The man says life everlasting. Then, when the child is no longer listening, she feels herself suddenly seized under her arms and lifted in the air. She is held over the box. She can see inside. A large doll is sleeping on a white satin bed. "Give grandma a kiss," she is told, and she is lowered toward the doll. Helplessly, she stiffens. "Go on now!" her mother's voice directs, "It's your last chance." But what if she falls inside the box into the arms of the dead grandma, whose kiss had been like a soft wet bite? At that moment she is roughly thumped down. At that moment she feels hot pee running down her thighs. Then the face above her crumbles in rage. "Shame! Don't you know enough not to pee, a girl your age?" And then is her own small face slapped with such ferocity that she falls to the floor.

◆

A tourist guide in khaki walks by with a red balloon raised over her head, and tourists shuffle after her. Lucy wedges herself into the open space and puts her forehead on the cool glass of the case. There is the golden mask of Agamemnon, dug up at Mycenae. Lucy draws her head slightly away, and reflected back at her are two deeply set eyes surrounded by hollows of darkness, thin lips, skin tightly stretched as if they had only so much and had to make do; in short, the face that three weeks ago she'd named Lucy Snowe. But what surprises Lucy now is the indifference with which it views her: something hard and rejecting in the face that she didn't see when she left the clinic, supposedly repaired. Who is she seeing? Lucy wonders. She stares at herself. She doesn't have a clue.

The day passes. Crowds thin. Lucy's beginning to feel sated. She's seen fragments of carved heads and half bodies from the pre-Palace period with the amulets they took to the grave, seals from Zacros—ritual objects like the bull's-head rhyton carved in black statite; its purpose is right there, in the booklet, and it turns out they poured their grief into it and let it drain back into the earth. It occurs to Lucy: How thoroughly they mourned.

When she hears the insistent clanging, she is standing in front of a large glass cube. Inside, she recognizes the "priceless original" of the lekythos she left on the sidewalk in Rhodes. The vase is painted in umber, black and red with a cream-colored background. There's a standing woman and a seated woman. What had made it so disturbing? Now the guard comes to say they're locking up. *They're in different worlds,* Lucy realizes as she's ushered out.

"Hotel Electra," she says, getting into the first taxi lined up outside. She leans back and looks through the streaked window, memorizing the city of Athens, knowing she's seeing it for the last time. Ancient buildings, stained and rotted, the stone chewed, as if by rodents, by pollution. Too many cars, the streets overcrowded, spoiled. And with no warning Lucy has a yearning to go home; she feels nostalgia for what she left, wherever that was. She considers going directly to the airport. There's nothing she really needs in the hotel room, just the white fur jacket and that's not even hers. But what would Cissy think? Lucy pictures her waiting in the lobby, attracting a lot of attention because there's power in beauty, and all the world knows it. "Why have you stopped here?" Lucy is grips the door handle.

A blue delivery van is stopped in front of the taxi, pulled half up on the curb, its door open. The driver of the van slides out and goes around front. Then he passes Lucy's window, awkwardly carrying a dog, a heavy dog, holding it at a distance from his body under its forepaws. A large dog, its limp body hanging. The man lowers the dog to the edge of the sidewalk. A semicircle of people have gathered. They stand a little apart.

Once they've driven off Lucy can't seem to let go of the scene. Was this the same yellow dog she'd seen sprawled on the roof top earlier, or a different dog? Embedded in the grime of her window she sees the dog—always the same dog—its stillness deeper than sleep. A thin line of red stains the soft, slack muzzle. Lucy stares, she begins to hyperventilate. She puts her arms around him, struggling to lift him. But she doesn't feel him as a weight, he seems part of herself. Heat comes from the cold and already rigid body; it passes now into her heart, stirring cold ashes, pumping love. She looks down. She is shocked to see that it's not a dog she's carrying. She sees the waxlike, expressionless face. The huge, soft wrinkled lids. The half-open mouth.

Pressing the door handle, Lucy calls out, "Stop here, please."

"WANT TO GRAB A CAB?" DANIEL ASKS HIS LAWYER when they've come down from her office and are out on the street.

"Let's walk," Marty says.

Devonshire Street is a dark narrow valley. Austere stone buildings rise on either side, space enough between them to conceal a mugger with a pipe wrench. The obligatory drunk lies curled in a doorway, asleep with a bottle in a bag. Daniel turns his eyes away; he couldn't tell if it was a man or woman. Unisex in everything, he thinks. When Cissy used to drink herself unconscious he'd put her in bed, couldn't risk a fall and damaging that face. It's probably about ten o'clock, but there's no traffic. Rain shines like tinfoil in the potholes; it must have come down hard while he was upstairs with Marty; funny, he didn't hear it. On the corners their two shadows loom reassuringly solid for a few seconds under the streetlights then flicker away like a moving target. There are no stars in the sky. A sliver of moon comes through the misty brown. Daniel glances up at the street sign, he doesn't recognize the name. Cabs splash on Salem Street. He isn't wearing a topcoat, and he feels cold. The rawness has attacked his stomach and he feels afraid. He has never in his life felt such dread. In New York, you'd have to be crazy to walk down a street like this at night, he thinks, glancing behind. Why does she do it? He lengthens his stride to stay abreast of Marty.

She walks fast, intrepidly slapping down her large, flat shoes.

Barging unaware through puddles. Before they left her office she had put on a rumpled tan raincoat with a thrown-back hood. Her hair is curling, baby fine. An uneven scoop of dress hangs below the coat to swing around her solid ankles. Yet she's not unattractive, Daniel finds himself thinking. There is something courageous and appealing about her thin shoulders, ridiculously erect, carrying the burden of all that unflattering clothing. Her fine nose is in the air, thrust forward like a bloodhound's.

"Do you like walking?" she asks. He's tense, she's sensed it; she's trying to put him at ease.

"Not particularly," he says. "I play tennis for exercise. At the Vertical Club."

"That doesn't heal," Marty debates. "It's not yin, it's yang."

"I'm doing fine, I don't need to heal."

"Right now," she tells him, "I want you to clear your head. Maybe you'll remember what you haven't told me. Forty blocks ought to do it." Her voice grates. The nasal accent is exclusive, he thinks, producible only by twelve years in the Chelsea public school system. It can't be faked—or erased.

There are four people at the bar along the wall at Arturo's. Just beyond it Marty climbs upstairs and clatters along the wooden floors between empty tables in the dining room. "Not fancy enough for tourists and too early for the regulars," she explains over her shoulder. "It gets busy around eleven." Daniel, following her, looks at the murals—crude realism of slickered fishermen, fishing dories trailing netted fish, a lighthouse on its stone island. Not his island; his island is New York, midtown—Woody Allen's Manhattan.

Marty says, when they're seated, "Ever come to the north end anymore?"

"No. Back Bay, once in a while. Cambridge. Some good Italian restaurants."

"That's not Italian," Marty snorts, "that's Italian decor."

"Do you ever get to New York?" Daniel challenges. "Matisse was at MOMA."

"When I go," she says, "I try to stay south of Twenty-second Street. That's where I lived when I went to NYU. If I need to go to Harlem on business, I go underground. Midtown is a swamp. As far as I'm concerned, the money stinks worse than the garbage." She's baiting him. Daniel remembers that she is sometimes disagreeable just for the fun of arguing. She has no sense of humor. He wonders why he's putting up with her.

"You're awfully thin," Daniel says, propping the one menu up between them. "How about the veal chop?"

"Don't take care of me," Marty snarls. "That didn't work when we were in law school and it won't work now. I'm a grown woman. I live alone because I like taking care of myself. I'll order when the waiter shows up."

"A bottle of wine?"

"Not unless you intend to drink it."

After a silence, he asks, "Why are you so angry at me, Marty? I want you to level the way I've leveled with you. If there's some way I've hurt you in the past, tell me." For the life of him he can't remember how they ended their relationship, which of them broke it off. Could she have loved him?

"Yes, you son of a bitch!" Her pupils get so close, they almost cross. "You're right, I'm damn angry with you! You were the poor kid who swore he was going to save the world from capitalism—and you sold out! You disappointed me." She looks up, smiling. "Linguine with clams, and chopped tomatoes and onions."

As soon as the waiter leaves, Daniel says, "I like doing what I do, and according to some people, I do it pretty well." His words come out with such humility, such sweetness, such decency. "Why are we arguing?" he asks, gazing straight at her, showing her everything: that he's honest, that he's scared, that he's vulnerable and that he needs her.

"Bullshit!"

Her lack of sympathy irritates and confuses him; he doesn't usually have trouble making people like him. "You disappointed me too," he tells her, getting back. "You were supposed to be a Supreme Court justice, and you settled for defending anarchists and big-name murderers."

"Like you?"

He grabs her shoulders; it's an unplanned response, like shaking a bad child that you'd really like to slap. But then he catches himself, ashamed. And instantly a warm feeling that he doesn't know what to do with surges through him. He looks to see if she feels it. Yes! They have sprung together the way a stretched rubber band does when one end is let go. And he's reeling from the impact. Round one is over, he thinks.

They eat their dinners. "We've established that we've grown apart," Daniel says, cautiously, after a time. "Not too far apart, I hope."

"We'll see," Marty grunts. "When you're finished we'll go back to the office."

"I guess I've missed the last shuttle. Where'll I stay?"

"The Park Plaza should have rooms."

Daniel laughs; he's seeing the girl the cops dragged out of the chancellor's office kicking and cursing, when the SDS occupied Memorial Hall. She is pig-headed, mercenary and determined to write the script herself. That could be an asset, he decides.

OUT ON THE STREET, LUCY STARTS RUNNING. SHE'S uncoordinated: sticklike legs flung out, arms flailing, clawed hand pommeling the air. She'll say good-bye to Cissy and head right for the airport; she's been to too many places she doesn't want to be in. A bell chimes; Lucy counts six strokes. She hurls herself against the rush-hour crowd; they seem a legion of the heartless. She churns against them as a swimmer might against the deadliest current.

Light is draining from the sky. HOTEL ELECTRA in pink neon blinks at indefinite intervals in the distance. On the boulevard cars, trucks, motorcycles mingle in one foul, toxic stream; backfire crackles like gunshot. From time to time Lucy is forced off the curb. Then suddenly she's hit. She lies on the ground blinded by headlights. A motorbike tears past, horn blaring, the driver never turning his globed head.

For a moment a bulky shadow pitches her into darkness, and then she feels herself being hauled up and flung like stone into the sea of ungiving bodies. Abruptly, she is dragged to her feet by a stranger whose expression is unforgiving. "Sober up," the man says in English, and barges on. From the back he is a businessman with a briefcase, walking rapidly, shoulders squared.

The deformed foot, missing its shoe, meets the pavement numb to pain. Lucy is jostled along. Most stores are closed and the hotel sign, the star she set her course by, is no longer visible. She tries to stay close to the buildings. Winded, she steps into the entranceway of a store. Her pants leg is ripped, and she's not surprised to see that she's bleeding. When she glances up there is a man not a foot away in the store window, perfunctorily removing the fur coats worn by the baldheaded mannequins. She taps the glass, but ignoring her, he vanishes through a door at the back with the hill of dead animals in his arms. A few minutes later he comes out to the street, walks right by Lucy; she narrowly escapes being crushed by the chain-link grate that crashes down. She limps on.

It's dusk. Lucy stops in front of a shoe store and raps on the glass. "I'd like to see those," she mouths to the saleswoman inside. She points to a pair of boots; the foot is silver mesh and looks as if it stretches. Lucy lifts her shoeless clubfoot in the air where the sales woman can see it.

Seated in the row of attached seats, Lucy has some trouble getting into one of the knee-high boots. Once she has it on, however, it expands. The boot is made of hundreds of tiny mirrors, held by elastic threads that glitter iridescently like fish scales. Lucy's uncertain; the young woman waiting on her smiles. Lucy crams her other foot in and, standing, goes unsteadily to the register. None of the bills she puts on the counter are returned. She minces with painful steps to the door. The saleswoman motions her back. Coming around the counter the woman knots around Lucy's waist a large, fringed shawl in vibrant colors. It reaches Lucy's knees. The woman steps back and rolls her large dark eyes theatrically. Before being bundled out the door, Lucy balances on one foot, and with her hand on the saleswoman's shoulder, wiggles out of her torn black pants. The woman locks up and links her arm through Lucy's.

As the two women sway down the street, the fringe of Lucy's shawl indifferently veils the bare flesh of her thighs; she can sense it brushing across her skin like a whisper in the dark. In the shawl and high boots, she must look like a whore, she thinks, mysterious, alluring. Darkness has fallen, the early, tense dark of an unforeseeable night. Traffic is a distant swish. The frosted hoods of cars cruise slowly by, all quiet and bathed in prescient magic.

They've stopped. "Here? What's in here?" Lucy asks. They're in front of an ornately carved wooden door fixed like a resolute mouth in the otherwise bland and flat marble face of a small building. The saleswoman adjusts the shawl on Lucy's hips. "*Cherete*," the woman says. "No," Lucy says, shaking her head. "Hotel Electra." They're unable to communicate and the woman is leaving her. Lucy goes to the curb and raises her arm. Taxis race by.

Lucy twists the brass key in the middle of the door, and a bell sounds. After a long time an eye plugs the peephole; a finger extrudes and points to the sign in English, Greek and Japanese: PRIVATE CLUB. MEMBERS ONLY. Lucy says she wants to use the phone. As the peephole starts to close, she holds up the hundred-dollar bill, American, that she kept in her bra for emergencies. This is an emergency. Fingers reach through the slot and pluck up the bill. The door swings in.

Lucy is in a square vestibule, with red flecked walls and a mirrored ceiling about thirty feet high that reflects the tiny top of her head. Seeing nobody, she puts her foot on the first step of the staircase carpeted in red, its nap like velvet. The clenched bones on her hand rest on the rounded banister; they ride up. Lucy's wondering if she ought to just turn around and get out of here. There's something odd about the mausoleumlike silence. What danger could there be in a private club? she rationalizes. But she's afraid. There's no reason, but she's still afraid.

Up, up, up a long flight. She is in a red-walled hall with a series of closed, unmarked doors. Lucy chooses arbitrarily, like the Lady did the tiger, she's thinking, and is startled to find herself abruptly face-to-face with a stranger. There is, as always, first the shock, then rejection, before she says mentally, *That's me.* She goes in, shuts the door and walks around the mirror, boot heels echoing. Quite alone in a large, shining-tiled locker room, musky smelling and spotless, Lucy assures herself, tentatively removing her shawl, that there's nothing to fear. There are stacks of invitingly thick towels on wire racks. Just what she needs before meeting Cissy. They'll have a drink before she leaves for the airport.

After her shower, Lucy sits down on the bench cushion tufted in red silk and squeezes into her boots. She hates to put on the same dirty clothes but she slips on her black jersey. Her bra is dropped in the wastebasket. For a few minutes Lucy scans the long table on which there's a hair dryer, a jar of combs soaking in antiseptic, little pots of color and soft crayons. Then she takes up a brush. She lines her eyes in black and daubs color on the lids. Passable, she thinks, standing and wrapping the fringed shawl around her waist, fastening it with a safety pin she found on the floor.

The red hall is empty. She looks both ways. Diffidently, she knocks, then carefully opens the next door, expecting to see treadmills, stationary cycles, free weights. Or if not a gym, maybe a lounge where you can have a drink, with a phone on one of the end tables. Something similar to the Sky Club at TWA—she was handed a courtesy card at Ben-Gurion.

The walls of the room are covered with rich, dark paintings of Moroccan design, tumbling couples with knotted limbs. Are they doing what she thinks they are?

She takes a step or two on the black marble floor, which has a hard gloss like a body of water; the rugs appear to be floating islands. Lucy wades out, stepping from one to the next. Around the edges there are couches, couches, Lucy begins to make out, that have bodies on them sprinkled with dots of color. The shifting splatter of colored particles is coming from a high, slowly revolving crystal ball. Now Lucy can hear muffled laughter; it's coming from the six or eight people in the center of the room, sitting or lying in the small, sunken pool of aquamarine water. One of them stands and comes up the few steps. He is not young, he's bald, but he looks fit. He is naked. In the split second before she has time to react, the man has gripped Lucy's hand and is going toward the pool, toward three women sitting waist deep, their breasts bare. The water ripples as if in anticipation, and Lucy spins around as if the building were on fire. Wrenching her hand free she runs to where the door was. But the door has disappeared and in its place is a huge painting that waves with force against her pummeling fists—it's not a painting, she realizes, groping, it's woven tapestry. New bodies she hadn't noticed before are emerging everywhere: on the rugs, on the couches, along the walls. Men with men, women with women, mingled groups each engaged dreamlike or perhaps drugged, in sex.

"WHAT AM I CHARGED WITH?" DANIEL DEMANDS.

Marty Simmering stands before him, an eyesore in a nondescript dress insufficiently covered by her raincoat, and bare legs in scuffed clogs. She has just bounced into police headquarters. Her soft, dry, nasal voice says, "Stay cool. We'll find out."

"We were scheduled to meet with Detective Lucas at ten," Daniel accuses her. "I've been waiting"—he glances at the clock over the high desk with three policemen lined up like the Three Stooges—"over two hours. Where the hell were you?"

"Upstairs," Marty says noncommittally; she sits down on the bench. "Sniffing around."

"Luckily they haven't called me."

"That's the system."

The enormous public area buzzes with the voices of confident, terribly smart women lawyers in power-shouldered jackets and miniskirts. Daniel lowers his voice, as if a man's voice would be too vulgar. "Why am I here, Marty?"

Taking his arm, she raises him and pulls him toward a pair of double swinging doors like those in a barroom. "Don't say anything," she warns just before they enter.

He shakes off her hand. "What do they suspect me of?"

She pushes him through.

"Hel-lo, Marty." Lucas springs up from his lounger. He pumps her hand, beaming. His blue eyes glitter. "Sit down. Sit down, please." Gallantly, he spoons Marty into the mission oak, first poking up the sunken seat cushion, and then indicates the canvas butterfly for Daniel. Daniel sinks down in the sling, close to the floor. Lucas lies back in his lounger. Beck stands.

For quite some time Lucas sits with his palms together and his index fingers under his chin in an attitude of meditation, if not prayer. Daniel, jackknifed well below the others, gazes around the room from the viewpoint, it occurs to him, of a dog. At eye level, for instance, leaning against the small tile fireplace is a very dim painting that wasn't there before, on which he can make out nothing but the dust accumulated on the cracked varnish. Beck, as Daniel's eyes glide up, could be a totem for all the animation in him. Still, he appears vigilant behind glasses that reflect the light and are thus opaque. Apparently in no hurry, Lucas at last lowers his hands and exposes his lips; he seems about to speak. Watching the lips for movement, Daniel is aware that their quite feminine fullness seems somehow at odds with the sharp blue eyes and lean, square jaw.

When the silence continues, during which Marty, his lawyer, smiles steadily at Lucas and he back, Daniel, from the sagging sling, says, "I'd like to get back to New York as soon as possible." He looks at Marty for support; she scowls as if annoyed by the remark, and furthermore had never set eyes on him before. "Can we get on with this?" he asks, despite Marty.

"Absolutely," Lucas says, as if grateful to be reminded. "Beck! The package, please."

Beck moves somnolently to the file cabinet. It is vintage 1968 gray metal; Daniel identifies it, he had one in graduate school that was moved to his mother's attic. He assumes it's still there. Grasping the rust-flecked handle, Beck pulls on the top drawer—it sticks halfway. He reaches in and lifts out the cat, drops her to the floor and closes the drawer with an ear-wounding scrape. After feeling around in the second drawer, Beck snatches out his hand and examines his fingers. From the third drawer down he removes a white plastic skull divided by blue lines into zones; craning his neck, Daniel catches above the left ear, *Destructiveness, Secretiveness and Sublimity*. Meantime, Beck has removed the steering column of a car, with the wheel twisted sideways like a spinning wheel, a football, a pair of flippers and at least four yards of black rubber tubing. While everything is going back in, Lucas keeps tossing his legs around impatiently. He is almost flat on his back, having slipped down. Finally, from the bottom drawer Beck brings out a poorly wrapped package. He sets this in Lucas's lap. Lucas draws himself erect and tugs the string, but the bow remains tied. With his nose up close he worries the knot, becoming more and more frustrated. Failing to undo the tangle, Lucas attempts to edge the string off one end—the package, having no shape of its own, compresses at his touch. After trying to bite it free, Lucas throws up his hands, and Beck instantly flashes a switchblade knife with the blade shot out. With an economical thrust he severs the string.

Lucas's knees are up under his chin and squeezed prissily together, the toes of his Top-Siders facing each other. He folds the brown wrapping paper back, and when the article lies exposed he lowers it carefully, as if it were of inestimable value, to the worn rug. Daniel leans forward in his chair with some difficulty.

Between his legs he can see a tan article of clothing that he doesn't recognize until, as Lucas begins to slowly raise it, the Burberry plaid lining is exposed. Then the heart in his chest gives a violent jump, as to resuscitate him.

Beck asks, "Look familiar?"

Marty answers before Daniel can, "Sure does, reminds me of mine."

The only similarity between the tailored, belted Burberry draped across Detective Lucas's thighs and the raincoat that covers Marty's shoes and a third of the rug like a pup tent is that both are in need of pressing. It gives Daniel's heart—now beating in his stomach—a terrible wrench to remember the day he bought it for Ursula. A light rain had been falling outside the Ritz-Carlton, where they'd gone for lunch. After lunch, they had checked in. When they came out in the late afternoon, the Common was the new green of spring and the doorman stood in the street flagging cabs. Daniel had taken Ursula's arm and hurried her across the street to the Burberry store. She'd seemed to him to look beautiful in every raincoat she tried. She chose one with the ubiquitous plaid lining and wore it, the belt buckled behind. They emerged into the shining sun, and a rainbow curved above the gold dome of the State House.

Now the coat is further surrendered toward Daniel without comment. Dark spots begin to appear. "What do you suppose that is?" Lucas finally asks, his eyebrows rising as if with genuine surprise.

"Dirt?" Daniel suggests cooperatively.

"Yes, you're right," Beck says, peering over Daniel's shoulder. "It certainly looks like dried dirt. But what about this?"

Daniel leans farther forward, unintentionally plunging out of the low chair. He catches himself just before landing on the evidence. "What is *that?*" he asks, looking up at Beck.

Lucas says loudly: "Blood."

"Blood?" The whole of the garment now held aloft by Lucas, who has stood up from his chair, seems to flutter—if anything that badly stained and stiffened by something a dark rust color can be said to flutter—above Daniel's head. Getting on his feet, Daniel steps back, horrified. "Are you sure? It doesn't look like blood."

"It's old, almost two years old," Lucas snaps back. He turns the raincoat slowly around and around, exposing an enormous, visible, unthinkable amount of discoloration; and Daniel begins to feel dizzy. He believes that he can smell Ursula's blood, menstrual blood—it had been a turn-on. He looks in confusion toward Marty. Her eyes are hard, emptied of the astigmatism, or whatever is wrong with them medically that makes them sometimes look misty; they are looking at him, and they reflect his tiny body in two clear, deep pools.

I N THE HOTEL ELECTRA LOBBY, THREE CLOCKS DISPLAY the time in New York, Paris and Athens, where it's six-twelve when Lucy asks at the desk to settle her bill and is issued her passport and wished a nice day. Looking around she sees that Cissy's not here yet.

Getting on the elevator, Lucy tugs the shawl over her bareness; and when it starts up she turns to the front and keeps her eyes on the lightening floor numbers. The elevator stops at five. A man and woman step on, dressed in evening clothes. They stand side by side, gauntly English, silently enduring the intimacy. Instead of rising, they all descend. The elevator stops again, more people get on. Lucy now wonders what the English couple think of the half-naked freak wearing silver boots like Mercury's. Then suddenly, she realizes that she doesn't care. She doesn't care what they think of her. She doesn't care what anybody thinks. She's leaving. As the couple get off the man turns toward Lucy and winks; he doesn't look embarrassed, he's actually smiling. If he noticed that her skin is like candle wax, he smiles anyway. Both of them smile. Plainly, they don't care how she looks, only how *they* look.

Stalking the corridor, a disquieting thought begins to repeat in a cadence to Lucy, like the sound of stones falling on wood, when the heavy, unrelenting earth is dumped, shoveled, thrown and settles forever on the coffin lid.

It's this: If she can never remember who she was, will she

have to wander forever among strangers, dependent on their benevolence? Lucy unlocks her door and turns on the electricity with her key. Pressing the door shut she leans her back against it. "God help me!" she says aloud.

It takes no time to clear her things from the bathroom. She puts on the dress she bought in Rhodes. There's little in the drawers, she doesn't bother emptying them. Opening the closet, she sees the white fur wrap curved around its solitary hanger. She lifts it and slips its shocking softness over her shoulders. The shawl will hang in its stead, she decides, sliding the shimmering rainbow onto the hanger; an effigy—it dangles, it nods. The reckless, abandoned fringe drags on the floor.

Sitting on the bed, Lucy unbuckles her tan bulky waist pack and dumps out receipts and a few remaining coins. She arranges her passport and ATM card, and the medical letter for when she buzzes through airline security. She buckles the money belt on again. You are packed, Lucy informs herself, and ready to go.

But go where? She gazes around, searching the blank walls of the room for a clue. Her eyes roll randomly until they burn, and at last they land on the mirror. There, Lucy encounters the phantom face; who else? The haunted stare, the reflection of the woman torn from her own learned image. She recalls that in order to be *someone* she took the name Lucy Snowe; and now she wears the name like the brand on the flank of a cow. It is her identity; she has become Lucy Snowe. How is this possible? she considers. Isn't there a *thing* that was her from her birth? Isn't there a thing that is the *self*, Lucy wonders, so axiomatic it is indescribable and fundamental from the beginning of life? And all one had to do was strive to be oneself. But her *self* is gone! What difference where she goes?

Restlessly, Lucy gets up and walks to the window. It's night outside and in the dark glass she sees an image. Quite undistorted. Lucy is being regarded by a cold, demanding stare. A harsh vertical crease between her eyes. Lucy goes closer to the glass. Mysteriously now, she has the sense of someone there she recognizes. Her own image overlays another's. Someone else's face is in the window, with the face of Lucy Snowe inexactly imposed upon it, quivering like a reflection in a black lake. Lucy puzzles over this likeness. It's a face she can almost recognize, a face she knows as well as her own. And she wonders now if the tracts of skin the doctors laid down like grass rugs, expecting them to root, had indeed finally rooted; and if her identity had been waiting as a bud does, in complete readiness to become the promised flower of its seed.

Her hand reaches up. "Mommy?"

She has been remade, it comes to Lucy, but the memory of her mother inflicts no less pain. She has surrendered her mind to blankness, her heart to emptiness, and always something has kept the pain alive. And when she thinks of her mother now, she cries inside not less. And crying, holds still more feeling in. Now "Mommy. Mommy!" cries out of her. For grief has come at last, and the realization that her mother is dead thrusts itself like a knife again and again into Lucy's body, ripping and ripping it.

◆

She steps out of the elevator in the lobby and Cissy stands up from the fan-back chair. She starts toward her, but falters, Cissy's face registering shock that falls just short of resentment: not because Lucy Snowe is wearing the thing itself, but because she can't forget that the white fur belongs with the life she gave up. And it's not transferable; she'd like to tell Lucy Snowe that.

Lucy notices the awkward moment of indecision and believes that she must look different to Cissy. She doesn't look like that wounded, scared Lucy Snowe anymore. No, and she isn't entirely the other Lucy either, the one Cissy has seen when Lucy gets rid of "that rigid, introverted snit." There must be something of both in her appearance—as if each personality had a grip on her hair, torn from its knot; and in the middle is the poor, askew face she saw in the dresser mirror, half stretched in a loose grin and the other half as mournful as death. Now Cissy is coming toward her as if she means to shake her; instead she says, "C'mon, Lucy. Let's get a drink."

Cissy leads the way; she seems to draw all the light in the room after her.

◆

Men stand two deep at the bar, as if they considered drinking a man's job that had to be done on your feet, like prizefighting. As Cissy crosses behind them, heads, in succession, turn as if choreographed. Cissy moves like a beam of light, intact, not stepping but floating. Tonight her hair is wound around her head and turned in on itself like a turban, smooth and secret; it's the soft, pale luxuriant hair of some rare, wild creature that men prey upon. She's wearing a belted jacket over a short leather skirt. However, now it strikes Lucy that there's a touch of bravado in the display, a touch of desperation.

Assembling herself at a small round table on a pedestal, Cissy signals the waiter. He bends over her shoulder. "Hi, Christiano," she says.

In a few minutes he comes with a silver ice bucket on its own spindly legs, stems of champagne flutes threaded through his fingers. He twists the wire, edges out the cork; there isn't much pop but foam spills. Cissy lifts her glass toward Lucy, her full, dark red lips proffered. Tentatively, Lucy raises her own champagne. "What are we toasting?"

"Survival."

Up close, there are imperfections. The cracked lips, furrows from the corners of her mouth to her chin. The jaw looks hinged. When Cissy doesn't say anything, Lucy wonders why Cissy was so intent on coming to Athens; she asks, "My survival?"

Cissy looks up and smiles. Her teeth are grainy, like a length of grayish grosgrain. The sulky lips have the look of something attached, appliquéd on, thinks Lucy.

Noticing Lucy's censorious eyes, Cissy clamps her mouth, as if she resented growing old and felt somehow to blame. After a few moments she touches Lucy's glass with her own and says, "Both of us survived."

They sit in silence. Cissy is making little wet circles on the glass tabletop. Her eyes dart, preoccupied, but vaguely compassionate toward the silver-footed boot jerking antically on the end of Lucy's crossed leg. Cissy looks right and left. "Before you go," she says, "I want to tell you something. It's something I haven't told anybody else. A secret."

Lucy doesn't want to hear any secrets, so she doesn't say anything.

Just at that moment a hush falls in the barroom. The only sound now is from the TV. The line of man-suited backs facing the mirror behind the bottles, and washed by the bright beam of color and shined by the high-mounted screen, all are attentive. The television screen above the bar glows cartoonishly bright and alive.

Between Doric columns a man is being hustled down broad steps. His raised-up arm shields his face. "What was the plea, Ms. Simmering?" a voice asks. The camera shifts to a round face, impassive, untroubled, confident. "Not guilty. No further comment. Please let us through." She gropes for the arm of the defendant, drags him along. Before the man can duck into the waiting car, he is caught in sunlight like a startled deer by head-lights. His narrow face appears stunned, as if he would, if not re-strained, throw himself headlong into the car's path.

Something heavy shifts in Lucy Snowe's heart, a slow churn-ing like a cold motor turning over. There is something about the man, something plaintive, shocked, tender, something fa-miliar. In a very real sense Lucy thinks she knows the shape—even the feel—of his full, soft lips. And as the thought goes through her mind that almost certainly she has seen this man before, a terrifying shock hits her, utterly without warning, with-out linkage, as in a nightmare. Lucy feels the sickening turbu-lence of falling, falling, heat against her face. She can feel hot liquid draining from her nose and the corners of her eyes, un-stoppably, as if the essence of her is pouring out. Lucy doesn't like this dream, it's too real, she wants to stop what she's feeling. And now a noise shatters her bones, a noise so interior that it threatens to blow her brain out of her head and leave it empty.

Swaying to her feet Lucy walks to the bar. The wall of men di-vides and she slides into the opening.

It is then that the photographs flash on the screen. The first is identified as the defendant, Daniel Dorfman. He wears a blue shirt; his wiry frame leans against the edge of a desk that has a silver-framed wife reflected at an angle in the glass top. The camera lingers lovingly on the woman's shiny-lipped smile and pale hair like spun sugar. One of the wife's arms hugs the mast of a sailboat; her body is full, round, colored starlet pink. A somber voice identifies, "Cecily Dorfman, Miss Tennessee of 1965, who died in the crash of a TWA jet." This picture is re-placed by a black-and-white snapshot slightly out of focus. A man and woman coming down the steps of a Victorian house. Both in profile, looking at each other. The man is the same man who was driven away from the courthouse a few minutes before.

The woman, the television voice says, is missing, presumed dead. Her body has never been found. She is Ursula Gant.

Lucy lifts one foot to the brass rail and steps up. Her left hand grips the rim of the bar. The fingers of her right hand, as gnarled and crooked as tree roots and the palms of the hand like bark, find the scar circling the edge of her face. She can only sense the touch of her own hand. So she closes her eyes and explores her face as if blind. The skin feels tight, pulling the eyes wide, making the jaw sharp. The nose is not the angular, narrow-bridged nose passed down by generations of Kornfield women; it has lost its reference, becoming small and snub. Lucy balances on the rail, leaning against the bulbous edge of the bar, and finally opens her eyes to see what has become of Ursula Gant.

◆

The space between them has cleared. The sound of the television is gone, the picture has turned to snow and the lights in the lounge have been turned off. "Well, now you've seen me on television," Cissy calls out from the table where she still sits, "what are you going to do about it?"

Ursula peers into the half dark. "Do?"

"Are you going to report Ah'm alive?"

All Ursula can make out is the dazzling white column of neck, aslant; then as Cissy approaches, her face blossoms pink and white, like a peony on its long stem. "Why should I?" asks Ursula.

"Y'all believe I should go back. Don't you?"

"Is that what you want to do?"

"If I don't he'll die for a crime he didn't commit."

"You don't think he killed her?"

Cissy laughs. "I know he didn't! Daniel doesn't let go of

things. He's a lover, not a hater. He loved that woman, and he needed her like he needed me." Confronting Ursula, she thrusts one leg forward and leans back on her other long, straight leg, like a compass. The mannerisms are there, thinks Ursula. But also signs of age, clear and ineradicable.

"You say he's innocent. But can you prove it?"

"Ah can," says Cissy. "I saw Ursula Gant at the airport. She was on the same plane as me. She died in the crash."

After a small interval, Ursula says, "You're responsible for clearing him, then." In an earlier phase, responsibility was something Ursula was an expert on.

Nervously, Cissy's two hands fly up, freeing her hair. She rakes it with the long, polished nails of one hand and with the other, she catches up the wiggly mane like a forelock spun of pure gold, tossing it back on her head. She's Daniel's wife, thinks Ursula, stepping down from the rail and sliding her hand along the lip of the bar; she's as unsuspecting and defenseless as the wife at the bottom of the spiral stair to the penthouse observatory.

"Don't give me away," Cissy pleads softly, groping for the knobbed knuckles of her friend's hand.

"But you've been on television," Ursula says. "People will recognize you."

"The beauty queen?"

So saying, Cissy begins to laugh as if she all at once realizes the triumph of her deception. The laugh bursts out of her, startling Ursula as it rises up the scale and explodes like a shower of sparks; and then, just as abruptly, Cissy stops, her laugh arrested by something she recognizes, an expression perhaps in the dark eyes opposite, suddenly magnified and individuated.

Cissy withdraws her hand, leaving Ursula's bare and lying there, unsightly, on top of the bar. "They're not looking for me,"

Cissy counters defiantly. "They think I'm dead. It's her they're looking for."

"Her?"

"Ursula Gant!"

With that, Cissy turns quickly and walks away, as if she has somewhere else to go, somewhere she's expected. After she's gone, Ursula can still see the shape of her body in the lit doorway. It is an image left on her retina. That image will always be there now.

◆

In the three-sided phone enclosure in the lobby, Ursula tells the automated voice, "Boston, Massachusetts. Information, please. A lawyer with the last name of Simmering." In response to the tone, she punches in the series of numbers. So far everything works, she realizes. Everything is swiftly sliding into place, as if the life of Lucy Snowe had been a fracture in time, a break in electricity that was a single instant. And now she's enabled again. The way she functions is exactly the same as before. But it doesn't feel the same. And she knows it will never feel the same again.

For several seconds static threads across an unfathomable distance, and then from the great echoing chamber comes a shrill, far ringing. A voice speaks quite intimately into her ear.

Ursula says, "Ms. Simmering? This is Ursula Gant speaking."

Halfway home is Zurich's stainless airport. Hurrying legs, blur of shadows on marble; tongues unknown—harsh and secret. Inscrutable faces, gazing up, moving on. Ursula sits on the bench below the clicking board of changing times and gate numbers, white fur on her shoulders, a book open in her lap. I am going home! keeps repeating inside, I am going home. What will she find? Her mother is gone, Daniel is gone, Brontë is gone. She thinks this and the sadness comes back. But if she is reaching for a book it will be there. If she is reaching for a memory it will be there. This is all she'll need. She had not been sure until now that it would be. Behind her on the wall there is a sudden, startling waterfall of slippage as the destinations change, followed by a gentle patter of renumbered departure times. She takes out a pencil and writes something in the margin of her book.

EPILOG

Days RISE FULLY LIT. DAWNLESS. JUST THE SAME HOT, clear day dropping into the screened flap of the tent like a slide on the wall. When Cissy exchanged her first-class return to New York for economy to Tanzania and $783 refund, she had already made the decision to move on. As soon as she'd identified Ursula Gant, Greece became uninhabitable; her lungs filled with the threat of suffocation and then she remembered the words Mimi had said. "Why don't you just walk?"

In Arusha, Cissy swapped her star-studded earrings for a secondhand tent and a used red Land Rover. The tent has no floor and there are spaces between the zippered doorway and the canvas sides; all night long insects buzz. The van's tires are bald, it has ninety-four thousand miles and a tape deck. She entered the Serengeti with a map of East Africa and the sun in her face. Animal country. This is the last place Daniel will look for her. Among the Disneyland animals, minding their own business. Being themselves in a way not possible for people.

The level earth grizzled with grayish-green sedge looks the same until the world's end, she thinks. Long grass and woodland, wild sisal and the flat-topped acacia trees. Heat. Sweat in the palms of her hands that hold the wheel. Clammy beads on the back of her neck. Shirt sticks. Rivulets down the sides of her nose, sunglasses sliding. Ankles feel tight. Fingers balloon. Sometimes a pair of ponderous elephants pad amicably past the car window, heavy-skinned and wrinkled. Well, just look at you! thinks Cissy. But that's all. Daniel had thought the gentle people in Morn-ingside Park were dangerous, hadn't he? How could he ever imagine her being here? She begins to laugh. Cissy is thinking, peering through the dirty windshield, that if there's an end to the earth, as they used to think, she's almost there.

Every morning she unzips the screen flap and wades into the calm as into a flowing river. Once she's on the road her thoughts float all day on the glittering surface. Sometimes, eyes watering against the glare of the daylight sky, she'll see the stage in Atlantic City where the most beautiful girl in Tennessee had stood with love pouring down from the lights and puddling around her feet. But there are other times, unlatching the door of the stinking outhouse at the Tarangire Main Gate—when she's caught sight of an older woman, the pieces of her face badly fitted, as if seen through a warped window. How can that be me? she thinks of protesting; but to whom? Down deep, she realizes that she's stood on the edge as long as she can, and maybe it's time now to take a deep breath and jump into dark-ness.

At the sign for Karatu town, Cissy slams on the brakes, and she's past the dozen shacks by the time the car stops. Ten minutes later, she walks out of the trading post in a length of bright-colored batik, knotted at the shoulder, and white sneakers. She marches purposefully down the empty road toward a squatting woman pounding something in a bowl between her spread knees. Raising her hand in greeting, Cissy holds up the Henri Bendel little black dress she wore to dinner with Daniel the night she left. She lays it wordlessly over the triangle of wooden sticks with unlit twigs and leaves beneath it, and sets her cosmetics case, open to the jars and the magnified lighted mirror, down in the red dust. Backing away, Cissy's eyesight blurs. Soon she can't see the shape of the dress any longer, all she can see is the ghost of Miss Tennessee, fading, disappearing in the hard, bright sun. "Enjoy wearing it," she calls out. That's what the saleswoman had said to her.

In the night table drawer at Ndutu Safari Lodge, on her first night, Cissy found two American tape cassettes, Tom Waits and the Doors. Now she pops in *Blind Love*. The singing van rocks along the bumpy, unwinding ribbon. No cars pass, none follow. Hot wind smacks her face and sucks her hair through the open window. She's going fast but the speedometer is stuck near forty. On land spread like a tablecloth she sees a pair of hippopotamuses standing stockstill like salt-and-pepper shakers. Through the roof hatch she feels the drilling, relentless heat; up ahead is the misted, surrealistic, clay-colored rim of the Ngorongoro Crater, suddenly there as if it had fluttered from the sky, a prop fashioned of papier-mâché. It looks abandoned, she thinks, as if the movie crew had left for L.A. Her mind's wandering, she knows that. All day the sun glitters without end. The sky remains an overall hue of blue. Night falls without warning with the moon tacked on.

The wind picks up. Suddenly the van rises and tilts like a spinning gyroscope. Cissy quickly rolls up her window; inside it's steamy, no air to breathe. Undulating banners of black dust spiral across the road; little bushes tumble. A tortoise flies at the car and its patterned underbelly is pasted for a moment directly in her view. Within seconds it slides off, legs flailing; blown sand coats the windshield, thick as smoke. Impenetrable, it leaves no holes; her headlights provide no opening. The earth invades the sky, colors it brown, seals her inside. A premature darkness has fallen. Wave after wave of flying debris roars up, smacks the hood. Gripping the wheel, Cissy keeps driving blind at undiminished speed. Finally, pumping the brakes, she reins in the sliding car; it seems to bump a mile before stopping. She backs up, looking through the rear window, which is plastered with dead insects. Then pulling off the narrow, rutted road, she cuts the engine. She spreads the map and tries to estimate distance, find a name, a location. A town, a campsite. Her back aches, her thighs stick to the baking seat, and she desperately has to pee.

Finally she forces the door open against the wind, puts her legs out and stands up. This is strictly forbidden; every game park has signs saying the animals are dangerous. She pulls down her shorts, leaning over and peeing on the tire like a dog. Blowing sand stings her ass, her hair turns inside out. Her face stings. Flies buzz in her ears, crawl on her flesh. Turning her head, Cissy sees the baking, putrid body of a dead buffalo with a jackal tearing at it. A vulture circles overhead. Cissy jumps back in the car, turns the key, pumps the gas. She filled the tank this morning. *Please, no!* But it's true. The great-deal car is dead.

Cissy takes a long slug from the bottle of Ultra Aqua that's been heating on the seat. Then reaching under the dashboard, she pops the hood. Sits, gathering courage. When she cracks the door open again, the wind whips it out of her grasp, back on its hinges, and throws her to the ground outside. Struggling to her feet, she doesn't look around. She inches forward, gripping the van like someone on the deck of a madly tossing ship, and steps up on the front bumper. Through a clot of tangled hair she searches the metal insides, surprised to find quite quickly two raggedly severed ends of a fat hose smelling of burnt rubber. You're a fucking genius, Cissy says to herself, jumping down.

Inside, Cissy presses down all four door buttons, climbs into the backseat, and sleeps at once.

Groping, she finds the light switch, and the dim globe on the ceiling comes on. She looks at her Cartier watch; it's never been off by so much as a minute. She unlatches the gold bracelet, holds it to her ear, shaking it. No use. She puts it back on. A little later she unlocks the roof hatch and boosts herself up into the dark. No moon, but stretching her neck Cissy sees a spectacular spatter of high stars. Nothing else. Finally she sits down again, leaving the hatch open; she needs to breathe, doesn't she? Tilting the rearview mirror she examines her face; it looks crusty, as if carved of the heavy African soil, cracked into wadis; eyes ringed in black like a bat-eared fox's, burning, half shut. She turns off the light.

Outside—does she imagine it?—she can hear elephants crunching, chewing, stomping. Taking her flashlight from the glove compartment, Cissy shines it though the closed window, half expecting to see a long, gray, flexible hose. An old vacuum hose that will reach into the hatch and suck her up between the tusks, vegetarian or not. All she sees is the blooming spiral. So now she pulls the knob and shoots the beam of her headlights into the blackness. And screams. Immediately before her, perhaps a few yards away, is a squatting man. Checking first to see that all the doors are locked, Cissy swiftly slams down the roof hatch and entombs herself. Terrified from her sweating palms to her bony, shaking knees, how is it that she cannot stay conscious?

Daylight wakes her. She has the feeling she's being watched, and rolls her eyes sidewise. Outside her window a thin, spear-carrying Masai, she vaguely remembers from the guidebook, is regarding her with suspicion. His unblinking gaze wanders over her body from her tangled hair to her unshod feet. The flattened tip of his nose is stuck like a wet leaf to the glass. With impressive violence Cissy raises up her hand and slams her palm against the pane. He's gone! Rolling down her window, she shouts through the crack, "My car's stuck, a hose is broken. Do you know where I can get it repaired?"

Now at eye level he prowls, circling the car twice. Moving rhythmically, but unhurriedly. Red, soft-looking cloth encircles his waist and is draped like a sarong over one shoulder; he is barefoot, with deeply brown and lustrous skin. He wears beaded bands around his ankles and a wide stiff collar of tiny red and yellow and white beads. His head is small and round; and his hair, thinks Cissy, looks like a very fine wool rug, lying flat. She takes in all this, feeling reassured by the beauty of his bearing, which affects her almost like a work of art. His small and delicate features, prominent cheekbones—the Masai face, smiling confidently, proudly, shyly. He motions for her to release the hood. She does as she's told and climbs out, stiff from sleeping in the car.

"See." Reaching forward, Cissy points to the torn hose. Without any warning the hood slams down. Cissy screams in pain and astonishment. Looking into the man's eyes for an explanation, she sees the dilated pupils roll with merriment. He clicks, showing sparse teeth.

Weakly, Cissy folds to the ground, eyelids closing. Her right arm languishes at her side, disconnected from will. Her left hand is lifted, the watch unfastened. The Masai removes his beaded girdle and binds her. Pulling Cissy to her feet, the man prods with the shaft of his spear, as if she were his tethered cow. Unresistingly, Cissy moves forward.

◆

Broken, Cissy informs herself. Her arm is wound in layers of warm green leaves and hung from her neck in a cradle of woven hairs; she sits up with difficulty. She is in a hut buzzing with flies, on a dung floor. Round, maybe five feet in circumference with a roof made of sticks and straw and littered with every kind of discarded trash. There are no windows, only a small hole in the roof. Empty oil cans, tin plates, plastic bottles, every kind of scavenged thing dangles from the walls; like a rat's nest, Cissy has it on the tip of her tongue to say. But who will she say it to? As her eyes adjust, she is startled to see that she's not alone. There is a crouched Masai. She is old, smiling without teeth; a metal snake winds her arm above the elbow, and heavy bead earrings hang from the top rims of her ears, bending them out from her shaved head. Scuttling forward she puts a tin dish down in front of Cissy. Cissy shakes her head; no, she cannot eat, the smell is too strange. The woman cups the plate in two weathered hands, bringing it to Cissy's lips, and Cissy sucks in her breath, for what is being offered looks like blood.

Cissy crawls to the doorway and lies like an old lioness in the shaft of sunlight. Blank and dull but not discontent is how Cissy seems to herself. This torpor she attributes to the pipe that the woman keeps filled with shreds of some weed. The two of them sit in the sun in companionable silence, smoking. At night she hears the guttural grunts that she knows are lions, the hyena's malicious laugh, the cries of baboons, shrill and crazed. The woman enters on flat feet, crouched like a monkey. Sometimes the domed head of a small child, its closed eyes massed with flies, its neck hung with beads, clings to the woman's round back. The old one sleeps on the other side of the glowing twigs. No sign of the man.

*   *   *

The hut is dim, the fire burns, the woman tends her. One night Cissy feels a soft breath in her hair; her body turns rigid with fright. A gentle hand soothes her, touching her head and neck, her shoulder, softly pressing. The hand continues to caress until Cissy can't stay watchful to attend her fear. If the hand pauses for a moment, she starts and wakes. And when the warm hand touches her again, Cissy imagines unseemly and impossible things. At forty-eight, hadn't she done with sex and longing?

◆

What's all this for? Cissy thinks, curious, weeks or maybe a month later, as the old one forces a wide stiff collar of beads strung on wire over her head. Cissy touches her head; it's close-clipped like the woman's. She is to ride the horned topi that lazes in front of the hut; across its bony rump provisions are suspended in cloth pouches. Both her legs are beaded round to the calf. The young warrior leading the animal away has on a loose garment of red plaid and a wide corset of beads banding his stomach. He carries his spear and on his arms wears three, no, four watches, one her own; she recognizes it. With a sudden jerk they set out. Where are they going? she wonders, her body rocking like a boat on the tilting sea. Swarming around her she hears the bawling and mewing of animals and the nasal trilling of the nomads' speech. She clutches the shorthaired hump below the goat's neck, pressing her knees into its bony sides, and looks back. Black smoke fills the air as the village they are leaving burns. And Cissy, part of the beastly procession, holds herself erect like the stately giraffe with its mute length of neck. Or the small-headed ostrich, she amends: flightless. She swallows dust; it stiffens her face. They proceed down the switchbacks ever descending toward the valley floor. The ghostly thunder of drums rolls closer.

*   *   *

Just before the black night seals them in, they stop. The Masai women begin to sway and sing: a shrill, discordant racket. Simultaneously, the bony, graceful figures of men, lined up, begin one by one to spring into the air, so that there is a constant popping up and down like exploding corks. The male dancers are crying out with sweaty, drugged intensity and the women stamp flatfootedly in a rapturous, orgiastic dance. The tempo increases; Cissy hesitates. The moment they begin to fall, spent, one upon another, she slides unheeded off the animal. Now she has a clear view. Halfway up a shoulder-high termite mound her abandoned red Land Rover—the doors flung open, "Light My Fire" spewing forth at top volume—sits with its front end in the air like a rhino on wheels.

The next day, picking her way among the high-stepping flamingos, who prance heads up, turning this way and that, and herons, and top-heavy storks (some rise in a fluttery flurry, but most take no notice) Cissy wades into the lake. The water is pea green with blooming algae, the shores are pink. She sloshes almost entirely across through water no higher than her knees. On the opposite shore a black-robed priest, a portly Anglican with a dark beard flecked with gray, pours a half-gallon plastic container of water over her head. Sodden as a river rat, Cissy stumbles out, smiling.

The priest leads the way to the mud-walled church. Cissy stands barefooted and dripping in front of the altar hung with votive offerings—mostly familiar-looking auto parts: a sideview mirror, the knob of a clutch, a blackened spark plug, a rusted, red-flecked door. The air in the church is heavy with incense. The priest, puffing from the exertion, lights the oil in two brass pots and sets them in motion. The lamps swing hypnotically back and forth in front of Cissy's face, giving her a moving glimpse of a woman she has not seen properly since she left civilization. She looks like a pagan goddess, she thinks. Glowing face, not young but with a certain style that so pleases her, she dances side to side, not letting her reflection out of her sight. Beside her, the Masai man, timid and exulant, kneels and with the pointy nail on his pinky scratches a double axe on the dirt floor. Suddenly gasping for air, she writes "Cissy," with the coil of wire the priest hands her. As they exit the church, a distant volcano puffs black ashes that fall around them like confetti.

All that night the Masai dance in firelight to the drums: humming, singing, crying, howling. Arms wave, they move with trancelike unawareness. Faces expressionless. Drugged out of their heads, Cissy decides, lying tensely on the back bench of the red Land Rover. It was as if a chemical had been released. For her, the air had changed during that ceremony in the church, slightly, but enough to give her the sensation of having fallen without realizing it into one of those deep pits with spikes on the bottom.

Ursula? Should I call you Ursula? I wanted to get in touch with you. I feel I owe you an explanation. You made me feel really good about myself, and confident. I don't want to lose that feeling.

You're fine. You're you.

I wish I hadn't had to leave. But I felt afraid. I'd gone through so much to be free of Daniel and that life I'd lived.

I wouldn't have given you away.

I couldn't chance it.

And now, how do you feel?

I'm still very shaken, but it's not as bad. I'm not in Greece anymore, you should know that. After a while I'll probably get over being bitter about you and Daniel, and stop hating you because you humiliated me. And then the time will come that I won't care either way very much and we might even be friends.

I'd like that. I've never had a friend.

The imagined conversation she has with Ursula ends with a bang. A solid object suddenly smashes the windshield. Glass flies, an apron of crystal covers Cissy's body. She stands up and looks out the roof hatch. Outside, the earth has begun to rock and rearrange. The warrior husband is nowhere in sight; he must be broadcasting the news, beating drums, lighting fires, drinking blood, thinks Cissy. It's not every day one purchases a bride. Under a massive baobab tree, Cissy's mother-in-law squats, gripping her bowllike pipe in her bristly jaw and complacently regarding her son's treasure. The surviving door falls off its surviving hinge. A whirling funnel of volcanic ash is hurrying toward Cissy, splitting the very ground apart, sucking everything in. A jagged running seam opens to the horizon. Vaulting into the front seat, Cissy releases the brake. The van, jiggling wildly, rolls backward off the termite hill. Cissy turns the key in the ignition.

It works!

Hours later, she crosses a wiggly one-lane bridge suspended by vines; the planks clatter under the tires. At the end a costumed inspector glances into the empty back seat. "Where am I?" she asks, barely pausing. He smiles without understanding and waves her on. Cissy squints as the van slithers across the bristly yellow field toward the rays of sun. She drifts past a kopje with a leopard sitting high in the branches of a sausage tree; he turns his head, his yellow eyes steely. A reminder. She'd endured Daniel's glare of contempt, and wherever she's going now, it's not back there. Finally, suddenly, magically, the dark and impersonal forces of old age don't scare her. Cissy hasn't felt this sure of anything, since she basked in the floodlight of happiness on the stage at Atlantic City.

Printed in the United States
by Baker & Taylor Publisher Services